Also by Jackie L. Smith

Echoes of 1969

The Customs Conspiracy

The Fractured Path to Emerald Vale

Echoes of Betrayal

Atlas Drummond: Fragments of Deceit

Hank Blankenship and the Longest Fall

Colby Utterback: Finding His Place

Brynn Thornwick: Guardian of the Crimson Crown

Wilbur Northcutt and the Boonesborough Fall

The Last Whisper of Innocence

The Last Whisper of Innocence

A Family Crime Thriller

By

Jackie L. Smith

Copyright Page

The Last Whisper of Innocence

Copyright © 2026 by Jackie L. Smith

All rights reserved.

No part of this publication may be reproduced, distributed, or transmitted in any form or by any means, including photocopying, recording, or other electronic or mechanical methods, without the prior written permission of the author, except in the case of brief quotations embodied in critical reviews and certain other noncommercial uses permitted by copyright law.

This is a work of fiction. Names, characters, businesses, places, events, and incidents are either the products of the author's imagination or used in a fictitious manner. Any resemblance to actual persons, living or dead, or actual events is purely coincidental.

Published by Jackie L. Smith

First Edition: 2026

Cover Design by: Jessica Stacey

ISBN: 979-8-9959280-4-1 (paperback)

Published and Printed in the United States of America

Dedication

For those who served, those who sacrificed, and those who never stopped believing that family is worth fighting for.

Epigraph

"The apple doesn't fall far from the tree, but sometimes the tree falls on the apple."

— Anonymous

Author's Note

This novel is a work of fiction set in Bakersfield, California. While the city and Kern County are real places, all characters, incidents depicted in this story are entirely imaginary. No resemblance to any actual person, living or dead or to any real organization or event is intended or should be inferred.

The Reapers Motorcycle Club is a fictional organization. Any similarity to actual motorcycle clubs, past or pevents, organizations, and resent, is coincidental.

The themes of family loyalty, addiction, and loss explored in this story are drawn from the universal human experience. If you or someone you know is struggling with substance abuse, please contact the Substance Abuse and Mental Health Services Administration (SAMHSA) National Helpline at 1-800-662-4357.

— *Jackie L. Smith*

PROLOGUE

"God Help Me"

October 19, 2024 — $0 — "Lorraine asked for $20,000. I said no. First time I've ever said no. She was angry. God help me."

The kitchen smelled like coffee and Pine-Sol, the way it always did on Saturday mornings. Cyril Butterworth sat at the desk in the corner of his bedroom — the oak rolltop Helen had bought him at an estate sale the year before she got sick — and opened the notebook.

It was nothing special. A black composition book, college-ruled, the kind you could buy at any drugstore for two dollars. He'd started it fourteen years ago, the first time Lorraine called about rent. He didn't know why he started keeping track. Maybe because Helen would have wanted to know where the money went. Maybe because writing it down made it feel like a decision instead of a surrender.

He turned to the next blank line. The pages before it told a story he never meant to write. Fourteen years of entries, each one the same: a date, a dollar amount, and a sentence or two that said less than he felt. He never wrote what he really wanted to say. That would have meant admitting things a father shouldn't have to admit about his youngest daughter.

He picked up the pen — a cheap Bic, blue ink, the same kind he'd used for forty years of facilities reports at the county building — and wrote the date.

October 19, 2024.

Then the amount.

$0.

He stared at the zero. In fourteen years, he had never written a zero. There had always been something — two hundred, five hundred, a thousand, three thousand that one terrible time she called from county jail. He'd never said no. Not once. Not when Archie told him he was enabling her. Not when Knox looked at him with those sad, knowing eyes. Not when his own gut told him the money wasn't going where she said it was going.

But twenty thousand dollars.

She'd called that morning. Her voice had that edge to it — the one that meant she hadn't slept, or had slept too much, or had done something to herself that she'd never call by its real name. She needed twenty thousand dollars. She said it was for a debt. She said people were pressuring her. She said she was scared.

He believed the scared part. He always believed the scared part.

But twenty thousand dollars was not rent. It was not a car repair. It was not textbooks for a semester she'd never finish. Twenty thousand dollars was something else, and for the first time in fourteen years, Cyril Butterworth heard his own voice say the word he'd been choking on since she was seventeen years old.

No.

He said it gently. The way Helen would have said it, if Helen had lived long enough to see what their daughter had become. "I can't keep doing this, sweetheart. I love you. But I can't."

The silence on the other end lasted long enough for him to hear his own heartbeat. Then she said things. Ugly things. Things a daughter says when the one person who never let her fall finally steps back. He let her say them. He held the phone away from his ear and looked at the framed photograph on the desk — Lorraine at five, gap-toothed, standing in the sprinklers in the backyard, laughing so hard she'd fallen down. His little star.

She hung up without saying goodbye.

Now he sat at the desk, pen in hand, and finished the entry.

"Lorraine asked for $20,000. I said no. First time I've ever said no. She was angry. God help me."

He closed the notebook. Put the pen on top. Pushed the chair back and walked to the kitchen where the retirement invitations sat on the counter in a neat stack — forty of them, stamped, addressed, ready to mail on Monday. Forty years at Kern County Facilities Management. Forty years of showing up. The party was two weeks away.

He poured himself a cup of coffee and stood at the window. The backyard was quiet. The grass needed cutting. The sprinklers hadn't run in weeks. He thought about calling Archie but didn't. Archie would ask about Lorraine, and Cyril didn't have the energy to defend himself tonight.

He drank his coffee. Washed the mug. Turned off the kitchen light. Checked the front door — locked. Checked the back door — locked. Left the porch light on the way he always did, in case one of his children ever came home late and needed to find their way.

Two weeks later, someone he trusted would walk through that door and kill him.

But tonight, the house was quiet. The coffee was good. The invitations were ready. And Cyril Butterworth went to bed believing that the hardest thing he would ever do was say no to his daughter.

He was wrong.

Contents of Contents

CHAPTER 1: "The Good Son"

The trading floor at Kessler-Braun Capital smelled like burnt coffee and ambition, and Archibald Butterworth was fluent in both.

He stood at his desk—nobody sat at Kessler-Braun, not during market hours—watching three monitors cycle through numbers that would have looked like chaos to anyone who hadn't spent a decade learning to read them like weather. Futures on the left screen. Equities in the center. Options flow on the right. The S&P was up fourteen points on a Fed rumor, and the Russell was lagging behind like it always did when institutional money got nervous about small caps.

Archie saw the gap before anyone else on the desk.

"Danny, you seeing this?" Archie called out without looking up. Muscle memory. Fingers already moving.

Danny Faulk, two stations over, glanced at his own screen. "The Russell lag?" Danny said. "Yeah, it'll correct in twenty minutes."

"It'll correct in eight," Archie said. He was already in. Three hundred contracts on the IWM, leveraged against a short position on the SPY that he'd built the day before when the market was pricing in a rate cut that wasn't coming. The trade was clean, fast, and visible—the kind of move that made the desk managers either love you or fear you, depending on whether they'd made the same bet.

Seven minutes and forty seconds later, the Russell corrected. Archie closed the position. Net gain: $387,000 for the firm. His cut would show up on Friday's P&L statement, but he already knew the number. He always knew the number.

Danny shook his head. "Eight minutes," Danny said. "You're a machine, Butterworth."

Archie didn't smile. He never did on the floor. Smiling after a win was a rookie tell—it said the win surprised you. Archie wasn't surprised. He'd spent four years in the Marines learning to read terrain, and Wall Street was just terrain with better lighting. You studied the ground. You identified the opportunity. You moved before the enemy knew you were there. The discipline was the same. The stakes were lower. Nobody bled on a trading floor.

He logged the trade and pulled up his portfolio summary. Net worth north of two million, not counting the condo in the Financial District or the retirement accounts. At thirty-five, he was exactly where his father's work ethic and the United States Marine Corps had built him to be. UC

Berkeley had given him the education. The Corps had given him the spine. The rest was execution.

Archie checked his phone. A text from Bella: "Still on for 7? I found a new place on Valencia. Thai."

Archie typed back: "I'll be there. Order me whatever you're having."

Bella replied: "Dangerous move, Marine. I like it spicy."

Archie sent back: "I know."

He pocketed the phone and spent the last hour of the trading day reviewing positions, answering emails, and pretending to listen to Danny talk about a crypto currency he'd bought that was going to change everything. At 4:15, the closing bell rang. Archie shut down his screens, grabbed his jacket, and walked out without saying goodbye to anyone. It wasn't rudeness. It was efficiency. He'd see them all tomorrow, same positions, same screens, same war fought with different numbers.

The restaurant was called Lemongrass, a narrow storefront on Valencia Street with mismatched chairs and a chalkboard menu that changed daily. Bella was already there when he arrived, sitting at a corner table with a glass of white wine and her reading glasses pushed up on her head. She was reviewing a case file, a yellow legal pad covered in handwriting so small and precise it looked like a code.

Arabella Castillo. Thirty-two. Immigration attorney. Mexican-American with roots in California's Central Valley so deep her grandmother still grew chiles in the backyard of a house in Delano that hadn't changed since 1968. Bella was smart in a way that made most men nervous—the kind of smart that saw through performance and asked questions that didn't have comfortable answers. She was beautiful in a way she didn't seem to notice, which made it worse.

They'd been together eight months. Long enough for Archie to know she was different from anyone he'd dated. Not long enough for him to let her all the way in. He was working on it. Working on it was the best he could do.

"You're early," Archie said, kissing her cheek and sliding into the chair across from her.

"You're late," Bella said without looking up from the legal pad. "I ordered the panang curry and the drunken noodles. Extra spicy. You said dangerous move."

"I did say that," Archie said.

She closed the file and took off her glasses. Her eyes were dark brown, almost black, and when she looked at him directly—which was always—it felt like being scanned by someone who already knew what she'd find.

"Good day?" Bella asked.

"Made the firm almost four hundred thousand on a seven-minute trade," Archie said.

"Should I be impressed?" Bella asked.

"You should be buying dinner," Archie said.

Bella laughed. It was the kind of laugh that started in her eyes before it reached her mouth, and it was the reason Archie had asked her out in the first place—at a fundraiser for a legal aid clinic, where she'd been arguing with a state senator about asylum policy and winning.

The food came. They ate. They talked about her case— a family from Guatemala fighting a deportation order, the kind of case Bella took for free because nobody else would. She talked about the Central Valley, about families who'd built lives from nothing and now lived in fear of a knock on the door. Archie listened. He was good at listening when he wasn't trying to control the conversation, which Bella had pointed out was a skill he needed to practice.

"How's your dad?" Bella asked, halfway through the drunken noodles.

The question landed differently than she intended. Archie set down his fork.

"He's good," Archie said. "Excited about retirement. Two weeks out. Forty years at Kern County and he's finally going to stop fixing other people's buildings."

"And Lorraine?" Bella asked.

She asked it the way she always did—carefully, like she was stepping around something sharp on the floor. Bella had never met Lorraine. She'd heard enough to know why.

"I don't know," Archie said. "Dad doesn't bring her up much anymore. Last time I asked, he changed the subject."

"That's not like him," Bella said.

"No," Archie said. "It's not."

He picked up his fork again. The noodles were good. The curry was better. The restaurant was loud enough to give them privacy, quiet enough to hear each other, and Archie thought—not for the first time—that this was the part of his life he'd been missing. Not the money. Not the discipline. This. A woman across a table who asked about his father and noticed when the answer was wrong.

He almost told her about Lorraine. The real version— not the sanitized one he'd offered on their third date, the one where his sister was "going through a rough patch." The real version involved meth, a motorcycle club, a revolving door at county jail, and a father who couldn't stop writing checks to a daughter who couldn't stop cashing them. But telling the real version meant opening a door he'd spent years keeping shut, and Archie Butterworth was a man who controlled his doors.

"She'll figure it out," Archie said. The lie tasted like nothing.

Bella looked at him for a long moment. She didn't push. That was the other thing about her—she knew when to wait. Eight months in, and she was still waiting for him to trust her with the ugly parts. He knew it. She knew he knew it. They both let it sit there, a quiet negotiation neither of them was ready to finish.

They split the check—Bella insisted, something about feminist principles and a four-hundred-thousand-dollar trade not needing her sympathy—and walked to her car. The October air in San Francisco was cold and clean, carrying fog from the bay. He kissed her goodnight on the sidewalk, longer than usual, and she pulled back with a look that said she'd noticed.

"You okay?" Bella asked.

"Yeah," Archie said. "Just—good night. That's all."

She studied him the way she studied case law—looking for the thing that didn't fit. Then she smiled, got in her car, and drove away.

His condo was on the thirty-second floor of a glass tower south of Market Street. Two bedrooms, two baths, a kitchen he barely used, and a view of the Bay Bridge that real estate agents described as "iconic" and Archie described as "useful for thinking." He'd bought it three years ago with cash, which his accountant said was inefficient and his Marine buddies said was the most Archie thing they'd ever heard.

He changed into sweats, poured two fingers of bourbon—Woodford Reserve, neat, the only indulgence he allowed himself on weeknights—and sat down at his home office desk to review the next day's positions. The market didn't sleep, and neither did the traders who wanted his seat.

The phone rang at 9:47 PM.

The screen said DAD.

Archie picked up on the second ring. "Hey, Pop," Archie said. "Late for you."

"Can't sleep," Cyril said. His voice was steady but thin, the way it got when he was tired or thinking too hard about something. "Just wanted to hear your voice."

"Everything okay?" Archie asked.

A pause. The kind of pause that carried weight.

"Your sister called today," Cyril said.

Archie closed his laptop. "What did she want?" Archie asked.

"Money," Cyril said. "A lot of it. More than I've ever—she asked for twenty thousand dollars, Archie."

"Tell me you said no," Archie said.

"I said no," Cyril said.

The words hung there, strange and unfamiliar. In fifteen years, Archie had never heard his father say those two words about Lorraine. Not when she dropped out. Not when she got arrested. Not when the excuses stopped making sense and the money kept disappearing into a life none of them were allowed to see.

"That must have been hard," Archie said, and meant it.

"Hardest thing I've ever done," Cyril said. "Harder than losing your mother, in a different way. Helen dying wasn't a choice. This was a choice. And she was angry, Archie. Real angry."

"She'll get over it," Archie said.

"Maybe," Cyril said. Another pause. "I just keep thinking—what if she doesn't call back? What if that's the last time I hear her voice and the last thing she said to me was—" Cyril stopped himself. "Never mind. I'm just tired."

"Dad," Archie said. "You did the right thing. You know that."

"I know," Cyril said. "I know I did." His voice shifted, reaching for lighter ground. "Archie, your brother's been coming around more. He's a good boy. That girl of his—Delaney—she's a good one. Reminds me of your mother."

"That's high praise," Archie said.

"It's the truth," Cyril said. His voice softened further. "How's your girl? The lawyer."

"Bella," Archie said. "She's good. We had dinner tonight."

"Bring her home sometime," Cyril said. "I want to meet the woman who got Archibald Butterworth to eat Thai food."

Archie laughed. A real laugh, the kind his father could still pull out of him when nobody else could. "I'll bring her," Archie said. "After your retirement party. We'll make a weekend of it."

"I'd like that," Cyril said. "I'd like that a lot."

"Get some sleep, Pop," Archie said.

"You too, son," Cyril said. "I love you."

"Love you too, Dad," Archie said.

He hung up. Set the phone on the desk. Picked up the bourbon and took a slow sip.

Something was off. Not in what Cyril said—in what he didn't say. Twenty thousand dollars. Lorraine had never asked for that much. The amounts had always been manageable—five hundred here, a thousand there, just enough to sound like rent or car trouble or some other fiction they all pretended to believe. Twenty thousand dollars wasn't a fiction. It was a signal. Something had changed in Lorraine's world, and the change was big enough to make her desperate and bold enough to ask for a number that even Cyril couldn't rationalize.

Archie stared at the Bay Bridge, lit up against the black water, and thought about calling Lorraine himself. He hadn't spoken to her in four months. The last conversation had ended the way they always did—her defensive, him frustrated, both of them talking past the ghost of the sister she used to be.

He didn't call.

He finished the bourbon. Brushed his teeth. Lay in bed staring at the ceiling while the fog pressed against the windows and the city hummed thirty-two stories below.

Something about that phone call was bothering him.

He didn't know it yet, but it was the last time he would ever hear his father's voice.

CHAPTER 2: "The Golden Child"

The apartment smelled like cigarettes and regret, and Lorraine Butterworth hadn't opened a window in three days.

She sat on the edge of the mattress in the one-bedroom unit on South Chester Avenue, the cheapest place she could find that didn't ask for a credit check. The sheets were tangled. The blinds were drawn. A half-eaten bag of gas station chips sat on the nightstand next to an ashtray full of cigarette butts and a lighter with a cracked casing. The television was on but muted — some daytime court show where people screamed at each other in silence.

Lorraine's hands were shaking. Not the big shakes, not the ones that meant trouble. The small ones. The ones that meant the last hit was wearing off and the next one was still a decision she hadn't made yet. She told herself she was in control. She always told herself that. It was the one lie she never got tired of believing.

She was thirty-one years old. She looked forty.

The mirror in the bathroom confirmed it every morning, and she'd stopped looking three weeks ago. The hollows under her cheekbones. The skin pulled too tight across her jaw. The eyes that used to be her best feature — dark brown like her mother's, wide and warm — now flat and dry and set too deep in a face that had forgotten how to rest.

Methamphetamine had done what a lifetime of bad decisions had started. It was finishing the job with the patience of a disease that knew it had time.

She picked up her phone. The screen was cracked from when she'd thrown it at the wall last Tuesday. Or was it Wednesday? The days blurred together when you slept in three-hour intervals and ate when you remembered to.

She pulled up her father's number. Stared at it. Put the phone down. Picked it up again.

The memories came whether she wanted them or not.

Lorraine at sixteen, standing in the wings of the Bakersfield High auditorium, waiting for the cast list for the spring musical. She'd auditioned for the lead. She'd practiced for weeks, singing in her bedroom with the door closed, imagining the standing ovation, imagining her father in the front row. The list went up. Her name wasn't on it. Not for the lead. Not for the chorus. Not anywhere. She'd walked home in the rain and didn't tell anyone for two days. Cyril found out from another parent. He drove to the school and spoke to the drama teacher. He came home and sat next to her on the bed and said, "Their loss, little star. You're my leading lady." She cried into his shoulder. He held her like she was made of glass.

Lorraine at twenty-one, fired from the insurance office where she'd worked for four months. Her boss said she was late too often, careless with files, distracted. Lorraine said her boss was a tyrant. Cyril wrote a check for $800 to cover her rent and said, "You'll find something better."

Lorraine at twenty-five, handcuffs behind her back, a county deputy guiding her into a patrol car outside a house in Oildale she should never have been inside. Possession. Misdemeanor. Cyril paid the bail. He didn't yell. He didn't lecture. He drove her home and made her a sandwich and sat across from her at the kitchen table with a look on his face that was worse than yelling — the look of a man who was watching something he loved disappear and couldn't figure out how to stop it.

Every failure had a check attached to it. Every fall had a net made of Cyril's money and Cyril's love and Cyril's inability to let his youngest daughter hit the ground. Lorraine knew it. She hated herself for needing it. She hated herself more for never being able to say thank you without it sounding like she was setting up the next ask.

She dialed the number.

Cyril answered on the third ring. "Hey, sweetheart," Cyril said. His voice was warm. It was always warm when he answered her calls, even when she knew he'd been dreading them.

"Daddy, I need help," Lorraine said. The word came out before she could stop it. Daddy. She was thirty-one years old and she still called him Daddy when she needed something. She knew what it did to him. She knew it was a weapon. She used it anyway.

"What kind of help?" Cyril asked.

"Money," Lorraine said. "Twenty thousand dollars. I know it's a lot. I know you're going to say it's too much. But I'm in trouble, Daddy. Real trouble. There are people who — I owe them, and they're not the kind of people who wait."

The silence on the other end stretched long enough for Lorraine to hear the hum of the refrigerator in Cyril's kitchen. She could picture him standing there, one hand on the counter, the other holding the phone, his forehead creased the way it creased when he was trying to find a way to say yes.

But he didn't say yes.

"I can't keep doing this, sweetheart," Cyril said. His voice was gentle. Gentle in a way that felt like a door closing. "I love you. You know I love you more than anything. But twenty thousand dollars — I can't do it. Not this time."

"You can't or you won't?" Lorraine asked. The edge was already in her voice. She could feel it rising like heat from pavement.

"Both," Cyril said. "I've given you everything I can give, Lorraine. For fifteen years. And it hasn't helped. I don't know what this money is really for, and I don't think you'd tell me if I asked."

"I told you what it's for," Lorraine said. "I owe people."

"What people?" Cyril asked.

"People," Lorraine said. "You don't know them. You don't want to know them."

"That's what scares me," Cyril said.

"So you're just going to let them hurt me?" Lorraine said. "Is that what a father does? Just walks away?"

"I'm not walking away," Cyril said. "I'm standing right here. But I can't keep writing checks to a problem I don't understand. Come home. Talk to me. Let me help you the right way."

"The right way," Lorraine said. She laughed, and the sound was ugly even to her own ears. "The right way is rehab. That's what Archie told you, isn't it? That's what the golden son thinks. Ship Lorraine off to some clinic and pretend she doesn't exist."

"Archie loves you," Cyril said.

"Archie loves himself," Lorraine said. "Archie loves his money and his fancy apartment and his perfect little life. He doesn't love me. He tolerates me because I'm your daughter and he doesn't want to disappoint you."

"That's not fair," Cyril said.

"None of this is fair," Lorraine said.

She said more after that. Ugly things. Things about Archie and Knox and the fact that Cyril had always loved them more, that she was the afterthought, the accident, the child who never measured up. She knew none of it was true. She knew Cyril loved her more than he loved the boys — had always loved her more, with a fierce and irrational devotion that defied every reason he had to pull away. She knew it and she used it against him because the rage was the only thing louder than the shame.

Cyril didn't argue. He let her finish. Then he said, "I love you, Lorraine. When you're ready, I'm here."

Lorraine hung up without saying goodbye.

She sat on the mattress, breathing hard, the phone still in her hand. The shaking was worse now. Not from withdrawal. From something deeper. From the sound of her father's voice saying no for the first time in her life, and the terrifying possibility that he meant it.

She needed to move. Sitting still would kill her. Sitting still meant thinking, and thinking meant facing the arithmetic of her life — the jobs lost, the chances wasted, the people who'd given up on her one by one until only Cyril was left. And now Cyril had said no.

She grabbed her keys off the counter, stepped over a pile of laundry she hadn't washed in two weeks, and walked out the door.

The drive to Cyril's house took eleven minutes. She knew the route with her eyes closed — south on Chester, west on Brundage, north on H Street, and into the quiet neighborhood off Columbus where her father had lived for thirty years. The house where she'd grown up. The house where Helen had died. The house where the sprinklers still ran on a timer because Cyril couldn't bring himself to change the schedule his wife had set.

Lorraine parked across the street, two houses down, under a jacaranda tree that blocked the streetlight. She turned off the engine and sat in the dark.

The kitchen light was on. Through the window, she could see Cyril standing at the sink. Washing dishes. He always washed dishes by hand, even though Helen had bought a dishwasher twenty years ago. He said he liked the routine. The hot water. The feeling of making something clean.

Lorraine watched him.

He looked old. When had he gotten old? In her memory, Cyril was the man who'd carried her on his shoulders at the Kern County Fair, the man who'd taught her to ride a bike in this same driveway, the man who'd held her hand on the first day of kindergarten and told her she was the bravest girl in the world. That man was gone. The man at the sink was sixty-five, stooped slightly at the shoulders, moving with the careful economy of someone whose body had started keeping score.

She sat there for twenty minutes. Her hands gripped the steering wheel until her knuckles went white. The rage hadn't left. It had just gone quiet, settling into something colder and more patient.

She thought about walking in. She knew the key was under the mat by the back door. She knew the alarm code — 0712, Helen's birthday. She could walk right in and scream at him. She could tell him what the twenty thousand dollars was really for. She could tell him about Dante. She could tell him everything and watch his face collapse.

She thought about it.

She didn't move.

Cyril finished the dishes. Dried his hands on the towel that hung from the oven handle. Turned off the kitchen light. The house went dark except for the porch light, which he always left on. Always. In case one of his children came home late.

Lorraine stared at that porch light until her eyes burned. Then she started the engine and drove away.

Dante Voss lived in a house on the east side of Bakersfield that looked respectable from the outside — beige stucco, chain-link fence, a pickup truck in the driveway. The respectability ended at the front door. Inside, the living room served as an office for the kind of business that didn't keep records, and the garage held things that Lorraine had learned not to ask about.

She didn't knock. She never knocked. Dante had told her not to.

He was in the living room, sitting in a leather recliner, watching a boxing match on a flat-screen television that took up half the wall. He was thirty-eight, built like a man who'd spent his twenties fighting and his thirties making other people fight for him. Dark hair pulled back in a knot. A tattoo on his neck — a skull with wings, the Reapers MC insignia. His eyes were the color of motor oil, and they tracked Lorraine the way they tracked everything: with the steady calculation of a man who measured people by their usefulness.

"He said no," Lorraine said. She was standing in the doorway, arms crossed, voice shaking.

"Sit down," Dante said. He didn't look away from the television.

"He said no, Dante," Lorraine said again. "Twenty thousand dollars and he said no. First time he's ever said no to me. Something's different. Archie's been in his ear. That self-righteous —"

"Sit down," Dante said again. This time he looked at her.

Lorraine sat.

"Tell me about the money," Dante said. "Not the twenty grand. The real money. Your old man's money."

"What about it?" Lorraine asked.

"How much has he got?" Dante asked. "Total. The house. The pension. The savings. All of it."

Lorraine shouldn't have answered. She knew she shouldn't have answered. But the rage was still there, sitting in her chest like a coal, and Dante was the only person in her life who didn't look at her with pity or disappointment. Dante looked at her like she was useful. In the absence of love, usefulness felt like enough.

"The house is paid off," Lorraine said. "It's worth maybe three hundred thousand. He's got a pension from the county — forty years, so it's full. And savings. He's always been a saver. Archie told me once it was close to two hundred thousand."

"Half a million," Dante said. He said it the way someone else might say a woman's name. Soft. Interested.

"Close to it," Lorraine said.

"And the house," Dante said. "The alarm. Does he set it?"

"The code is 0712," Lorraine said. "He never changes it. It's my mother's birthday."

"Keys?" Dante asked.

"There's one under the mat by the back door," Lorraine said. "He's kept it there for twenty years. Everyone in the family knows."

"When's he home alone?" Dante asked.

"Every night," Lorraine said. "He lives alone. Has since my mother died."

Dante nodded. He turned back to the boxing match. A fighter was on the canvas, trying to get up. The referee was counting.

Lorraine didn't register what she'd done. Or she did and the meth and the rage and the fifteen years of shame had built a wall between the knowing and the feeling. She'd given Dante the alarm code, the key, the schedule, and the money. She'd drawn him a map to her father's front door.

Later — days later, weeks later — she would try to tell herself she didn't know what Dante would do with that information. She would try to believe it. She would almost succeed.

Dante reached into the side table drawer and pulled out a small plastic bag. Crystal. He tossed it to Lorraine. "Relax," Dante said. "I'll take care of it."

Lorraine caught the bag. She looked at it for a long moment. Then she went to the bathroom, closed the door, and did what she always did when the world was too loud and her own voice was the worst sound in it.

She got high. And the thinking stopped. And the porch light faded from her memory like a dream she'd already forgotten.

CHAPTER 3: "The Peacemaker"

Knox Butterworth stood at the front of his classroom at Bakersfield High School and watched thirty-two tenth graders pretend to care about the Missouri Compromise.

"So here's the question," Knox said. He leaned against the edge of his desk, arms crossed, the way he always did when he was trying to make history feel like a conversation instead of a lecture. "You've got a country that says all men are created equal, and you've got that same country drawing a line across a map and saying slavery is fine on one side and not on the other. How do you hold those two ideas in your head at the same time?"

Silence. The kind of silence that meant half the class was thinking and the other half was hoping someone else would answer.

A hand went up in the third row. Maria Espinoza, one of his best students. "You don't," Maria said. "That's why it fell apart. You can't compromise on something that's either right or wrong."

"Good," Knox said. "But they tried. For thirty years, they tried. And the people who brokered that compromise thought they were saving the country. They thought holding it together — even with a lie at the center — was better than letting it break." Knox paused. "Were they right?"

Another hand. Jaylen Carter, back row, football jersey, the kid who never talked unless the question hit him in the chest. "Depends on who's paying the price for the compromise," Jaylen said. "Easy to hold things together when you're not the one being held down."

Knox felt the sentence land in a place that had nothing to do with 1820. He thought about his father. He thought about Lorraine. He thought about the compromise he'd been making for two years — holding the family together by keeping his mouth shut about things he'd seen and people he'd noticed and a motorcycle parked outside his sister's apartment that had no business being there.

"That's exactly right, Jaylen," Knox said. "Write that down. That's your thesis for the essay."

The bell rang. Thirty-two backpacks scraped against thirty-two chairs. Knox stood at the door the way he always did, nodding at students as they filed out, calling a few by name. He liked this part. The small recognitions. The way a kid's face changed when a teacher remembered their name and used it like it mattered.

When the room was empty, Knox sat down at his desk and stared at the stack of ungraded quizzes he'd been avoiding for three days. He picked up a red pen. Put it down. Picked up his phone instead.

No missed calls from Cyril. No texts from Lorraine. The silence from both of them was louder than any conversation.

Knox was twenty-eight years old, the youngest of the three Butterworth children, and he had spent his entire life in the space between Archie and Lorraine — the buffer zone, the middle ground, the kid who learned early that his job was to keep the peace. Archie was the achiever. Lorraine was the crisis. Knox was the one who showed up for Sunday dinners and asked the right questions and never made anyone choose sides.

It was exhausting. It was also the only thing he knew how to do.

Delaney Park was sitting on the couch in their apartment when Knox got home, her laptop open and a stack of construction paper on the coffee table. She was cutting out paper leaves — orange, red, yellow — for a fall bulletin board at the kindergarten where she taught. She looked up when he came in, and her face did the thing it always did — a quick scan, the kind that looked casual but wasn't.

"How was your day?" Delaney asked.

"Fine," Knox said. He dropped his bag by the door, kissed the top of her head, and went to the kitchen for a glass of water. "Jaylen Carter said something brilliant in fourth period. Almost made me forget that Tyler Regan threw a paper airplane at the back of my head during second."

"Did you catch it?" Delaney asked.

"Caught it midair," Knox said. "Didn't break eye contact with the class. Best teaching moment of the week."

Delaney laughed. It was the laugh that had made him fall in love with her three years ago — bright and sudden, like a window opening in a quiet room. Delaney was thirty, Korean-American, born in Fresno, raised in a family that valued education the way some families valued religion. She was kind in a way that wasn't soft — the kind of kindness that came with backbone and clear eyes and the willingness to say hard things when they needed saying.

They'd been engaged for four months. The wedding was set for March. Small ceremony, outdoor venue, Delaney's mother handling the flowers with a precision that bordered on military planning. Knox was happy about it. He was happy about most things in his life — the teaching, the apartment, the woman cutting paper leaves on the couch. The happiness sat on top of something else, something heavier, and most days he could pretend the weight wasn't there.

"Your dad called," Delaney said. "About an hour ago. I told him you were still at school."

"What did he want?" Knox asked.

"Just to talk," Delaney said. "He sounded tired. He asked about the wedding. He wanted to know if we'd picked a cake yet."

"We haven't picked a cake yet," Knox said.

"I know," Delaney said. "I told him we were leaning toward lemon."

"Are we leaning toward lemon?" Knox asked.

"We are now," Delaney said. She smiled, but the smile faded as she watched him. "Knox, he sounded off. Not sad, exactly. Just — heavy. Like he was carrying something."

Knox set the glass of water on the counter. "I'll go see him tonight," Knox said. "I haven't been over there in a week. He's got the retirement party coming up. Probably just stressed about that."

"Probably," Delaney said. She didn't push. She was good at not pushing. But she was also good at remembering, and Knox knew she'd come back to this conversation later, when the paper leaves were finished and the apartment was quiet and there was nowhere to hide from the questions she was too smart not to ask.

Cyril's house looked the same as it always had — a single-story ranch on a tree-lined street, white paint, brown trim, a lawn that was always mowed and hedges that were always trimmed. Cyril believed in maintenance. He'd spent forty years maintaining buildings for Kern County, and he maintained his own home with the same steady, unglamorous discipline. The porch light was on. The driveway was clean. The retirement invitations sat in a neat stack on the kitchen counter, stamped and ready.

Knox let himself in through the front door. "Dad?" Knox called out.

"Kitchen," Cyril called back.

Knox found his father at the kitchen table, a plate of leftover meatloaf and mashed potatoes in front of him, a glass of iced tea, and the Bakersfield Californian folded open to the crossword puzzle. Cyril looked up and smiled, and the smile reached his eyes but not all the way — it stopped somewhere around the bridge of his nose, like it had run out of energy.

"Hey, son," Cyril said. "Sit down. You hungry? There's meatloaf."

"I'm good," Knox said. He pulled out a chair and sat across from his father. "Delaney said you called."

"I did," Cyril said. "Just wanted to hear a friendly voice. How's school?"

"Good," Knox said. "We're on the Missouri Compromise this week. A kid in my class said something that might be smarter than anything I learned in grad school."

"That's teaching," Cyril said. "You plant seeds. Sometimes they surprise you." Cyril took a bite of meatloaf, chewed slowly, set his fork down. "Your brother called last night. We had a good talk."

"How's Archie?" Knox asked.

"Archie's Archie," Cyril said. "Making money. Dating that lawyer girl. He sounds happy. I think she's good for him."

"Bella," Knox said. "He talks about her like she's a case study he hasn't figured out yet."

Cyril laughed. "That's your brother," Cyril said. "Can't just feel something. Has to analyze it first. Gets that from me, I think. Your mother would have just grabbed his face and said, 'Stop thinking and kiss her.'"

They both laughed. Helen Butterworth had been dead for eight years, and she was still the funniest person in the room.

The laughter faded. Cyril picked up his fork and put it down again. He looked at the crossword puzzle like the answer he needed wasn't in the grid.

"Your sister called me today," Cyril said.

Knox felt the weight shift. The heavy thing beneath the happiness pressed upward, like water rising.

"What did she want?" Knox asked.

"Money," Cyril said. "A lot of it. I said no."

"You said no?" Knox asked.

"I said no," Cyril said. "First time. Twenty thousand dollars, Knox. I don't even — I don't know where a number like that comes from. Not rent. Not car trouble. Not any of the stories she's told me before."

Knox knew where the number came from. He knew exactly where it came from. The knowledge sat in his chest like a stone, and he'd been carrying it for two years.

He'd first seen Dante Voss eight months ago. He'd driven past Lorraine's apartment on a Saturday afternoon — not checking on her, just passing through, or that's what he told himself — and there it was. A Harley-Davidson Road King, black and chrome, parked outside her building. The patches on the saddlebags were Reapers MC. Knox was a history teacher, not a cop, but you didn't grow up in Bakersfield without knowing what those patches meant. Meth. Violence. The kind of people who solved problems with baseball bats and shallow graves.

He'd seen the motorcycle three more times after that. Once at her apartment. Once at a gas station on Union

Avenue, Lorraine climbing off the back. Once in the parking lot of a bar on Edison Highway, at 2 AM, when Knox was driving home from a friend's house and took the wrong turn. Each time, he told himself it wasn't what it looked like. Each time, he knew it was exactly what it looked like.

He'd almost told Cyril. Twice. The first time was at Thanksgiving, when Lorraine didn't show up and Cyril spent the evening pretending he wasn't watching the door. The second time was at Christmas, when Lorraine showed up two hours late, thin and jittery, and excused herself to the bathroom three times in forty-five minutes. Both times, Knox had looked at his father's face — the hope in it, the fragile architecture of denial — and couldn't bring himself to knock it down.

He told himself he was protecting Cyril. He told himself knowing about Dante would only add to the pain. He told himself it was Lorraine's life, Lorraine's choice, and that intervening would only push her further away.

But sitting across from Cyril now, watching his father's hands wrapped around a glass of iced tea, the hands of a man who'd spent forty years fixing things and couldn't fix this — Knox knew the truth. He wasn't protecting Cyril. He was protecting himself. From the conversation. From the fallout. From the look on his father's face when the last illusion about his daughter finally broke.

"Maybe she'll come around," Knox said. The words tasted like cowardice.

"Maybe," Cyril said. "I keep the porch light on. You know that. Every night. In case she comes home."

"I know, Dad," Knox said.

"Your mother used to say I loved Lorraine too much," Cyril said. "She didn't mean it as a criticism. She meant it as a warning. She said you can love someone so hard you break them, because they never learn to stand on their own. Helen was smart that way. Smarter than me."

"Mom was smart about everything," Knox said.

"She was," Cyril said. He looked at Knox with an expression that was half-smile, half-plea. "You and Delaney — you're building something good. The teaching. The wedding. A real life. I'm proud of you, Knox. I don't say it enough."

"You say it enough, Dad," Knox said.

"Not enough," Cyril said. "Not nearly enough."

Knox stayed for another hour. They finished the crossword together — Cyril got 14-across and Knox got 23-down, and they both missed 31-across, which turned out to be "palindrome." They talked about the retirement party. Cyril wanted barbecue. Knox suggested a caterer. Cyril said caterers were for people who didn't know how to cook. Knox didn't argue.

At the door, Cyril hugged him. A real hug, the kind that lasted three seconds longer than normal. "Take care of Delaney," Cyril said. "She's a keeper."

"I know," Knox said. "Goodnight, Dad."

"Goodnight, son," Cyril said.

Knox drove home the long way. He didn't mean to. He just missed the turn on Brundage and kept going south, and then he was on Chester Avenue, and then he was passing Lorraine's apartment building without having decided to pass Lorraine's apartment building.

The Harley was there.

Parked in the same spot it always occupied — right side of the building, near the stairwell, chrome catching the streetlight. The Reapers patches on the saddlebags were visible even from the road. The apartment window on the second floor was dark, but a thin line of light leaked from under the blinds.

Knox slowed the car. He didn't stop. He looked at the motorcycle for three seconds — long enough to confirm what he already knew, short enough to pretend he hadn't — and kept driving.

His phone sat on the passenger seat. He could call Archie. He could call the police. He could turn around and bang on Lorraine's door and tell Dante Voss to stay away from his sister.

He didn't do any of those things.

He drove home. He parked in his usual spot. He sat in the car for five minutes, listening to the engine tick as it cooled, feeling the weight of everything he wasn't saying press down on his chest until it hurt to breathe.

Delaney was asleep when he came in. The paper leaves were finished, spread across the coffee table in neat rows of orange and red and yellow. Knox stood in the dark living room and looked at them. Beautiful, fragile things, cut by hand with the kind of care that believed the world was still worth decorating.

He got into bed. Delaney stirred but didn't wake. He stared at the ceiling and thought about his father sitting alone in that house with the porch light on, and his sister in a dark apartment with a man who wore a skull on his jacket, and the twenty thousand dollars that wasn't for rent or car trouble or any of the old lies.

Knox Butterworth, the peacemaker, the middle ground, the boy who never made anyone choose sides, closed his eyes and prayed for sleep. It didn't come.

CHAPTER 4: "Tuesday Night"

The market had been flat all day, and Archie Butterworth didn't trust it.

Flat markets were liars. They looked calm on the surface — the S&P drifting sideways, volume low, the VIX sitting in the basement like a dog that hadn't barked in a week. But underneath, the money was moving. It always moved. You just had to know where to look.

Archie stood at his desk at Kessler-Braun Capital and watched the screens cycle through their afternoon rhythm. No trades worth making. No gaps worth exploiting. Danny Faulk had left early for a dentist appointment, which meant the desk was quieter than usual, which meant Archie had nothing to do but think.

He didn't like having nothing to do. Idle time was dangerous time. It was the space where the things you'd been ignoring found room to breathe.

He'd been thinking about his father's phone call for two weeks. Not constantly — he wasn't the type to obsess. But in the quiet moments, between trades and meetings and the daily machinery of a life built on discipline, the conversation would surface like something caught in a current. Twenty thousand dollars. Cyril saying no. The pause in his father's voice that said more than the words did.

Archie had called Cyril twice since then. Both conversations had been normal — retirement party plans, the weather in Bakersfield, a plumbing issue in the guest bathroom that Cyril was determined to fix himself despite being sixty-five years old and having no business under a sink. Neither conversation mentioned Lorraine. The silence around her name was so complete it had its own weight.

He'd thought about calling Lorraine. He hadn't.

At 4:15, the closing bell rang. Archie logged out, grabbed his jacket, and took the elevator down to the lobby. The October air — no, November now, the calendar had turned without him noticing — was sharp and gray, the fog already rolling in from the bay. He walked three blocks to his building, nodded at the doorman, and took the elevator to the thirty-second floor.

The condo was quiet. He changed into sweats, poured a glass of water instead of bourbon — he'd been cutting back, a decision he'd made without examining too closely — and sat down at his home office desk. He had a stack of research reports to review, a quarterly performance summary to draft, and an email from his firm's compliance department about a new trading regulation that he needed to read and probably wouldn't.

He worked for two hours. Ordered takeout — pad see ew from a place on Folsom that delivered in twenty minutes.

Ate at his desk. Checked his phone. No messages from Bella. She was in court all week on the Guatemala deportation case, working sixteen-hour days, and they'd agreed to give each other space until Friday. He missed her. He didn't say so. He wasn't good at saying so.

At 9:30, he closed his laptop and moved to the couch. Turned on the television. Flipped through channels without landing on anything. Turned it off. Picked up a book — a biography of Jim Simons that Danny had recommended — and read three pages without absorbing a word.

The apartment was too quiet. The city hummed outside the windows, thirty-two stories of distance turning San Francisco into a muffled heartbeat, and Archie sat in the middle of it feeling something he couldn't name. Not anxiety. Not fear. Something lower and slower, like the pressure change before a storm that hasn't arrived yet.

His phone rang at 11:47 PM.

The screen said KNOX.

Knox never called this late. Knox was a teacher. Knox went to bed at 10:30 on school nights because he believed in routine and because Delaney enforced it with the gentle authority of a woman who'd spent her career managing five-year-olds. A call from Knox at 11:47 PM meant something was wrong.

Archie picked up on the first ring. "Knox?" Archie said.

"Archie." Knox's voice was wrong. Flat and hollow, like someone had scooped out the center of it and left only the edges. "Archie, you need to come home."

"What happened?" Archie asked. He was already standing. His body had started moving before his brain caught up — a Marine reflex, the autonomic response to a voice that carried the frequency of bad news.

"It's Dad," Knox said.

"Is he hurt?" Archie asked. "Is he in the hospital?"

"He's dead, Archie," Knox said. "Someone killed him."

The words entered Archie's ears and traveled to a place in his brain that refused to process them. He stood in his living room, barefoot on the hardwood floor, the phone pressed to his ear, and the city lights blurred through the window like a photograph taken by a shaking hand.

"What did you say?" Archie asked.

"Dad is dead," Knox said. His voice cracked on the last word, a fracture that spread through the sentence like a line through glass. "I came over to drop off some retirement party stuff. The front door was unlocked. I found him in the living room. There's blood, Archie. There's — I called 911. The police are here. You need to come home."

"I'm coming," Archie said. "I'm coming right now. Don't touch anything. Don't move anything. Stay on the porch and don't talk to anyone until I get there."

"Archie —" Knox started.

"I'm coming," Archie said again, and hung up.

He stood still for three seconds. Three seconds was all he allowed himself. In those three seconds, the world rearranged itself around a single fact — Cyril Butterworth was dead — and everything that had mattered five minutes ago stopped mattering entirely. The research reports. The compliance email. The quarterly summary. The pad see ew container on the desk. All of it became scenery from a life that had just ended.

On the fourth second, he moved.

He pulled on jeans, a sweatshirt, and running shoes. Grabbed his wallet, his keys, and his phone charger. He booked a flight on his phone while he rode the elevator down — the last flight to Bakersfield was long gone, but there was a red-eye to LAX at 1:15 AM. He'd rent a car and drive the two hours north. He'd be there by sunrise.

In the Uber to SFO, he called Bella. She answered on the fifth ring, her voice thick with sleep.

"Archie?" Bella said. "It's midnight. What's wrong?"

"My father's been murdered," Archie said. He said it the way he'd say a market number — flat, factual, stripped of everything that would make it real. If he let it be real, he'd stop functioning. And he couldn't stop functioning. Not now.

"Oh my God," Bella said. "Archie, oh my God. What happened?"

"I don't know yet," Archie said. "Knox found him. I'm on my way to the airport. Red-eye to LA, then driving to Bakersfield."

"I'm coming with you," Bella said.

"You're in court all week," Archie said.

"I'm coming with you," Bella said again, and the way she said it left no room for discussion. "I'll get a flight in the morning. I'll be there by noon. Where should I go?"

"Cyril's house," Archie said. "1847 Columbus Street. I'll text you the address."

"Archie," Bella said. "I'm so sorry."

"I know," Archie said. "I have to go."

He hung up. The Uber driver glanced in the rearview mirror but didn't say anything. Archie stared out the window at the dark freeway and felt nothing. Absolutely nothing. The grief was there — he could sense it the way you sense a wave building offshore, a wall of water still too far away to hear but close enough to feel in the change of pressure. It would hit him eventually. But right now, his body was running on the old programming, the Marine wiring that said grief is a luxury and the mission comes first.

The mission was getting to Bakersfield. The mission was finding out who killed his father. Everything else could wait.

He landed at LAX at 2:40 AM. The rental car counter was a blur of fluorescent light and paperwork. He was on the I-5 by 3:15, driving north through the dark San Joaquin Valley, past the oil fields and the feed lots and the flat agricultural land that stretched to the horizon like a table set for no one. The Grapevine rose and fell beneath his tires. Bakersfield appeared in the distance at 5:20 AM — a scatter of lights in the valley floor, ordinary and indifferent.

He pulled onto Columbus Street at 5:47 AM. The neighborhood was quiet in the pre-dawn gray, the kind of quiet that belonged to people who hadn't been woken by the worst phone call of their lives. Cyril's house sat in the middle of the block, and Archie saw it before he was ready.

Police tape. Yellow, bright, stretched across the front porch and the driveway. Two cruisers parked at the curb, their lights off but their presence loud. A crime scene van in the driveway. Neighbors on porches in bathrobes and bare feet, standing in clusters of two and three, watching the

house the way people watch a building that's on fire —
unable to look away, unable to help.

Knox was sitting on the porch steps, outside the tape.
He was wearing the same clothes he'd been wearing when he
found Cyril — khakis and a blue button-down, the teacher
uniform. There was blood on his right sleeve. He was staring
at the lawn with the fixed, empty expression of a man who
had seen something his brain was still trying to reject.

Archie parked. Got out. Walked across the lawn. Knox
looked up, and his face collapsed.

"Archie," Knox said. He stood, and his legs nearly
buckled. Archie caught him. They held each other on the
front lawn of their father's house, under the yellow tape, in
the gray light, and neither of them spoke. There was nothing
to say that the holding didn't already cover.

After a moment, Archie stepped back. He held Knox at
arm's length and looked at him. "Tell me," Archie said.

"I came by around ten," Knox said. His voice was
steadier now, held together by the structure of Archie's
presence. "I had the guest list for the retirement party. The
front door was unlocked. The lights were off. I called out and
he didn't answer. I went into the living room and —" Knox
stopped. He swallowed hard. "He was on the floor. By the
fireplace. Blunt force trauma. That's what the paramedics
said. Someone hit him. Multiple times."

"No forced entry?" Archie asked.

"No," Knox said. "The door was unlocked. The alarm was off. The back door was locked from inside. Whoever it was, Dad let them in. Or they had a key."

Archie looked at the house. The porch light was still on. Cyril had left it on. He always left it on.

"Where's Lorraine?" Archie asked.

"I've been calling her," Knox said. "It goes straight to voicemail."

A woman stepped out the front door, ducking under the police tape. She was mid-forties, athletic build, dark hair pulled back, wearing a blazer over a white blouse. A badge hung from a lanyard around her neck. Her face was the kind of face that had learned to look neutral in rooms full of grief — not cold, but controlled.

"Mr. Butterworth?" the woman said, looking at Archie.

"Yes," Archie said.

"I'm Detective Rina Salcedo," Salcedo said. "Bakersfield PD, Homicide. I'm the lead on your father's case. I'm sorry for your loss."

"Thank you," Archie said. "What do you know?"

"It's early," Salcedo said. "What I can tell you is that your father suffered blunt force trauma. The medical examiner will determine the exact cause and time of death, but based on the scene, we're looking at sometime between 9 and 11 PM last night. No forced entry. No sign of a struggle. Your father appears to have been in the living room, possibly seated, when he was attacked."

"Someone he knew," Archie said.

"Or someone he wasn't afraid of," Salcedo said. She watched him as she said it. Archie felt the weight of her observation — she was measuring him. His calm. His composure. The way he asked questions instead of breaking down. She was filing it away.

"Where were you last night, Mr. Butterworth?" Salcedo asked. "I have to ask."

"San Francisco," Archie said. "Home alone. I took a red-eye to LAX at 1:15 AM and drove here."

"We'll need your boarding pass and the rental agreement," Salcedo said. "Standard procedure."

"You'll have them today," Archie said.

Salcedo nodded. She looked at Knox. "Mr. Butterworth, you mentioned a sister. Lorraine?"

"She's not answering her phone," Knox said.

"Do you have an address for her?" Salcedo asked.

Knox gave her the address on South Chester Avenue. Salcedo wrote it down. "We'll send someone to check on her," Salcedo said. "In the meantime, I'd like both of you to come to the station later today for formal statements. Take some time. Get some rest if you can."

Salcedo went back inside. Archie watched her go. He turned to Knox.

"She thinks I did it," Archie said.

"She's doing her job," Knox said.

"She thinks I did it," Archie said again. "I can see it. I'm too calm. I flew in from out of state in the middle of the night. I'm asking questions instead of crying. She's already building a profile."

"Archie —" Knox started.

"We need to find Lorraine," Archie said. "We need to find out where she was last night. And we need to find out who Dad let into this house."

Knox didn't answer right away. He looked at the house. He looked at the porch light. He looked at the blood on his own sleeve.

"Come inside," Knox said. "Not the living room. The kitchen. I'll make coffee. Dad would want us to have coffee."

They walked around to the back of the house. The kitchen door was unlocked — the police had cleared this part of the home. They stepped inside, and the kitchen was exactly as it always was. The retirement invitations on the counter, stamped, addressed, never mailed. The crossword puzzle from the Bakersfield Californian, half-finished, Cyril's pen sitting on top of it. The iced tea glass, washed and drying in the rack.

Knox made coffee. Cyril's coffee, from the can in the pantry, the same brand he'd been buying for thirty years. The machine gurgled and dripped, and the kitchen filled with a smell that belonged to every morning of Archie's childhood.

Archie stood at the counter and looked at the retirement invitations. Forty of them. Forty years of service. Two weeks from a party he'd been planning for months.

He picked one up. Turned it over. Read the back. Cyril had handwritten a note on each one: "Hope to see you there." The same message, forty times, in the careful, slanted handwriting of a man who believed showing up mattered.

Archie put the invitation down. He pressed both hands flat on the counter and leaned forward, his head bowed, his eyes closed. The wave was coming. He could feel it building, the grief he'd been outrunning since Knox's phone call, and he couldn't let it hit. Not yet. Not here. There was too much to do.

He stood up straight. He took a breath. He accepted

the coffee Knox held out to him and drank it black, the way Cyril had always drunk it.

"We'll find who did this," Archie said.

"I know," Knox said.

"And we'll find Lorraine," Archie said.

Knox looked at his brother over the rim of his coffee mug. His eyes were red. His hands were shaking. The blood on his sleeve had dried to a dark brown stain that he couldn't stop looking at.

"Yeah," Knox said. "We'll find Lorraine."

The kitchen was quiet. The coffee was bitter. The porch light was still on. And somewhere in Bakersfield, their sister wasn't answering her phone.

CHAPTER 5: "Suspects"

Bella had called at 8:00 AM. Her flight landed at 11:30. She rented a car and drove straight to Columbus Street. She arrived at the house in a gray blazer and flat shoes, her hair pulled back, her face set in the expression Archie had seen her wear in court — composed, alert, ready. She hugged Archie on the front porch. He held on longer than he meant to.

"I'm here," Bella said. "Whatever you need."

"Right now I need you to stay at the house," Archie said. "Knox and I have to go to the station. Formal statements."

"Do you have a lawyer?" Bella asked.

"I don't need a lawyer," Archie said. "I didn't do anything."

"That's not what I asked," Bella said. Her voice was steady but firm, the immigration attorney cutting through the grieving boyfriend with surgical precision. "Do you have a lawyer?"

"No," Archie said.

"Get one," Bella said. "Before you walk into that station. Promise me."

Archie looked at her. She looked back. She wasn't going to blink.

"I'll think about it," Archie said.

"Think fast," Bella said.

He thought about it in the car on the way to the station. He thought about it in the parking lot. He decided Bella was right, but not yet. Walking into a police station with a lawyer the day after your father's murder sent a message, and the message was guilt. He'd give his statement first. Clean, honest, nothing to hide. If things changed, he'd lawyer up.

It was the first miscalculation Archibald Butterworth had made in a long time.

The Bakersfield Police Department sat on Truxtun Avenue like a building that had been designed to discourage conversation.

Beige walls, fluorescent lighting, the kind of industrial carpet that absorbed sound and hope in equal measure. Archie walked through the front entrance at 2:00 PM with Knox beside him and the taste of Cyril's coffee still on his tongue.

They hadn't slept. After the kitchen, after the coffee, they'd sat in Cyril's backyard on the patio chairs their father had bought at a Home Depot clearance sale twelve years ago and watched the sun come up over the valley. Neither of them spoke much. The silence wasn't uncomfortable — it was the silence of two men who didn't have words big enough for what had happened and were smart enough not to try.

Detective Salcedo met them in the lobby and led them down a hallway to a room that wasn't an interrogation room but felt like one. A table, four chairs, a recorder, and a window that looked out on the parking lot. The fluorescent lights buzzed overhead with the faint, persistent hum of a government building that had been underfunded since the last century.

"We'll do this one at a time," Salcedo said. "Mr. Butterworth —" She looked at Archie. "You first. Knox, there's coffee in the break room. Officer Daniels will show you."

Knox looked at Archie. Archie nodded. Knox left.

Salcedo sat across from Archie and opened a notebook. A second detective — a heavyset man in his fifties with a gray mustache and a tie that had seen better decades — sat in the corner. Salcedo didn't introduce him. He didn't speak. He watched.

"For the record, this is a voluntary statement," Salcedo said. "You're not under arrest. You're not a suspect. You're free to leave at any time. Do you understand?"

"I understand," Archie said.

"Tell me about your father," Salcedo said.

Archie told her. Cyril Butterworth. Sixty-five. Facilities manager for Kern County, forty years. Widower. Helen died of cancer eight years ago. Three children — Archie, Lorraine, Knox. The house on Columbus Street, paid off. A pension. Savings. A man who showed up every day, did his job, and came home to a house that got quieter every year.

"Your father's will," Salcedo said. "Do you know the terms?"

"I'm the executor," Archie said. "The estate splits three ways. Equal shares. Me, Lorraine, Knox."

"What's the estate worth, roughly?" Salcedo asked.

"The house is probably three hundred thousand," Archie said. "Savings around two hundred. The pension pays out a survivor benefit but it's modest. Call it half a million total, split three ways."

"A hundred and sixty-seven thousand each," Salcedo said. She wrote the number down. "That's a meaningful amount of money."

"Not to me," Archie said. "I make more than that in a good quarter."

"But it might be meaningful to someone else in the family," Salcedo said.

Archie saw the line she was drawing. He chose not to follow it. "You're asking me if someone in my family killed my father for money," Archie said.

"I'm asking you to help me understand the financial picture," Salcedo said. "No forced entry. No sign of a break-in. The alarm was disarmed. Your father let someone in, or someone had access. That narrows the field."

"The key under the back mat," Archie said. "Everyone in the family knew about it. Friends too. Neighbors. Dad wasn't secretive about it. He grew up in a time when people didn't lock their doors."

"The alarm code," Salcedo said. "Who had it?"

"All three of us," Archie said. "Me, Knox, Lorraine. Possibly some of Dad's close friends. He wasn't careful with it."

"What's the code?" Salcedo asked.

"0712," Archie said. "My mother's birthday. July 12th."

Salcedo wrote it down. "Let's talk about last night," Salcedo said. "Walk me through your evening."

Archie walked her through it. Left work at 4:15 PM. Walked home. Changed clothes. Worked at his desk. Ordered takeout — pad see ew from the place on Folsom. Ate at his desk. Read. Watched television briefly. Received Knox's call at 11:47 PM. Booked a flight. Uber to SFO. Red-eye at 1:15 AM. Landed LAX at 2:40. Rental car. Drove to Bakersfield. Arrived at 5:47 AM.

"You were home alone all evening," Salcedo said.

"Yes," Archie said.

"No one came by? No phone calls? No video calls?" Salcedo asked.

"No," Archie said. "Bella — my girlfriend — was working late on a case. We'd agreed to give each other space this week."

"So between approximately 5:00 PM and 11:47 PM, no one can verify your location," Salcedo said.

"My cell phone can," Archie said. "Check the tower data. I was in my condo in San Francisco."

"We will," Salcedo said. She made a note. "Mr. Butterworth, I have to tell you that cell tower data in urban areas can be imprecise. Your condo's tower coverage may overlap with the airport, and SFO to Bakersfield is a short flight."

Archie felt something shift in the room. A temperature change. Salcedo wasn't just asking questions. She was building a geometry — drawing lines between points, measuring distances, testing whether the spaces in between were big enough for a man to fly from San Francisco to Bakersfield, kill his father, and fly back before anyone noticed.

"I didn't kill my father," Archie said.

"I'm not saying you did," Salcedo said. "I'm mapping the timeline. That's my job."

"Your job is to find who did this," Archie said. "Not to map me into a theory."

"Right now, Mr. Butterworth, the two might be the same thing," Salcedo said. "Let me be straight with you. No forced entry. Family had access. The estate is worth half a million dollars. You're the executor. You have the alarm code, you know about the key, and you were home alone with no verifiable alibi during the window when your father was killed. I'm not accusing you. But I'd be lying if I said you weren't on the board."

The detective in the corner shifted in his chair. Salcedo's pen hovered over the notebook.

"I want to help you," Archie said. "Ask me anything. I'll take a polygraph. I'll give you my phone, my laptop, my bank records. Whatever you need."

"We may take you up on that," Salcedo said. "Let's talk about your sister."

"Lorraine," Archie said.

"She hasn't returned our calls," Salcedo said. "Officers went to her apartment this morning. No answer. A neighbor said she left yesterday afternoon and hasn't been back."

"That's not unusual for Lorraine," Archie said.

"Tell me about her," Salcedo said.

Archie paused. This was the door he'd been keeping shut for years — the one he hadn't opened for Bella at dinner, the one he kept closed out of family loyalty and the stubborn belief that Lorraine's problems were Lorraine's problems. But Cyril was dead. The door didn't matter anymore.

"Lorraine has a drug problem," Archie said. "Methamphetamine. It's been going on for years. She's been in and out of trouble — a DUI, a possession charge, jobs she couldn't hold, apartments she couldn't keep. My father supported her financially for fifteen years. He couldn't say no to her."

"Until recently," Salcedo said.

"Until two weeks ago," Archie said. "She asked him for twenty thousand dollars. He told me he said no. First time ever."

"How did she react?" Salcedo asked.

"He said she was angry," Archie said. "Real angry. His words."

Salcedo wrote for a long time. "Anyone else who might have had a conflict with your father?" Salcedo asked. "Neighbors? Coworkers? Anyone who owed him money or had a grudge?"

"My father didn't have enemies," Archie said. "He was a facilities manager. He fixed buildings. He went to church on Sundays. He did crossword puzzles. He was the least complicated man I've ever known."

"Everyone's complicated, Mr. Butterworth," Salcedo said. "Some people are just better at hiding it."

Knox went in next. Archie sat in the break room and drank bad coffee from a Styrofoam cup and stared at a vending machine that offered twelve varieties of disappointment. He thought about what Salcedo had said. On the board. He was on the board. He'd walked into this station as a grieving son and he was walking out as a name on a whiteboard in a homicide detective's office.

Knox came out forty-five minutes later. His face was pale, his jaw tight. They walked to the parking lot in silence.

"How was it?" Archie asked once they were in the car.

"She asked about the will," Knox said. "The money. The alarm code. Where I was last night."

"Where were you?" Archie asked.

"Home with Delaney," Knox said. "We watched a

movie. Delaney fell asleep around nine. I went over to Dad's at ten to drop off the guest list. That's when I found him."

"Delaney can confirm you were home until ten?" Archie asked.

"She was asleep," Knox said. "She knows I was there when the movie started. She doesn't know exactly when I left. I didn't wake her."

"So there's a gap," Archie said.

"There's a gap," Knox said. He stared out the windshield. "Archie, she asked me about you. About your relationship with Dad. About money."

"What did you say?" Archie asked.

"I told her the truth," Knox said. "That you and Dad were close. That you never fought about money. That you didn't need Dad's money."

"Did she believe you?" Archie asked.

"I don't know," Knox said. "She writes everything down and her face doesn't move. It's like talking to a wall that takes notes."

"What about Lorraine?" Archie asked. "Did she ask about Lorraine?"

"Yes," Knox said. "I told her what you told her. The drugs. The money. The twenty thousand."

Knox paused. He was gripping the door handle with his right hand, squeezing and releasing in a rhythm that matched his breathing. Archie watched and waited.

"There's something I didn't tell her," Knox said.

"What?" Archie asked.

Knox shook his head. "Not here," Knox said. "Not yet. I need to think about it."

"Knox —" Archie started.

"Not yet," Knox said. "Please."

Archie looked at his brother for a long moment. Knox's eyes were wet, his jaw clenched, his shoulders pulled up around his ears like a man bracing for impact. Whatever he was carrying, it was heavier than grief.

Archie started the car. "When you're ready," Archie said. "But don't wait too long. We don't have the luxury of time."

They drove back to Columbus Street in silence.

Lorraine surfaced at 4:00 PM. She showed up at the police station on her own, unannounced, wearing jeans and a sweatshirt that was too big for her. Salcedo called Archie to let him know.

"Your sister came in voluntarily," Salcedo said. "She gave a statement. She says she was at a friend's house last night. She doesn't have the friend's full name. She says she didn't know about your father until she saw the news this morning."

"Do you believe her?" Archie asked.

"I'm not in the business of believing," Salcedo said. "I'm in the business of verifying. Right now, her story has holes. But so does everyone's."

"What did she say about me?" Archie asked.

Salcedo paused. The pause was a fraction of a second too long. "She mentioned that you and your father had disagreements about money," Salcedo said. "She said there were tensions in the family about the will."

"That's not true," Archie said. "There were no disagreements about money. There were no tensions about the will. She's lying."

"Noted," Salcedo said. "Mr. Butterworth, I'd recommend you get yourself an attorney. That's not an accusation. It's advice."

The line went dead.

Archie set the phone on the kitchen counter. Bella was standing in the doorway, watching him. She'd been at the house all day — cleaning, organizing, fielding calls from Cyril's friends and neighbors. She'd answered the door eleven times. She'd accepted four casseroles, two pies, and a basket of fruit. She'd handled it all with the quiet competence of a woman who understood grief as a logistical problem that required management.

"That was Salcedo," Archie said. "Lorraine came in. She gave a statement. She told them I had disagreements with Dad about money."

Bella's expression didn't change, but something behind her eyes hardened. "That's a lie," Bella said.

"I know it's a lie," Archie said. "But it's on the record now."

"Call a lawyer," Bella said. "Right now. Tonight."

"I know," Archie said.

"Archie," Bella said. "I am not asking."

He looked at her. She looked back. The immigration attorney, the woman who fought for people who had no one else to fight for them, was standing in his dead father's kitchen and telling him to wake up.

"Okay," Archie said. "I'll make the call."

He picked up the phone and called the only criminal defense attorney he knew — a name Bella had given him that morning, written on a napkin in her precise handwriting. Marcus Hale, Esq. Former public defender, fifteen years in criminal law, known for being smart and impossible to rattle.

The phone rang three times. A voice answered — gruff, tired, the voice of a man who'd been woken from a nap or hadn't slept in a day.

"Marcus Hale," Hale said.

"Mr. Hale, my name is Archibald Butterworth," Archie said. "My father was murdered last night. The police think I did it. I need a lawyer."

"Where are you?" Hale asked.

"Bakersfield," Archie said. "My father's house."

"Don't talk to the police again," Hale said. "Don't talk to anyone. I'll be there in the morning."

"Thank you," Archie said.

"Don't thank me yet," Hale said.

Archie hung up. He looked at Bella. She nodded once, a small motion that carried the weight of everything she hadn't said all day.

He walked to the window. The porch light was still on. He hadn't turned it off. He didn't know if he ever would.

Somewhere in Bakersfield, Lorraine had just planted a seed in a detective's notebook. And the soil was ready.

CHAPTER 6: "Aftermath"

Lorraine Butterworth had known her father was dead for eighteen hours before she walked into the police station, and every minute of those eighteen hours had been a performance.

Dante had called her at 11:15 PM on Tuesday night. She'd been in his bathroom, sitting on the tile floor, the high still buzzing behind her eyes like a fluorescent light that wouldn't stop flickering. Her phone vibrated on the edge of the sink. She picked it up.

"It's done," Dante said. His voice was flat, businesslike, the voice of a man placing an order at a drive-through.

"What's done?" Lorraine asked. But she knew. She knew before the words left her mouth. She knew the way you know a car is going to crash in the second before it does — the physics already decided, the outcome already sealed, and your body flooding with the sick awareness that you set the whole thing in motion.

"Your old man," Dante said. "It's handled. Don't call me. Don't call anyone. When the money comes through from the estate, we split it. Fifty-fifty."

"Dante —" Lorraine started.

"Don't," Dante said. "Don't say anything on this phone. Don't say anything to anyone. You were at a friend's house tonight. You don't know anything. You found out from the news. Say it back to me."

"I was at a friend's house," Lorraine said. Her voice sounded like it was coming from the bottom of a well. "I don't know anything. I found out from the news."

"Good," Dante said. "Go home. Stay off the phone. I'll find you when it's time."

The line went dead.

Lorraine sat on the bathroom floor for a long time. She didn't know how long. Time had become elastic, stretching and compressing in ways that had nothing to do with clocks. The tile was cold against her legs. The fluorescent light above the mirror hummed. The meth was still in her system, which meant her heart was racing and her thoughts were moving too fast and the thing she was trying not to think about kept rushing at her from every direction like water finding cracks in a wall.

Her father was dead.

Her father was dead because she'd told Dante about the money. The house. The alarm code. The key under the mat. She'd drawn a map and handed it to a man who wore a skull on his neck and she'd told herself she was just venting, just talking, just angry — and now Cyril Butterworth was dead on the floor of the house where he'd raised her, two weeks before a retirement party he'd spent months planning, and the last words she'd said to him were ugly words she could never take back.

She threw up in Dante's toilet. Twice. Then she washed her face, looked at herself in the mirror, and began the process of becoming someone who didn't know.

It was easier than she expected. That was the worst part.

She drove home at 3:00 AM. The apartment on South Chester Avenue was dark and cold and smelled the way it always smelled — cigarettes, stale air, the faint chemical residue of a life lived in short, desperate intervals. She sat on the mattress and stared at the wall. She didn't cry. Crying would have meant feeling, and feeling would have meant acknowledging what she'd done, and acknowledging what she'd done would have broken something inside her that she needed intact to survive the next twenty-four hours.

Instead, she built a story. The story was simple: she was at a friend's house. She didn't have the friend's last name — just Carla, a woman she'd met at a meeting she'd stopped attending months ago. Carla's apartment was on the east side, no fixed address that Lorraine could remember. They'd watched television. Lorraine had fallen asleep on the couch.

She'd woken up, driven home, and found out about her father from the morning news.

The story had holes. She knew it had holes. But Lorraine had spent fifteen years lying to the one person who loved her most, and if she could look Cyril Butterworth in the eye and tell him the money was for rent when it was really for meth, she could look a detective in the eye and say she was at Carla's house.

Knox called at 6:00 AM. She let it go to voicemail. He called again at 6:30. And 7:15. And 8:00. Each time, she watched the screen light up with his name and felt the vibration in her hand like a small electric shock. She didn't answer. She wasn't ready. She needed to rehearse. She needed the story to feel like a memory before she could sell it as one.

Archie called at 9:00 AM. She let that go to voicemail too.

At 10:00 AM, she turned on the television. The local news carried the story on the half-hour: Kern County facilities manager found dead in his Bakersfield home. Apparent homicide. Police investigating. A photograph of Cyril filled the screen — his county employee ID photo, the one where he was wearing the blue polo shirt he kept specifically for picture days because Helen had once told him he looked handsome in blue.

Lorraine stared at the photograph. Her father smiled back at her from the television, the patient, tired, hopeful smile of a man who never stopped believing that love was enough.

She turned off the television. She showered. She put on clean clothes — jeans, an oversized sweatshirt, no makeup. She wanted to look like a woman who'd been blindsided by grief, not a woman who'd been rehearsing her alibi for nine hours.

She knew her brothers had already been to the station. Knox had left a voicemail at 8:00 AM saying he and Archie were going in that afternoon to give statements. If the police had already talked to Archie, they'd already heard his version of the family. She needed to get her version on the record before Archie's story hardened into the only story.

At 3:30 PM, she drove to the Bakersfield Police Department and walked in through the front door.

The officer at the front desk was young, polite, and clearly uncomfortable around a woman who said her father had just been murdered. He made a phone call. Three minutes later, Detective Rina Salcedo came down the hallway.

Salcedo was not what Lorraine expected. She'd expected a man — older, gruff, the kind of detective she'd seen on television shows. Instead, she got a woman in her mid-forties with sharp eyes and a calm voice and the kind of posture that said she'd been standing in rooms full of liars for a long time and had stopped being surprised by any of them.

"Ms. Butterworth?" Salcedo said. "I'm Detective Salcedo. I spoke with your brothers earlier today. Thank you for coming in. I'm sorry about your father."

"Thank you," Lorraine said. She let her voice crack on the second word. Not too much. Just enough.

Salcedo led her to the same room where Archie and Knox had sat hours earlier. The table, the chairs, the recorder, the window overlooking the parking lot. The fluorescent lights humming the same institutional hum. A second detective sat in the corner — the same heavyset man with the gray mustache who had watched Archie give his statement. He nodded but didn't speak.

"This is voluntary," Salcedo said. "You're not under arrest. You can leave at any time. Do you understand?"

"I understand," Lorraine said.

"When did you learn about your father's death?" Salcedo asked.

"This morning," Lorraine said. "I saw it on the news. I couldn't believe it. I still can't believe it." She pressed her fingers to her temples, the gesture of a woman overwhelmed.

"Knox left me voicemails, but I — I wasn't in a place to answer. I couldn't face it. When I finally listened to his messages and realized it was real, I knew I had to come here."

"Where were you last night?" Salcedo asked.

"At a friend's house," Lorraine said. "Carla. She's someone I know from — from a support group I used to go to. We were watching TV. I fell asleep on her couch. I drove home this morning."

"Carla's last name?" Salcedo asked.

"I don't know her last name," Lorraine said. "We're not — it's not that kind of friendship. She's just someone who understands what I've been through."

"Address?" Salcedo asked.

"East side," Lorraine said. "I can't remember the exact street. I could find it if I drove over there, but I wasn't paying attention to the address."

Salcedo's pen moved across the notebook in short, precise strokes. Her face remained neutral, the same expressionless mask she'd shown Archie hours before. But behind the mask, wheels were turning. Lorraine could feel them.

"Your brothers both gave statements today," Salcedo said. "They told me about the family. Your father's career, the estate, the will. I'd like to hear your perspective. Tell me about your relationship with your father."

"He was everything to me," Lorraine said. And for the first time since she'd walked into the station, she wasn't lying. "He was the only person who never gave up on me. I've had — problems. I'm not going to pretend I haven't. Drugs. Jobs. Legal trouble. But my dad was always there. Always."

"Were you close with your brothers?" Salcedo asked.

"With Knox, yes," Lorraine said. "Knox is sweet. He doesn't judge. He just shows up." She paused. She knew Archie had already sat in this chair. She knew he'd told Salcedo about the drugs, the money, the twenty thousand dollars. She had to get ahead of whatever picture Archie had painted — not by denying it, but by reshaping it.

"Archie is different," Lorraine said.

"Different how?" Salcedo asked.

"Archie and my dad had a complicated relationship," Lorraine said. "Archie loves — loved — our father. But there were tensions. About money, mostly. Archie thought Dad spent too much on me. He thought Dad was enabling me. They argued about it. Not screaming arguments, but the cold kind. The kind where someone stops calling for a month."

"When was the last time they argued?" Salcedo asked.

"I don't know exactly," Lorraine said. "But it was recent. Dad told me Archie called him and told him to stop giving me money. Dad was hurt by it. He felt like Archie was trying to control him."

The lie was precise, layered, and built on a foundation of just enough truth to make it difficult to disprove. Archie had told Cyril to stop giving Lorraine money — that part was real. The rest — the arguments, the cold silences, Cyril feeling controlled — was invention. But it was the kind of invention that sounded like something that could have happened, which made it more dangerous than a pure lie.

Salcedo wrote for a long time. She'd already heard Archie's version — the clean one, the one where there were no arguments and no tensions. Now she had two versions. Two siblings telling different stories about the same family. One of them was lying. Her job was to figure out which one.

"Your father's estate," Salcedo said. "Are you aware of the terms of his will?"

"I know it splits three ways," Lorraine said. "Equal shares."

"A hundred and sixty-seven thousand dollars, approximately," Salcedo said. "Is that a significant amount of money to you?"

"I'm not rich," Lorraine said. "But I'm not — I didn't kill my father for money, if that's what you're asking. He was the only person in the world who still loved me. Why would I destroy that?"

The question hung in the air. Salcedo looked at her for a long moment, and Lorraine held the gaze without blinking. She'd learned that trick from Dante — the steady eye contact of someone who has nothing to hide, which is the same steady eye contact of someone who has everything to hide.

"Thank you, Ms. Butterworth," Salcedo said. "That's all for now. We may need to speak with you again."

"Of course," Lorraine said. "Whatever you need. I want to find who did this to my dad."

She stood. She walked to the door. She stopped with her hand on the handle and turned back. This was the part she'd rehearsed the most — the parting shot, the seed planted as an afterthought, the kind of thing a worried sister might say on her way out the door.

"Detective?" Lorraine said.

"Yes?" Salcedo said.

"My brother Archie — he's a good person," Lorraine said. "He loved our father. But he has a temper. And he has a way of making things look like they're under control even when they're not. I just — I thought you should know that."

She left the room. She walked down the hallway and through the lobby and out the front door into the Bakersfield afternoon, where the sun was too bright and the air smelled like diesel and the parking lot stretched out before her like an empty stage.

In her car, she sat behind the wheel and gripped it with both hands. The performance was over. The mask was off. And underneath, the thing she'd been holding at arm's length since 11:15 PM last night finally reached her.

Her father was dead. She had done this. Not with her hands, not with a weapon, but with her mouth and her rage and her fifteen years of taking and taking and taking until there was nothing left but a man at a desk writing zeros in a notebook and a daughter who told the wrong person where the key was hidden.

She started the car. She drove to the east side of Bakersfield, to a house she knew, to a man who had something that would make the feeling stop. She bought a bag. She drove home. She locked the door and closed the blinds and did what she always did when the truth got too close.

She got high. And the truth retreated. And the porch light — the one Cyril left on every night, the one he'd left on for her — burned in her memory like a sun she couldn't look at directly, even with her eyes closed.

What Lorraine didn't know — what she wouldn't learn until it was too late — was that Detective Rina Salcedo was not a woman who was easily redirected.

Salcedo sat in the interview room after Lorraine left and stared at her notes. She now had three statements from three siblings, taken in the same room on the same day. Archie's story was clean — no arguments, no tensions, a father and son who loved each other without complication. Lorraine's story contradicted it — cold arguments, financial control, a father caught between his children. Knox's story fell somewhere in the middle, careful and measured, the statement of a man who loved both his siblings and didn't want to hurt either one.

Someone was lying. Salcedo's job was to determine who.

The story about Carla had no bones. The emotional display was calibrated a fraction too perfectly. And the parting comment about Archie's temper — that was a tell. People who were genuinely grieving didn't leave breadcrumbs about their siblings on the way out the door.

But Salcedo had her own pressures. Her supervisor, Lieutenant Ray Garza, had already been in her office twice that morning. Garza was a numbers man — clearance rates, case timelines, budget allocations. He wanted the Butterworth case closed quickly. High-profile victim, forty years of county service, the media already circling. A clean arrest, a clean narrative, a press conference before the end of the month.

And the clean narrative pointed at Archie. No alibi. Financial motive. Cell tower data that was ambiguous enough to leave room for doubt. A sister who said there were tensions about money. A former Marine with the discipline to plan and execute and the composure to sit across from a detective and never flinch.

Salcedo had been burned before. Two years ago, she'd pursued an alternative suspect theory in a domestic homicide — convinced the husband's business partner was involved, followed the trail for three weeks, presented it to the DA, and watched it collapse at trial when the partner produced an alibi she'd missed. The husband walked. Garza had put a note in her file. The note was still there.

She wasn't going to chase shadows again. She was going to follow the evidence, and right now the evidence said Archie Butterworth. If it changed, she'd change with it. But she wasn't going to change first.

She closed her notebook. She stood up. She walked to the whiteboard in the squad room and wrote two names at the top.

ARCHIE BUTTERWORTH.

KNOX BUTTERWORTH.

She underlined Archie's name twice.

CHAPTER 7: "The Arrest"

One week after Cyril Butterworth's murder, the case against his eldest son was building like a storm system that nobody could see from the ground.

Archie knew pieces of it. Marcus Hale knew more. But the full picture — the one taking shape on Salcedo's whiteboard and in the DA's office and in the conversations happening in rooms Archie wasn't invited to — was worse than either of them imagined.

It started with the cell tower data.

Hale called on Thursday morning, four days after the murder. "We have a problem," Hale said. His voice carried the specific gravity of a man who delivered bad news for a living and still hadn't gotten used to it.

"What kind of problem?" Archie asked.

"Your cell phone," Hale said. "The tower data from the night of the murder. Your condo's coverage overlaps with SFO. The prosecution can argue you were at the airport, not at home, during the window when your father was killed."

"I was at home," Archie said.

"I believe you," Hale said. "But believing isn't evidence. Did you use your home Wi-Fi that night? Stream anything? Order anything online with a timestamp?"

Archie thought. The pad see ew. He'd ordered it through an app. "I ordered takeout," Archie said. "Around 7:30. Delivery app. It would have pinged my location."

"That helps for 7:30," Hale said. "Your father was killed between 9 and 11. What about after the food arrived?"

Archie searched his memory. He'd eaten at the desk. Reviewed positions. Read. Watched television. None of it left a digital footprint. He hadn't sent a text, made a call, or logged into anything between 8:00 PM and Knox's call at 11:47.

"Nothing," Archie said.

"Three hours and forty-seven minutes of dead air," Hale said. "That's the gap they'll drive a truck through."

"I was reading a book, Marcus," Archie said. "I was sitting on my couch reading a biography of Jim Simons. People do that. People sit in their homes and read books and don't generate digital evidence of their existence."

"People who aren't accused of murder do that," Hale said. "You don't have that luxury anymore."

Then came the witnesses.

On Friday, Salcedo interviewed Graham Whitfield, a former business partner Archie had cut ties with three years ago after Whitfield made a series of trades that skirted the edge of insider dealing. Archie had reported him to compliance. Whitfield had been fired. He'd never forgiven Archie for it.

Hale obtained a summary of Whitfield's statement through discovery channels. "He told Salcedo that you 'always talked about your father's money,'" Hale said. "His exact words. He said you described the estate as 'your inheritance' and that you were 'impatient' for your father to retire so the assets could be distributed."

"That's a lie," Archie said. "I never said any of that. Whitfield hates me because I reported him. This is revenge."

"I know it's a lie," Hale said. "But it's on the record. And it corroborates what your sister told Salcedo about tensions over money."

"Lorraine is lying too," Archie said.

"Two liars telling the same lie starts to look like the truth," Hale said. "That's the problem."

On Saturday, another name surfaced. Derek Yoon, a college friend from Berkeley who had asked Archie for a fifty-thousand-dollar loan two years ago to fund a tech startup. Archie had said no. The startup failed. Yoon blamed Archie for not backing him. They hadn't spoken since.

Yoon told Salcedo that Archie was "cold" and "transactional" and that he "treated relationships like investments — if the return wasn't there, he cut you off."

Yoon added that Archie had once said his father was "too soft" and "couldn't say no to people who didn't deserve it."

"Did you say that?" Hale asked.

"I said my father had trouble setting boundaries," Archie said. "I was talking about Lorraine. I was frustrated. It was a private conversation over drinks two years ago."

"Private conversations become public testimony when you're the suspect in a homicide," Hale said.

On Sunday, a neighbor on Columbus Street — Margaret Fenn, three houses down — told Salcedo she'd seen a dark SUV parked near Cyril's house on the night of the murder. She couldn't identify the make or model. She couldn't identify the driver. But she remembered it was dark-colored, possibly black, and that it had been parked on the street sometime between 9 and 10 PM.

Archie drove a black Audi Q7.

"Half the SUVs in California are dark-colored," Archie said when Hale told him.

"And one of them is yours," Hale said. "Which was parked in the garage of your building in San Francisco at the time. We can prove that with the building's security footage. But Salcedo hasn't asked for it yet, which means she's holding the neighbor's statement in reserve. She's building a narrative, Archie. Piece by piece."

"A false narrative," Archie said.

"They're all false until a jury says otherwise," Hale said.

On Monday, Archie tried to work.

He'd flown back to San Francisco on Saturday, at Hale's suggestion. "Go home," Hale had said. "Go to the office. Be visible. Every day you're in Bakersfield hovering over the investigation, you look like a man with something to manage. Go be a trader. Let me be the lawyer."

So Archie went back to Kessler-Braun. He stood at his desk. He watched the screens. The numbers moved the way they always did, and for the first time in his career, they meant nothing. The S&P climbed twelve points on an earnings surprise and Archie stared at it like a man watching rain through a window — aware of the movement, unable to feel it.

Danny Faulk tried to make conversation. "Good to have you back, Butterworth," Danny said. "Sorry about your dad."

"Thanks, Danny," Archie said.

"If you need anything —" Danny started.

"I'm fine," Archie said. The words came out harder than he intended. Danny nodded and went back to his screens. The desk was quieter than usual. Archie could feel people not looking at him, which was worse than if they'd stared.

At 2:00 PM, his managing director called him into a glass-walled office overlooking the trading floor. Sandra Caldwell. Mid-fifties, silver-streaked hair, the kind of woman who'd survived three decades on Wall Street by being smarter and harder and more patient than every man who'd underestimated her. "Archie," Sandra said. "Close the door."

Archie closed the door.

"I'm going to be direct," Sandra said. "The firm has been contacted by a detective in Bakersfield. She's requesting your employment records, compensation history, and trading logs."

"She's investigating my father's murder," Archie said. "I'm cooperating."

"I know," Sandra said. "And the firm will comply with whatever legal requests are made. But I need you to understand the position this puts us in. We're a publicly traded brokerage. Our clients trust us with their money. If a senior trader is involved in a homicide investigation — even as a witness —"

"I'm not a witness," Archie said. "I'm a suspect. That's what you're trying to say."

Sandra looked at him for a long moment. "The firm would like you to take a leave of absence," Sandra said. "Paid. Full benefits. Effective immediately. Until the investigation is resolved."

"And if I say no?" Archie asked.

"Then we have a harder conversation," Sandra said. "One that involves the legal department and the board. I don't want that conversation, Archie. And neither do you."

Archie stood in the glass office and looked out at the trading floor. His desk. His screens. The world he'd built over ten years, trade by trade, relationship by relationship, the careful architecture of a life designed to be unshakable. And it was shaking.

"I'll take the leave," Archie said.

"I'm sorry," Sandra said. And she meant it. Archie could tell. She was sorry the way people are sorry when they're protecting something bigger than the person in front of them.

He cleared his desk in fifteen minutes. Laptop, personal files, the photograph of Cyril he kept in the top drawer — the one from last Christmas, Cyril standing in the backyard with a spatula in one hand and a beer in the other, grinning like a man who had everything he needed. Archie had kept it at his desk because it made him smile. He put it all in a cardboard box that a junior analyst brought him without making eye contact.

He walked out of Kessler-Braun Capital at 2:47 PM. The security guard held the door. The October — November — air hit his face. The city moved around him, indifferent.

He was halfway to his car when his phone rang. Hale.

"Don't go home," Hale said.

"Why?" Archie asked.

"Salcedo just called me," Hale said. "She's obtained a warrant for your arrest. Murder in the first degree. She's sending officers to your condo."

Archie stopped walking. He stood on the sidewalk with the cardboard box in his arms and the phone pressed to his ear and the world shrinking to the size of a single sentence.

"Tell me what to do," Archie said.

"Go to the Bakersfield PD," Hale said. "Turn yourself in. I'll meet you there. We control the narrative. We walk in together. No perp walk, no handcuffs in front of the cameras if we can help it."

"I'm in San Francisco," Archie said.

"Then get on a plane," Hale said. "I'll stall. I'll tell Salcedo you're en route and cooperating. But, Archie — do not talk to anyone. Not Bella. Not Knox. Not your doorman. You call me and only me from this point forward."

"Marcus," Archie said. "I didn't do this."

"I know," Hale said. "Now let's go prove it."

He didn't make it to Bakersfield first.

Two plainclothes officers were waiting at his building when he arrived to drop off the box. They were standing in the lobby, badges visible, the doorman's face frozen in the expression of a man who'd been told to stay calm and wasn't succeeding.

"Archibald Butterworth?" the first officer said. He was young, broad-shouldered, with the careful posture of someone who'd been trained to expect resistance.

"Yes," Archie said.

"I'm Officer Reyes with the San Francisco Police Department," Reyes said. "We're acting on a warrant issued by Kern County. You're under arrest for the murder of Cyril Butterworth. Please set down the box and turn around."

The box. The laptop. The framed invitation. Cyril's retirement party. Archie set it on the lobby floor, next to the doorman's desk, on the marble tile that he'd walked across every day for three years.

He turned around. The handcuffs were cold. They clicked twice — left wrist, right wrist. The sound was small and final, like a lock engaging on a door that only opened from the outside.

"You have the right to remain silent," Reyes said. "Anything you say can and will be used against you in a court of law. You have the right to an attorney. If you cannot afford an attorney, one will be provided for you. Do you understand these rights?"

"I understand," Archie said.

They walked him through the lobby. The doorman looked away. Two residents in the elevator bank stared, then looked at the floor. Outside, a patrol car waited at the curb. No sirens. No lights. Just a black-and-white Crown Victoria and the quiet efficiency of a system that had decided Archie Butterworth was a killer.

He ducked into the back seat. The door closed. The car pulled away from the building, and Archie watched his condo tower recede in the window — thirty-two floors of glass and steel and a view of the Bay Bridge that had been useful for thinking and was now useful for nothing.

The cardboard box sat on the lobby floor where he'd left it. His laptop, his files, and the photograph of his father grinning with a spatula. The doorman would hold it behind the desk for three days before Bella came to pick it up.

His phone was in his pocket. They hadn't taken it yet.

He had one call before they processed him.

He didn't call Hale. Hale already knew.

He didn't call Bella. Bella would find out.

He didn't call Knox. Knox couldn't help him.

He called Reece Calloway.

The phone rang twice. A voice answered — calm, measured, the voice of a man who'd spent a decade in Marine intelligence and had learned that the first thing you do in a crisis is lower your heart rate.

"Archie," Reece said. "Talk to me."

"I've been arrested," Archie said. "Murder one. My father."

Silence. One second. Two seconds. Three.

"Where are they taking you?" Reece asked.

"San Francisco PD first," Archie said. "Then transfer to Kern County."

"Lawyer?" Reece asked.

"Marcus Hale," Archie said. "He's good."

"We're coming," Reece said.

"Reece, I didn't —" Archie started.

"I know you didn't," Reece said. "We're coming. All of

us. Don't say another word to anyone until Hale is in the room. Copy?"

"Copy," Archie said.

"Sit tight, Marine," Reece said. "The cavalry's on the way."

The line went dead. The patrol car turned onto the freeway. San Francisco blurred past the window — the skyline, the bridge, the fog rolling in from the Pacific like a curtain being drawn across a stage.

Archie leaned his head back against the seat. The handcuffs pressed into his wrists. The grief he'd been outrunning for a week was still there, patient and heavy, waiting for a moment when his guard was down. He didn't give it one. Not yet. There was too much to do.

Somewhere in Sacramento, Reece Calloway was making phone calls.

Somewhere in Bakersfield, Tommy Fuentes was checking his gear.

Somewhere in Fresno, Wes Draper was pouring the last of a bottle down the sink, looking in the mirror, and saying something to himself that only Marines say when the mission is bigger than the damage.

They were coming. All of them. Because that's what Marines do. You call one, you call all.

Archie closed his eyes. The patrol car hummed beneath him. The city disappeared behind him. And for the first time since Knox's phone call on Tuesday night, Archie Butterworth allowed himself to feel something that wasn't grief or rage or the cold discipline of a man holding himself together by force.

He felt hope. Small, stubborn, unreasonable hope. The kind that shows up in handcuffs.

CHAPTER 8: "The Cavalry"

The Kern County Superior Court smelled like floor wax and bad decisions, and Archie Butterworth was standing in the middle of both.

He'd been transferred from San Francisco to Bakersfield on Wednesday, processed through the Kern County jail system with the efficient indignity of a machine that didn't care who you were or what you'd done. Fingerprints. Mugshot. Orange jumpsuit. A cell with a metal toilet and a mattress that smelled like bleach and the man who'd slept on it before him. Archie had spent four years in the Marines sleeping on worse, but the Marines had never locked the door from the outside.

Marcus Hale had been waiting for him at the Kern County courthouse on Thursday morning, standing in the hallway outside Department 12 in a rumpled gray suit and a tie that looked like it had been knotted in the dark. He was shorter than Archie expected — five-eight, maybe five-nine — with thinning brown hair, wire-rimmed glasses, and the kind of face that juries trusted because it looked like it belonged to a man who'd rather be fishing.

"Mr. Butterworth," Hale said, extending his hand. "Marcus Hale. We spoke on the phone."

"Thank you for being here," Archie said.

"That's what the retainer's for," Hale said. "Let's talk about bail. The DA is going to ask for remand — no bail. I'm going to argue for release. You've got no prior record, deep community ties through your father, a stable career, and no passport since your military discharge. You're not a flight risk. But the charge is murder one, which means the judge has discretion, and discretion means money."

"How much?" Archie asked.

"I'm guessing half a million," Hale said. "Can you cover it?"

"Yes," Archie said.

"Good," Hale said. "Now, the DA is going to paint you as a wealthy man with the means and motive to kill his father for an inheritance. She's going to use your composure against you — too calm, too controlled, too Marine. My job is to make the judge see a grieving son, not a calculated killer. Your job is to stand there, say nothing, and look like a man whose father just died. Can you do that?"

"My father did just die," Archie said.

"Then it shouldn't be hard," Hale said.

The courtroom was half full. Reporters in the back rows, notebooks open. A sketch artist in the corner. Knox and Delaney in the second row — Knox in a sport coat he never wore, Delaney holding his hand with both of hers.

Bella was behind them, alone, her back straight, her face composed in the way Archie had come to recognize as her war face — the expression that said she was terrified and had decided terror was not going to win.

Lorraine was not there.

The judge was the Honorable Patricia Moreno — mid-sixties, silver hair, reading glasses perched on the end of her nose. She had the bearing of a woman who'd been on the bench long enough to have seen every performance the human species was capable of and was no longer impressed by any of them.

The assistant district attorney was a man named Craig Jessup — late thirties, sharp suit, the kind of prosecutor who treated the courtroom like a stage and every case like an audition for the next rung on the ladder. He stood at his table with a file two inches thick and the confidence of a man who believed he was holding a winning hand.

"The People request remand, Your Honor," Jessup said. "The defendant is charged with first-degree murder. He has significant financial resources, no family ties that would prevent flight — his father is deceased, his mother is deceased, his siblings are adults. He maintains residences in San Francisco and has the means to flee the jurisdiction."

"Your Honor," Hale said, rising from his chair with the unhurried posture of a man who'd done this a thousand times, "my client is a decorated Marine veteran with an honorable discharge, a graduate of UC Berkeley, and a senior financial professional with no criminal record of any kind — not a parking ticket, not a speeding violation, nothing. He turned himself in voluntarily when he learned of the warrant. He has deep roots in this community through his father, who served Kern County for forty years. He is not a flight risk. He is a grieving son who wants to bury his father and clear his name."

"The defendant's net worth exceeds two million dollars," Jessup said. "He could be in any country in the world within twenty-four hours."

"My client does not hold a passport," Hale said. "He hasn't had one since his military discharge. He's prepared to submit to electronic monitoring, regular check-ins, and any travel restrictions the court deems appropriate."

Judge Moreno looked at Archie over her reading glasses. She studied him for a long moment — the kind of moment that felt like an hour and lasted three seconds.

"Bail is set at five hundred thousand dollars," Judge Moreno said. "Cash or bond. Defendant will surrender all travel documents, submit to GPS monitoring, and remain within Kern County for the duration of the proceedings. Any violation and I revoke without a hearing. Is that clear, Mr. Butterworth?"

"Yes, Your Honor," Archie said.

"We're adjourned," Judge Moreno said.

Archie posted bail within two hours. Hale had arranged it in advance — a cashier's check drawn against Archie's brokerage account, the kind of financial transaction that most people would never make and that the DA's office would later cite as evidence of a man with too much money and too little conscience.

Outside the courthouse, Knox was waiting on the steps. He hugged Archie without saying a word. Delaney stood beside him, her eyes red, her hand on Knox's back. Bella was at the bottom of the steps, car keys in her hand, already thinking three moves ahead.

"Where are we going?" Bella asked.

"Dad's house," Archie said. "I need to be in Dad's house."

They drove to Columbus Street in Bella's rental. The yellow tape was gone. The cruisers were gone. The crime scene van was gone. The house sat on its lot the way it always had — white paint, brown trim, lawn mowed, hedges trimmed. The porch light was on. Archie had asked Knox to leave it on, and Knox had understood without being told why.

Inside, the house was clean. Bella and Delaney had

spent two days scrubbing, organizing, and removing anything that reminded anyone of what had happened in the living room. The carpet had been replaced. The furniture rearranged. The kitchen was stocked. The guest rooms were made up.

Archie stood in the hallway and breathed. The house smelled like Pine-Sol and Cyril's coffee and something else — something underneath, faint and permanent, that no amount of cleaning could reach. The absence of a man who'd lived here for thirty years.

"Thank you," Archie said. He looked at Bella. He looked at Delaney. "For doing this."

"You don't have to thank us," Delaney said.

"Yes, I do," Archie said.

Two days passed. Archie stayed in the house, wore the GPS monitor on his ankle like a leash, and tried to make sense of a world that had stopped making sense. Hale came by each morning to review the case. The evidence was circumstantial but stacking — the cell tower gap, Whitfield's statement, Yoon's statement, the neighbor's dark SUV, Lorraine's seed about money tensions. No murder weapon had been recovered. No DNA. No fingerprints. The prosecution's case was built on inference and narrative, and the narrative was compelling: a wealthy son, a modest estate, a family full of secrets.

"They don't have enough to convict," Hale said on Saturday morning, sitting at Cyril's kitchen table with a legal pad and a cup of coffee. "But they have enough to indict, and an indictment in Kern County means a trial, and a trial means a jury, and a jury means twelve people who've never made four hundred thousand dollars in seven minutes deciding whether a man who has is capable of killing his father for a third of that."

"So what do we do?" Archie asked.

"We find the real story," Hale said. "And we do it without breaking any laws, contaminating any evidence, or giving the DA a reason to revoke your bail."

The doorbell rang at 11:00 AM.

Archie opened the front door. Three men stood on Cyril's porch. They looked like they'd driven through the night, which two of them had.

Reece Calloway was first. Thirty-six, lean, close-cropped hair going gray at the temples. He wore a black polo shirt and khakis and carried a laptop bag over one shoulder. His eyes swept the street behind him before he looked at Archie — a habit from Marine intelligence that had never switched off.

"Archie," Reece said. He extended his hand, and when Archie took it, Reece pulled him into a one-armed embrace.

Brief, tight, the kind of contact that said everything words couldn't.

Tomas "Tommy" Fuentes was next. Thirty-four, stocky, built low to the ground like a man designed for carrying heavy things long distances. He wore jeans and a flannel shirt and work boots that had seen every back road in the Central Valley. He'd driven from across town — Tommy had never left Bakersfield. He gripped Archie's hand and nodded once.

"Sorry about your pops, brother," Tommy said. "He was a good man."

"He was," Archie said.

Wes Draper arrived last. He came up the walkway with the careful gait of a man measuring each step, and Archie saw it immediately — Wes looked rough. Thinner than the last time they'd been together, which was eighteen months ago at a reunion barbecue in Sacramento. His face was drawn, the lines deeper, the skin around his eyes carrying the bruised, hollow look of a man who hadn't been sleeping well or had been sleeping with the help of things that didn't help. His hands had a tremor — subtle, almost invisible, but Archie had spent four years watching Wes's hands fieldstrip weapons in the dark, and those hands didn't shake.

"Wes," Archie said.

"Archie," Wes said. His voice was steady even if his hands weren't. He gripped Archie's hand and held it. His eyes were bloodshot but present — the eyes of a man who was falling apart and had decided to fall apart later. "I look like hell. I know. Don't say it."

"I wasn't going to," Archie said.

"Yeah, you were," Wes said. "It's fine. I'm going through a divorce. I'm not sleeping. I'm drinking more than I should. But I'm here. And I'm functional. Mostly."

"Mostly is enough," Archie said.

"Damn right it is," Wes said.

They came inside. All four of them in Cyril's living room — the new carpet, the rearranged furniture, the ghost of a man who'd raised one of them and been claimed by all of them. Bella was in the kitchen making coffee. Knox was on the couch, quiet, watching these men fill his father's house with a presence that was entirely different from anything the Butterworth family had ever contained. Military. Purposeful. Dangerous in a way that had nothing to do with violence and everything to do with competence.

Hale arrived ten minutes later. He looked at the three Marines standing in the living room and his expression shifted from professional composure to something closer to alarm.

"Who are these people?" Hale asked.

"My brothers," Archie said.

"Your biological brother is sitting on the couch," Hale said. "These men are not your brothers."

"Yes, they are," Archie said.

"Mr. Hale," Reece said, stepping forward with his hand extended. "Reece Calloway. Former Marine intelligence. I run a private security consulting firm in Sacramento. I'm here to help."

Hale shook the hand but didn't relax. "Help how?" Hale asked.

"Digital intelligence," Reece said. "Background research. Financial forensics. The things the police should be doing but aren't because they've already decided Archie did it."

"And you?" Hale asked, looking at Tommy.

"Tommy Fuentes," Tommy said. "I know this town. Every street, every back road, every bar where the wrong people drink. If someone local was involved in this, I'll find out."

"And you?" Hale asked, turning to Wes.

"Wes Draper," Wes said. "Former Marine MP. I'm a bail bondsman in Fresno. I know the criminal justice system from every angle — defendant, investigator, and the guy who drags you back when you skip. I'm here to make sure Archie doesn't do anything stupid, and to advise on how the prosecution thinks."

Hale looked at all three of them. Then he looked at Archie. "If any of these men get arrested," Hale said, "it torpedoes my case. Everything they find becomes fruit of the poisonous tree. Every piece of evidence gets challenged. Every argument I make in front of a jury gets undermined by the prosecution pointing at your personal army and saying you thought you were above the law."

"Then we won't get arrested," Wes said.

Hale stared at Wes. Wes stared back. The silence lasted four seconds.

"Fine," Hale said. "But I set the boundaries. Nothing illegal. Nothing that could be construed as witness tampering, obstruction, or intimidation. You find something, you bring it to me. Not to the police. Not to the press. To me. Understood?"

"Understood," Reece said.

"Crystal clear," Tommy said.

"You're the boss, counselor," Wes said. He said it with just enough respect to be sincere and just enough edge to make clear that he'd follow the rules until the rules stopped making sense.

Hale sat down at the kitchen table. The Marines pulled up chairs. Bella brought coffee. Knox listened from the couch. And for the next two hours, they built a plan.

Reece would handle digital intelligence — Cyril's financial records, Lorraine's digital footprint, any shell companies or unusual transactions connected to the family. Tommy would work the streets — the Reapers' territory, the clubhouse on the south side, the warehouse in the agricultural corridor. He already knew the landscape. Wes would coach on criminal justice strategy — how Salcedo was likely building her case, where the weaknesses were, what the prosecution needed and didn't yet have.

Bella had her own angle. Her immigration practice connected her to a network of Central Valley contacts — farmworkers, community organizers, legal aid workers — who knew things the police didn't. She would pull those threads quietly.

Knox sat and listened. He hadn't told Archie about Dante Voss yet. The weight of that silence was crushing him, and every minute he spent in this room — watching these men plan and strategize and put themselves at risk for his brother — made the weight heavier.

"Two tracks," Reece said, standing at the kitchen counter with a notepad. "Bella's Central Valley contacts and our tactical intelligence. We move parallel. We share everything. We find the real killer and we hand it to Marcus on a silver platter."

"And if we find the killer before the police do?" Tommy asked.

"Then we call Marcus," Reece said. "And Marcus calls the police. We don't play cop. We play intelligence."

"Agreed," Hale said. "Now get to work. And for the love of God, don't get arrested."

The meeting broke up. Reece set up his laptop at Cyril's desk. Tommy left to drive the south side. Wes poured himself a coffee and sat on the back porch, staring at the yard where Cyril had taught Archie to throw a football.

Archie walked Hale to the door. "You trust these guys?" Hale asked.

"With my life," Archie said.

"That might be exactly what you're doing," Hale said. He shook Archie's hand and left.

That night, after the house had quieted and the Marines had settled into the guest rooms and Knox had driven home with Delaney, Archie stepped onto the front porch for air. The street was dark. The neighbors' houses were buttoned up for the night. The porch light cast its yellow circle on the concrete steps.

Something was tucked under the windshield wiper of his rental car.

Archie walked to the curb. He pulled it free. A folded piece of paper, no envelope. He opened it under the porch light.

Block letters. Black marker. Five words.

STOP ASKING QUESTIONS ABOUT DADDY.

No signature. No fingerprints that he could see. Just the message, blunt and clear, left sometime between sunset and now on a quiet street in a neighborhood where Cyril Butterworth had lived for thirty years without anyone ever threatening his family.

Archie carried the note inside. He set it on the kitchen table. Reece came out of the guest room in a T-shirt and sweatpants, saw Archie's face, and looked at the note.

"When?" Reece asked.

"Tonight," Archie said. "On my car."

Tommy came down the hall. Wes appeared from the back porch. All three Marines looked at the note. Then they looked at each other.

The kind of look that didn't need words. The kind of

look that said the mission had just changed.

"They know we're here," Tommy said.

"Good," Wes said. "Now they know what's coming."

Reece picked up the note by the corner, slid it into a plastic bag from the kitchen, and set it on the counter. "Evidence," Reece said. "We give this to Marcus in the morning."

Archie looked at the three men standing in his father's kitchen at midnight, and for the second time since his arrest, he felt that stubborn, unreasonable hope. Not because the note didn't scare him. It did. But because the men standing around that kitchen table had been scared before — in places with worse lighting and higher stakes — and they hadn't quit then either.

"Get some sleep," Archie said.

"You too," Reece said.

"I will," Archie said.

He didn't. He sat at Cyril's kitchen table with the porch light burning through the window and the threatening note sealed in a plastic bag three feet away, and he thought about his father, and his sister, and the men who'd shown up without being asked, and the long fight ahead.

The hunt had begun.

CHAPTER 9: "The Other Side"

The parallel investigation began on Sunday morning with Archie sitting at Cyril's kitchen table, staring at a stack of bank statements that told a story his father had never wanted anyone to read.

Reece had pulled Cyril's financial records through legal channels — Archie was the executor of the estate, which gave him access to everything. The records went back five years. Before that, Reece had requested archived statements from the bank, which would take a few days. But five years was enough to see the pattern.

Small cash withdrawals. Irregular amounts. $200 here. $500 there. $1,200 in August. $3,000 in March. None of them matched any bill, mortgage payment, or regular expense in Cyril's meticulous budget. They were ghost transactions — money that left Cyril's account and vanished into a world that didn't generate receipts.

"He was giving her cash," Archie said. He was sitting across from Reece, the statements spread between them like a map of his father's private heartbreak. "On top of everything else. On top of the checks, the bail money, the rent payments. He was pulling cash and handing it to her."

"Over the last five years, the withdrawals total approximately forty-three thousand dollars," Reece said. He had his laptop open, a spreadsheet already built, every transaction logged and categorized with the precision of a man who'd spent a career turning raw data into intelligence. "That's in addition to whatever he gave her by check or direct transfer. And these are only the records we have access to right now. If the pattern goes back further, we could be looking at a lot more."

"Forty-three thousand dollars," Archie said. He said it the way you say a number that hurts more than it should. "And that's just what we can see. He was bleeding for her, Reece. For years. And nobody stopped it."

"We don't know where the money went," Reece said. "We know he was giving her cash off the books. We don't know who else was in her life or where the money ended up. The withdrawals tell us Cyril was supporting Lorraine in ways nobody saw. But that's motive for her to keep him alive, not kill him. Someone else is in this picture. We just can't see them yet."

"Then we find them," Archie said, tapping the bank statements. "Follow the money."

"That's the plan," Reece said. "Tommy's working the streets. If someone local was involved, he'll find the trail."

Tommy had left before sunrise. He knew the Reapers' territory the way he knew the engine of every truck he'd ever towed — from the inside out. The clubhouse was on South

Union Avenue, a cinder-block building with blacked-out windows and a parking lot full of Harleys. The warehouse was east of town, in the agricultural corridor between Bakersfield and Lamont, surrounded by almond orchards and cotton fields. Tommy had towed trucks out of that corridor for years. He knew which roads were paved, which were dirt, and which ones dead-ended at fences with no-trespassing signs that meant something worse than a fine.

He called at noon. "The clubhouse is quiet," Tommy said. "Sunday morning, most of these guys are sleeping off Saturday. But the warehouse is active. Two trucks came in this morning — unmarked panel vans, California plates. I got the numbers. Three guys unloading crates. Agricultural supplies on the outside. I couldn't see what was inside."

"Stay back," Reece said. He was on speakerphone in the kitchen. "Log everything. Plates, times, faces if you can get them. Don't engage."

"I know how to run surveillance, Reece," Tommy said. "I did it in Fallujah. This is just Fallujah with better tacos."

"And worse backup," Wes said from the couch, where he was reviewing the Kern County criminal code on his phone. "In Fallujah, you had a platoon. Here, you've got a bail bondsman with bad knees and a security consultant who irons his khakis."

"I don't iron my khakis," Reece said.

"You absolutely iron your khakis," Wes said.

Archie almost smiled. Almost. The banter was familiar — the rhythm of men who'd shared a barracks and a war and the specific kind of humor that grows in the space between danger and boredom. It sounded like the old days. It sounded like safety.

But the old days were gone, and Cyril was dead, and the banter faded the way it always did — quickly, without ceremony, replaced by the work.

That afternoon, Archie confronted Knox.

He'd been putting it off. The conversation with Knox in the car after the police station — the one where Knox said "there's something I didn't tell her" and then refused to say more — had been sitting in Archie's chest like a splinter, working its way deeper with every passing day. Knox had been quiet since the Marines arrived. Too quiet. He came to the house in the mornings, sat in the living room, listened to the briefings, and left in the evenings without contributing anything. He looked like a man standing at the edge of a diving board, staring at the water, unable to jump.

Archie found him in the backyard, sitting in one of Cyril's patio chairs, staring at the lawn.

"Knox," Archie said. "We need to talk."

"I know," Knox said.

"What didn't you tell Salcedo?" Archie asked.

Knox didn't answer immediately. He picked at the armrest of the patio chair — a nervous habit Archie remembered from childhood, Knox's fingers finding seams and edges and loose threads whenever the world got too tight.

"Lorraine has a boyfriend," Knox said. "His name is Dante Voss. He's a member of the Reapers Motorcycle Club."

Archie stood very still. "How long have you known this?" Archie asked.

"Eight months," Knox said. "I first saw his motorcycle outside her apartment in March. Harley Road King. Reapers patches on the saddlebags. I've seen it three more times since then. Once at her place. Once at a gas station — she was on the back of it. Once in a bar parking lot on Edison Highway at two in the morning."

"Eight months," Archie said. The number landed like a stone dropped from a height. "You've known for eight months that our sister is involved with an outlaw motorcycle club, and you didn't tell anyone."

"I didn't know what to do," Knox said. "If I told Dad, it would have destroyed him. If I told you, you would have gone to war. I thought — I thought maybe it would end on its own. I thought she'd come to her senses."

"She didn't come to her senses, Knox," Archie said. His voice was rising. He could feel the anger climbing his spine like a vine, wrapping around his ribs, tightening. "She went to Dante Voss's house and told him about Dad's money. She told him the alarm code. She told him about the key under the mat. And Dad is dead."

"You don't know that," Knox said.

"I know enough," Archie said. "And so do you. You've known enough for eight months to have done something — anything — and you chose to protect Lorraine instead."

"I was protecting Dad," Knox said. His voice cracked. "I was trying to keep the family together. That's what I've always done. That's what I've always been asked to do — stand in the middle and hold everyone together while Archie charges ahead and Lorraine falls apart. That's my job. That's the only job anyone ever gave me."

"Your job," Archie said, "was to tell the truth. And you didn't."

"The way you told the truth?" Knox said. He stood up from the chair, his face flushed, his eyes wet. "You moved to San Francisco and built your empire and called Dad once a week and told yourself that was enough. You knew about Lorraine. You knew about the drugs. You knew Dad was bleeding money. And what did you do? You told him to stop giving it to her and then you hung up the phone and went back to your trading floor. Don't lecture me about telling the truth, Archie. You told the truth from a safe distance. I was here."

The words hit Archie in a place he didn't know was exposed. He stood in his father's backyard, looking at his younger brother, and for the first time in his life, he didn't have a response. Because Knox was right. Not completely — keeping quiet about Dante Voss was indefensible. But the accusation underneath it — that Archie had loved his father from arm's length and called it enough — that was true. And the truth of it burned.

They stood in silence for a long moment. The backyard was quiet. The sprinklers hadn't run in weeks. The grass was starting to brown at the edges.

"I should have told you," Knox said. His voice was smaller now, the anger spent. "I should have told Dad. I should have told someone. Every day since Tuesday night, I've been thinking — if I'd said something, would he still be alive? And I don't know the answer. And I can't live with not knowing."

"You can't change it," Archie said. "Neither can I. We can only go forward."

"Forward means what?" Knox asked.

"Forward means we tell Reece about Dante Voss,"

Archie said. "Right now. Today. Everything you know."

Knox nodded. He wiped his eyes with the back of his hand. "Okay," Knox said. "Let's go inside."

They walked into the kitchen. Reece was at the table. Wes was on the couch. Archie looked at Reece.

"Knox has something to tell you," Archie said.

Knox sat down across from Reece and told him everything. The motorcycle. The Reapers patches. The gas station. The bar on Edison Highway. Dante Voss. Eight months of silence and the guilt that had been eating him alive since the moment he found his father's body on the living room floor.

Reece listened without interrupting. When Knox finished, Reece opened his laptop and typed for two minutes. Then he looked up.

"Dante Voss," Reece said. "Age thirty-eight. Two priors — assault and possession with intent. Known associate of the Reapers MC, Bakersfield chapter. He operates out of the clubhouse on South Union and a property in the agricultural corridor east of town."

"The warehouse Tommy's been watching," Archie said.

"The same one," Reece said. "Tommy reported Voss's

truck in the lot this morning. Black Dodge Ram, lifted, custom plates. He's there regularly."

"So Lorraine's boyfriend is running operations out of the same warehouse the Reapers use for distribution," Wes said from the couch. He hadn't moved, but his voice had changed — sharper, focused, the bail bondsman replaced by the former military policeman. "And Lorraine told this boyfriend about Cyril's money, the alarm code, and the key. Two weeks before Cyril was murdered."

"We don't have proof of that last part," Reece said. "We have Knox's knowledge of the relationship and Archie's knowledge of the money request. The connection between Voss and the murder is inference."

"It's more than the police have," Wes said. "Because the police aren't looking."

"Then we make them look," Archie said.

Reece shook his head. "Not yet," Reece said. "We bring suspicion to Hale, Hale takes it to Salcedo, and Salcedo dismisses it as a defense attorney throwing alternative suspects at the wall. We need evidence. Hard evidence. The kind that makes Salcedo turn her head whether she wants to or not."

"What kind of evidence?" Knox asked.

"Financial," Reece said. "A money trail between Lorraine and Voss. Phone records showing contact around the time of the murder. A connection between Voss and whoever actually entered that house. Tommy's surveillance is the start. But we need more."

"Then we get more," Archie said.

Late that night, Archie found Wes on the back porch.

Wes was sitting in Cyril's chair — the wooden rocker with the frayed cushion that Cyril had refused to replace because Helen had picked it out. A bottle of bourbon sat on the railing, a third of it gone. Wes held a glass in his right hand. His left hand rested on his knee, the tremor visible in the porch light.

Archie sat down in the chair beside him. He didn't say anything about the bottle. He didn't ask how Wes was doing. He already knew the answer, and Wes already knew he knew.

They sat in the dark for a while. The neighborhood was quiet. A dog barked somewhere down the block. The air smelled like cut grass and dust and the faint petroleum edge that Bakersfield never quite shook.

"My wife said I love the Corps more than I love her," Wes said. He didn't look at Archie. He looked at the yard. "She might be right. I came home from my last deployment and I couldn't — I couldn't turn it off. The alertness. The readiness. She'd ask me to take out the trash and I'd clear the garage like it was a hostile building. She said it wasn't funny. She was right. It wasn't funny."

"Have you talked to anyone?" Archie asked.

"A guy at the VA," Wes said. "Twice. He gave me a pamphlet about coping strategies and a prescription I never filled. The system's not built for guys like me. It's built for paperwork."

"You're here," Archie said.

"Yeah," Wes said. He took a sip of the bourbon. "I'm always here for you bastards. That might be the problem. I can't show up for my wife. I can't show up for myself. But you call and I'm in the car before I hang up the phone." Wes set the glass down. "What does that make me, Archie?"

"It makes you a Marine," Archie said.

"It makes me a mess," Wes said. "But I'm your mess. So let's catch whoever killed your old man and then I'll go back to Fresno and figure out the rest."

"Deal," Archie said.

They sat on the porch until the bottle was empty and the stars came out over the valley. Neither of them spoke again. They didn't need to. The silence between Marines who've served together is a different kind of silence — it doesn't need filling. It just needs company.

Archie went to bed at midnight. He didn't sleep well. But he slept. And in the morning, the work would start again, and the two tracks — Bella's Central Valley contacts and the Marines' tactical intelligence — would push deeper into the darkness that had swallowed his family.

The other side was out there. They just had to find it.

CHAPTER 10: "Dante"

The clubhouse smelled like motor oil and stale beer and the kind of cigarette smoke that had seeped so deep into the walls it had become part of the architecture. Lorraine Butterworth sat on a torn leather couch in the back room and watched Dante Voss count money.

He did it the way he did everything — with his hands steady and his face blank and his attention divided between the task in front of him and the six or seven things happening behind it that nobody else could see. The bills were twenties and hundreds, stacked in rubber-banded bundles on a card table under a bare bulb. How much, Lorraine didn't know. She'd stopped counting Dante's money a long time ago. Counting it meant understanding where it came from, and understanding where it came from meant admitting things about her life that she wasn't ready to admit.

The clubhouse was on South Union Avenue, a cinder-block rectangle set back from the road behind a chain-link fence and a parking lot that held between eight and fifteen motorcycles depending on the day. From the outside, it looked like an auto repair shop that had given up. A faded sign above the door read "Reapers MC — Bakersfield" in red and black. No one who drove past it on their way to work or the grocery store gave it a second look. That was the point.

The Reapers didn't advertise. They didn't need to. Everyone in this part of Bakersfield knew what happened behind the blacked-out windows, and everyone in this part of Bakersfield knew better than to talk about it.

Inside, the clubhouse was divided into three rooms. The front room was a bar — pool table, dartboard, a refrigerator full of beer, a television mounted on the wall that was always tuned to either boxing or football. The middle room was where business happened — the card table, the money, the phones, the maps and ledgers that tracked the movement of methamphetamine from Central American suppliers through agricultural properties in the valley and into the veins of a county that had been losing the drug war for two decades. The back room was storage, and Lorraine had been told on her first visit that the back room was not her business and would never be her business and that asking about it was the kind of mistake a person only made once.

Lorraine had not asked about the back room.

Two other Reapers were in the middle room — a man called Buckle, who was fifty and shaped like a barrel and whose real name Lorraine had never learned, and a younger man named Pike, who was twenty-six and had the empty, watchful eyes of a dog that had been hit too many times and had learned to bite first. Neither of them acknowledged

Lorraine. She was Dante's girl. That meant she existed in the space between furniture and person — present, tolerated, not spoken to unless Dante said otherwise.

She'd been with Dante for fourteen months. She'd met him at a bar on Edison Highway, back when she was still pretending that going to bars was social and not pharmaceutical. He'd bought her a drink. He'd listened to her talk. He'd looked at her with an expression that wasn't pity or disappointment or the careful neutrality of someone trying not to judge — it was interest. Plain, unfiltered interest. As if she were a person worth paying attention to.

Nobody had looked at her like that in years. Her brothers looked at her with concern. Her father looked at her with hope. The few friends she'd kept looked at her with the cautious distance of people waiting for the next crisis. Dante looked at her like she mattered. In the absence of everything else, mattering was enough.

It took her three months to realize that Dante's interest had a price tag. By then, she was too deep to climb out. He gave her meth when she needed it. He gave her a place to stay when her apartment felt like a coffin. He gave her the feeling of belonging somewhere, even if the somewhere was a cinder-block building on South Union Avenue that smelled like motor oil. And in return, he owned her. Not legally. Not on paper. But in the way that mattered

— the quiet ownership of a man who knows your weakness and feeds it just enough to keep you close.

Dante finished counting. He stacked the bundles in a metal lockbox and closed the lid. Then he looked at Lorraine for the first time since she'd walked in.

"Your brother's been busy," Dante said.

"Which one?" Lorraine asked.

"The Marine," Dante said. "Archie. He's got friends in town. Three of them, from what I hear. Staying at your old man's house on Columbus."

Lorraine felt something cold move through her stomach. "How do you know that?" Lorraine asked.

"I know everything that happens in this town," Dante said. He said it without arrogance, the way a weatherman says it will rain. A fact. Not a boast. "One of them's been driving the south side. Tow truck. Big guy. He was parked near the warehouse this morning."

"Tommy," Lorraine said. She didn't mean to say it. The name just came out, pulled from a memory she hadn't thought about in years — a barbecue at Cyril's house, three or four years ago, when Archie had brought his Marine friends home for a weekend. Tommy Fuentes, the one from Bakersfield. He'd helped Cyril with the grill. He'd made

Lorraine laugh. She'd been sober that weekend, or close to it, and for two days she'd felt like a person instead of a problem.

"You know him?" Dante asked. His voice didn't change, but his eyes did. The interest sharpened into something harder.

"He's one of Archie's friends," Lorraine said. "From the Marines. He lives here in town. He runs a tow truck business."

"A tow truck operator doing surveillance on my warehouse," Dante said. "That's not a tow truck operator. That's a problem."

"Maybe he's just driving around," Lorraine said. "Maybe it's a coincidence."

"There's no such thing as coincidence," Dante said. "Your brother is out on bail for killing your father, and his Marine buddies show up the next week and start watching my operation. That's not coincidence. That's a plan."

Lorraine didn't say anything. She pulled her knees up to her chest on the leather couch and wrapped her arms around them and tried to make herself small. It was a reflex from childhood — the posture of a girl who wanted to disappear from a conversation that had gotten too loud or too sharp. It hadn't worked when she was twelve and it didn't work now.

"Here's what's going to happen," Dante said. He leaned forward in his chair, his elbows on his knees, his voice low enough that Buckle and Pike couldn't hear. "Your father's estate is going to settle. You're going to get your third. And when that money comes through, you're going to give me half. That was the deal."

"I know the deal," Lorraine said.

"Good," Dante said. "Because the deal depends on your brother going down for this. If Archie beats the charge, the whole thing gets complicated. The estate gets tied up. Lawyers get involved. Questions get asked. I don't like questions."

"Archie didn't kill Dad," Lorraine said. The words came out before she could stop them, and the moment they were in the air, she wished she could pull them back.

Dante looked at her. The look lasted five seconds. Five seconds of silence that felt like a hand around her throat.

"I know Archie didn't kill your dad," Dante said. "You know that. I know that. But the police don't know that, and as long as they don't know that, everything works. So your job — your only job — is to keep your mouth shut and let the system do what it does."

"And if the system doesn't work?" Lorraine asked. "If Archie's friends find something?"

"Then I'll deal with it," Dante said.

"What does that mean?" Lorraine asked.

"It means if your brother doesn't back off, someone's going to teach him a lesson," Dante said. "Him and his Marine buddies. This isn't San Francisco. This is my town. And nobody runs surveillance on my operation and walks away thinking it was a good idea."

"Don't touch him," Lorraine said. The words came out harder than she expected — a flash of something old and protective, the sister she used to be before the meth and the money and the man sitting across from her turned her into someone she didn't recognize. "He's my brother, Dante. Whatever else is happening, he's my brother."

"Then make sure he stops," Dante said.

He stood up. He walked to the refrigerator, pulled out two beers, and handed one to Buckle. He didn't offer one to Lorraine. He didn't offer one to Pike. The hierarchy was clear — you drank when Dante decided you drank.

Lorraine sat on the couch and felt the walls of her life contracting. Two weeks ago, she'd had a father who loved her and a habit she couldn't break and a debt she couldn't pay. Now she had a dead father, a brother in handcuffs, a secret that could put her in prison for the rest of her life, and a man who owned her standing six feet away, drinking a beer and talking about teaching her brother a lesson.

She thought about Knox. Sweet, quiet Knox, who never judged, who showed up for Sunday dinners, who was probably sitting in his apartment right now grading papers and trying to hold himself together. She almost called him. She picked up her phone and pulled up his number and stared at it for ten seconds. Then she put the phone down.

She couldn't call Knox. Calling Knox meant talking, and talking meant the possibility of truth, and truth was the one thing she couldn't afford right now. Truth would unravel everything — the alibi, the deal with Dante, the carefully constructed fiction that Lorraine Butterworth was a grieving daughter who didn't know anything about anything.

She left the clubhouse at 9:00 PM. Dante didn't walk her out. He never did. She was useful, not precious, and the distinction had stopped hurting a long time ago.

She drove home through the dark streets of Bakersfield — past the high school where Knox taught, past the corner where Cyril used to pick her up when she was little, past the church where Helen's funeral had been held eight years ago. The city moved past her windows like a slideshow of a life she'd wasted.

At her apartment, she locked the door and closed the blinds. She sat on the mattress and opened the small plastic bag Dante had given her before she left. Crystal. Enough for two days, maybe three if she stretched it. Dante always sent her home with something. It wasn't generosity. It was maintenance. You keep the machine running so the machine keeps working for you.

She thought about her father. Not the dead version — the living one. Cyril in the kitchen on a Saturday morning, making pancakes with the radio on, singing along to Motown in a voice that was terrible and joyful and completely unselfconscious. Cyril in the driveway, teaching her to ride a bike, running beside her with his hand on the seat, saying, "I've got you, little star. I've got you." Cyril at the kitchen table, writing a check, sliding it across to her with a look on his face that said he knew it wouldn't help and couldn't stop himself from trying.

The grief hit her in the dark, the way it always did — not the clean grief of a daughter who'd lost a father, but the contaminated grief of a daughter who'd helped kill one. It came in waves, each one carrying a different piece of wreckage — his voice, his hands, the smell of his kitchen, the porch light he left on every night in case she came home.

She used. The needle of crystal caught the light from the lamp on the nightstand, and she watched it the way a drowning person watches the surface of the water — knowing which direction salvation was and swimming the other way.

The meth hit fast. The grief retreated. The thinking slowed and then stopped and then turned into the flat, buzzing nothing that was the closest thing to peace Lorraine Butterworth had felt in years.

She lay on the mattress and stared at the ceiling and let the drug do what the drug did — erase everything, for a little while, so she could pretend she was someone who hadn't destroyed the only person who ever loved her without condition.

The porch light burned in her memory. She closed her eyes against it. But it was still there. It would always be there.

CHAPTER 11: "Threads"

Arabella Castillo had spent six years fighting for people who had no voice, and she had never once been afraid of the work. Until now.

She sat in her rental car outside a community center in Delano, forty minutes north of Bakersfield, reviewing the notes she'd taken during a phone call that morning with a woman named Rosa Medina. Rosa ran a farmworker advocacy group in the Central Valley — a small operation, three staff members and a donated office, funded by grants that arrived late and ran out early. Bella had worked with Rosa on immigration cases for two years. They trusted each other. Trust was currency in the Valley, and Rosa spent hers carefully.

"There's something moving through the agricultural corridor," Rosa had said on the phone. Her voice was low, the voice of a woman who'd learned that walls had ears and phones had memories. "Meth. A lot of it. Coming through the packing houses and the labor camps. The workers are scared. They won't talk to police because half of them are undocumented and the other half don't trust the system. But they talk to me."

"What are they saying?" Bella asked.

"They're saying there's a motorcycle club running the

pipeline," Rosa said. "The Reapers. They use agricultural operations as cover — shell companies, labor contractors, transport trucks that look like they're hauling produce. The workers see things. Crates that don't match the manifests. Men who show up at night and leave before sunrise. Cash payments that don't go through payroll."

"Have you heard the name Dante Voss?" Bella asked.

Rosa paused. The pause was long enough to answer the question before she spoke. "Where did you hear that name?" Rosa asked.

"I can't tell you that," Bella said. "But it matters. It matters a lot."

"Dante Voss is the man the workers are afraid of," Rosa said. "He's not the boss — there's someone above him, connected to suppliers in Central America. But Voss is the one they see. He runs the local operation. The clubhouse, the warehouse east of town, the distribution. He's got people inside the labor camps — enforcers who make sure nobody talks. Two workers disappeared last year. One turned up in Fresno with broken ribs. The other hasn't turned up at all."

"Rosa, I need to ask you something," Bella said. "And I need you to think carefully before you answer. Is there any connection between Voss and a man named Cyril Butterworth?"

Another pause. "The county worker who was murdered?" Rosa asked.

"Yes," Bella said.

"I don't know of a direct connection," Rosa said. "But I know Voss has been spending money lately. New truck, new equipment at the warehouse. And one of my workers — a man named Ernesto — told me that Voss was talking about a payday. Something big coming through. This was about three weeks ago. Before the murder."

Bella wrote it down. Three weeks ago put it right around the time Lorraine asked Cyril for twenty thousand dollars. Right around the time Cyril said no.

"Rosa, can Ernesto talk to me?" Bella asked.

"Ernesto is undocumented," Rosa said. "He won't talk to anyone connected to the legal system. Not a lawyer, not a cop, not anyone with a badge or a briefcase. He barely talks to me."

"I'm not a cop," Bella said. "I'm an immigration attorney. I protect people like Ernesto. That's what I do."

"I know what you do, Bella," Rosa said. "But Ernesto doesn't know you. And right now, he's more afraid of Dante Voss than he is of ICE. That should tell you something."

"It tells me a lot," Bella said.

"I'll talk to him," Rosa said. "No promises. But I'll try."

Bella drove back to Bakersfield with the windows down and the November air cutting through the car. The Central Valley stretched out on both sides of Highway 99 — flat, vast, the patchwork geometry of almond orchards and cotton fields and oil pumps nodding like mechanical birds against the sky. She'd grown up in this landscape. Her grandmother still lived in Delano, in the same house where Bella had spent her summers eating tamales and listening to stories about the grape strikes and the men who'd marched with Chavez. The Valley was in her blood. She knew its beauty and its cruelty, and she knew that the two were often the same thing.

Her phone rang. The screen showed the number for Castellano & Reyes, the immigration firm where she'd worked for four years. She answered.

"Bella," the voice said. It was David Castellano, the senior partner. Sixty years old, silver-haired, the kind of lawyer who'd built his practice on handshakes and reputation and the belief that doing good and doing well weren't mutually exclusive. Bella respected him. She also knew the tone he was using, and it wasn't the tone of a man calling to chat.

"David," Bella said. "What's going on?"

"I need to talk to you about something uncomfortable," Castellano said. "The Hernandez family —

the deportation case you've been working. Their hearing is next week."

"I know," Bella said. "I've been preparing the brief."

"From Bakersfield," Castellano said. "Where your boyfriend has been arrested for murder."

The sentence sat in the air like a stone dropped into still water. Bella pulled the car onto the shoulder of the highway and stopped.

"David, my personal life has nothing to do with the Hernandez case," Bella said.

"I agree with you," Castellano said. "But the Hernandez family doesn't. Maria Hernandez called this morning. She's worried. She's seen the news. She asked me — and these are her words, Bella, not mine — whether her attorney was in trouble and whether that trouble could affect her case."

"That's absurd," Bella said.

"It's fear," Castellano said. "And fear is the only language these families speak. They've been let down by every system they've ever trusted. They can't afford to trust a system that's letting them down again."

"I'm not letting anyone down," Bella said.

"I know that," Castellano said. "But I have to think about the firm. We represent vulnerable people, Bella.

People who are one bad headline away from losing everything. If opposing counsel finds out that our lead attorney on a high-profile deportation case is personally involved with a murder defendant — even as a girlfriend, even tangentially — they'll use it. Not legally. Strategically. They'll use it to distract, to discredit, to create noise."

"So what are you saying?" Bella asked.

"I'm saying I need you to come back to San Francisco," Castellano said. "I'm saying the Hernandez hearing needs to be handled by someone who isn't in the middle of a homicide investigation. I'm not firing you, Bella. I'm protecting the client."

"You're protecting the firm," Bella said.

The silence that followed was the silence of two people who respected each other enough to let an honest sentence exist without argument.

"Both," Castellano said. "I'm protecting both. And I'm sorry."

"I'll think about it," Bella said.

"Don't think too long," Castellano said. "The hearing is in six days."

The line went dead. Bella sat on the shoulder of Highway 99 with the engine idling and the Valley stretching out in every direction and the weight of a choice she didn't want to make pressing down on her chest. Go back to San Francisco. Save the Hernandez case. Leave Archie alone in Bakersfield with his dead father's house and a murder charge and three Marines who were good at fighting but couldn't navigate the Central Valley the way she could.

Or stay. Lose the case. Possibly lose her standing at the firm. Risk the professional reputation she'd spent six years building, case by case, family by family, in a system that gave second chances to almost nobody.

She pulled back onto the highway. She drove south toward Bakersfield. She didn't call Castellano back. She didn't call Archie. She made the decision in silence, the way her grandmother had made every important decision — alone, with her hands on the wheel and her eyes on the road and the knowledge that the right choice and the easy choice were almost never the same.

She was staying.

She met Reece at Cyril's house that evening. Knox was at school. Wes was reviewing case law on the couch. Tommy was out running surveillance. Archie was in the backyard, sitting in Cyril's chair, staring at the grass the way he'd been staring at it for days — not seeing it, just using it as a surface for the thoughts he couldn't put anywhere else.

Bella spread her notes on the kitchen table. Reece sat across from her with his laptop open.

"Here's what I have," Bella said. "The Reapers are running meth through the agricultural corridor east of town. Shell companies, labor contractors, transport trucks disguised as produce haulers. Dante Voss is the local operator. He's connected to Central American suppliers — someone above him, identity unknown. A farmworker named Ernesto told my contact that Voss was talking about a big payday about three weeks before Cyril's murder."

Reece typed as she talked. "That tracks with what I've found," Reece said. He turned the laptop so Bella could see the screen. "I've been pulling corporate records for agricultural properties in the corridor. Three of them are registered to shell companies with overlapping addresses — a PO box in Lamont and a registered agent in Fresno. The agent is a law firm that specializes in business formation. They churn out LLCs the way a factory churns out widgets. No real clients, no real operations. Just paper."

"Money laundering," Bella said.

"Almost certainly," Reece said. "The shell companies lease equipment, hire contractors, and generate invoices for services that may or may not exist. Cash goes in dirty, comes out clean. Classic agricultural corridor operation — you hide the drug money inside the farm money and nobody can tell the difference because the volumes are similar."

"And Lorraine?" Bella asked.

Reece pulled up another file. "Lorraine's arrest record," Reece said. "Possession charge, March 2020. She was arrested at a house in Oildale. The police report lists a male companion who was not charged — description matches Voss, but no name on the report. He was released at the scene."

"So the police had Voss in their hands four years ago and let him walk," Bella said.

"He wasn't the target," Reece said. "Lorraine was a low-level possession bust. Nobody was looking at the companion."

Bella leaned back in her chair. The picture was forming — not complete, not provable, but forming. Lorraine connected to Voss. Voss connected to the Reapers. The Reapers connected to meth distribution through the agricultural corridor. Cyril's money flowing to Lorraine. Lorraine's debt flowing to Voss. And somewhere in the middle, a murder that the police were pinning on the wrong Butterworth.

"This is good," Bella said. "But it's circumstantial. Every piece of it. A farmworker who won't testify. Shell companies that could belong to anyone. An arrest report with a nameless companion. We need the link between Voss and the night Cyril died."

"I know," Reece said. "Tommy's working on it. He's been logging traffic at the warehouse — plates, faces, schedules. If Voss is connected to the killer, the connection runs through that warehouse."

"And if Tommy gets caught?" Bella asked.

"Tommy won't get caught," Reece said.

"That's not an answer," Bella said.

"It's the best one I've got," Reece said.

Bella looked at Archie through the kitchen window. He was still in the chair, still staring. The GPS monitor on his ankle caught the porch light. She thought about Castellano's phone call. She thought about the Hernandez family. She thought about the career she was putting on hold for a man she'd been dating for eight months and a family she'd never met until two weeks ago.

She didn't regret it. But she felt the cost. The cost was real and it was hers and nobody was going to reimburse her for it.

"Everything I'm finding points in one direction," Bella said, looking back at Reece. "And it's not the direction the police are facing. They're building a case against Archie while the real trail leads through the Reapers and that warehouse."

"I'm looking," Reece said. "We all are."

Bella left the house at 10:00 PM. She was staying at a motel on Rosedale Highway — a clean, anonymous place that charged by the night and didn't ask questions. She'd been there for a week, living out of a suitcase, eating takeout, working the case during the day and lying awake at night thinking about the distance between the life she'd planned and the life she was living.

She was halfway to the motel when she noticed the car.

Silver sedan. Tinted windows. Two car lengths behind her, matching her speed. She'd first noticed it when she turned off Columbus Street. Now she was on Rosedale, and it was still there.

Bella changed lanes. The silver sedan changed lanes.

Bella slowed down. The silver sedan slowed down.

Her heart rate climbed. She gripped the steering wheel with both hands and forced herself to think like a lawyer, not a victim. Options. She could drive to the police station. She could call 911. She could pull into a gas station with bright lights and cameras and let the sedan decide whether it wanted to be seen.

She chose the gas station. A Chevron on the corner of Rosedale and Coffee, lit up like a stage, two other cars at the pumps. She pulled in, parked near the entrance, and watched the rearview mirror.

The silver sedan slowed as it passed the station. It didn't stop. It didn't turn in. It rolled past at thirty miles an hour, and through the tinted windows, Bella saw nothing — no face, no features, just the dark shape of a driver who wanted her to know he was there.

The sedan turned left at the next intersection and disappeared.

Bella sat in the gas station parking lot for five minutes. Her hands were shaking. She'd fought for families facing deportation, argued with federal judges, stared down ICE agents in detention centers — and none of it had prepared her for the simple, primitive fear of being followed by someone who meant her harm.

She didn't tell Archie. Not tonight. If she told him, he'd pull her off the investigation. He'd say it was too dangerous. He'd try to protect her by taking away the one thing she could do to help. And she wasn't ready to give that up.

She drove to the motel. She locked the door. She checked the window twice. She lay in bed with the lights on and her phone on the pillow beside her and the memory of the silver sedan playing on a loop behind her eyes.

She didn't sleep well. But she slept. And in the morning, she would go back to work, because that's what Arabella Castillo did. She showed up. Even when showing up was the hardest thing in the room.

CHAPTER 12: "The Teacher's Burden"

Knox Butterworth stood in front of his fourth-period class and couldn't remember what he was supposed to be teaching.

The whiteboard behind him said "The Compromise of 1850" in his own handwriting, which meant he'd written it at some point that morning, probably during the ten-minute gap between second and third period when he'd been running on autopilot and caffeine. The thirty-one students in front of him were waiting — some patiently, some not — for him to say something about Henry Clay or Daniel Webster or the Fugitive Slave Act, and Knox was standing at the front of the room with a dry-erase marker in his hand and absolutely nothing in his head.

"Mr. B?" Maria Espinoza said from the third row. "You okay?"

"I'm fine," Knox said. "Sorry. Where were we?"

"The Fugitive Slave Act," Maria said. "You were about to tell us why it made everything worse."

"Right," Knox said. "The Fugitive Slave Act. Yes." He turned to the whiteboard and wrote the words FUGITIVE SLAVE ACT in block letters, and his hand was shaking badly enough that the letters came out jagged, like the handwriting of a man on a moving train.

He taught the rest of the period on muscle memory. The words came out — Clay's compromise, Webster's betrayal, the Northern outrage, the Southern demands — but they came from a place in his brain that operated independently of the part that was currently drowning. He'd been teaching for five years. He could lecture on the antebellum period in his sleep. Today, he was doing something close to it.

When the bell rang, the students filed out. Jaylen Carter stopped at the door.

"Mr. B," Jaylen said. "I heard about your dad. I'm sorry."

"Thank you, Jaylen," Knox said.

"My uncle got killed when I was twelve," Jaylen said. "Shot on the east side. Nobody got arrested for three years. It messes with your head. But they got the guy eventually."

Knox looked at the seventeen-year-old standing in his doorway, offering the kind of wisdom that no teenager should have to carry, and felt something crack inside his chest.

"I appreciate that, Jaylen," Knox said. "More than you know."

Jaylen nodded and left. Knox sat down at his desk and put his head in his hands. The classroom was empty. The fluorescent lights buzzed. The whiteboard said FUGITIVE SLAVE ACT in shaky letters, and Knox Butterworth, the peacemaker, the middle ground, the man who'd spent his whole life holding things together, was falling apart.

He'd told Archie about Dante Voss four days ago. The relief he'd expected hadn't come. Instead, the guilt had shifted shape — from the guilt of keeping a secret to the guilt of having kept it too long. If he'd told Archie in March, when he first saw the motorcycle. If he'd told Cyril at Thanksgiving, when Lorraine didn't show up. If he'd called the police, or confronted Lorraine, or done anything other than drive past her apartment and keep his mouth shut. The conditional tense was a torture device, and Knox was strapped to it every waking hour.

His phone buzzed. A text from Delaney: "Coming home early. Department meeting canceled. Want me to pick up dinner?"

Knox typed back: "Sure. Whatever you want. Love you."

Delaney replied: "Love you too. You sound tired in text form. That's impressive."

He almost smiled. Almost.

He left school at 3:30 and drove home the long way — not past Lorraine's apartment, not anymore, but through the neighborhoods he'd grown up in, past the park where Cyril had coached his Little League team, past the church where Helen's funeral had been held. The city looked the same. It shouldn't have. A man had been murdered, and the streets didn't care. The traffic lights changed on schedule. The gas stations were open. The world continued its business as if Cyril Butterworth's death was a footnote in a story the city wasn't reading.

He parked in his usual spot at the apartment complex — a two-bedroom unit on the second floor of a building on Stockdale Highway, nothing fancy, teacher's salary, but clean and close to school and big enough for two people who didn't need much space. He climbed the stairs and reached for his keys.

The door was unlocked.

Knox stopped. His hand hovered over the knob. He always locked the door. Delaney always locked the door. It was one of the small non-negotiable rituals of their shared life — lock the door, check the stove, set the alarm on both phones. Delaney had grown up in a family where security was a habit, not an option, and she'd transferred that habit to Knox within a week of moving in.

He pushed the door open.

The apartment looked normal. The living room was tidy — Delaney's throw blanket folded on the couch, the coffee table clear except for a stack of graded worksheets and a mug she'd left that morning. The kitchen was clean. The bedroom door was open. Nothing was missing. Nothing was broken. Nothing was out of place.

Except one thing.

On the nightstand, next to the bed, Delaney kept a framed photograph — the two of them at the beach in Pismo, from last summer, wind in her hair, Knox squinting into the sun, both of them laughing at something he couldn't remember. The photograph was always on the left side of the nightstand, next to the lamp. Delaney was precise about these things — everything had a place, and everything stayed in its place.

The photograph had been moved to the right side. Turned slightly. Facing the door instead of the bed.

Knox stood in the bedroom doorway and stared at it. A photograph that had been moved three inches. That was all. No broken windows. No ransacked drawers. No message written on the wall. Just a framed picture of the woman he loved, repositioned so that anyone walking through the front door would see her face first.

The message was clear. Someone had been inside his home. Someone had touched Delaney's photograph. Someone wanted Knox to know that the people he loved were within reach.

He picked up the photograph. His hands were shaking — not the small shakes of a man who hadn't slept, but the deep, involuntary shakes of a man whose body understood a threat before his mind could process it. He checked every room. The closets. The bathroom. Under the bed. The windows were all locked from inside. The back slider was locked. Whoever had come in had come through the front door, moved one object, and left. Nothing stolen. Nothing damaged. Just the quiet announcement that they could get to him whenever they wanted.

Knox set the photograph back on the left side of the nightstand. He sat on the edge of the bed and tried to breathe. His phone was in his hand. He could call the police. He could call Archie. He could call Reece or Tommy or Wes.

He didn't call the police. The police thought his brother was a killer. The police weren't looking for motorcycle club enforcers who broke into apartments to send messages.

He called Archie.

Archie answered on the second ring. "Knox," Archie said. "What's wrong?"

"Someone was in my apartment," Knox said. He heard his own voice and it sounded wrong — thin and hollow, the same way it had sounded the night he called Archie to tell him their father was dead. "The front door was unlocked.

Nothing's missing. But they moved Delaney's picture. On the nightstand. They moved it so it faces the door."

Silence. Three seconds.

"Get out of the apartment," Archie said. "Take Delaney and come to Dad's house. Now."

"Delaney's not home yet," Knox said. "She's on her way."

"Call her," Archie said. "Tell her to meet you at Dad's house. Don't go back inside. Lock the door and leave."

"Archie, it's just a photograph," Knox said. "Maybe I'm overreacting. Maybe Delaney moved it this morning."

"Delaney didn't move it," Archie said. "You know she didn't. Someone is sending you a message. The same people who left a note on my car. Get out. Now."

Knox locked the apartment door and went downstairs. He sat on the bench outside the building's laundry room and called Delaney.

"Hey," Delaney said. She sounded cheerful, normal, a woman whose biggest concern was what to pick up for dinner. "I'm thinking Thai. Or maybe that new —"

"Delaney," Knox said. "I need you to listen to me. Don't come home. Drive to my dad's house on Columbus Street. I'll meet you there."

"What's going on?" Delaney asked. The cheerfulness drained from her voice in a single breath.

"I'll explain when I see you," Knox said. "Just go to the house. Please."

"Knox, you're scaring me," Delaney said.

"I know," Knox said. "I'm sorry. I'll explain everything. Just go to Columbus."

"Okay," Delaney said. "I'm going."

He hung up. He sat on the bench and waited for his hands to stop shaking. They didn't.

At Cyril's house, Knox told them everything. Archie, Reece, Tommy, Wes — all four of them standing in the living room, listening to Knox describe an unlocked door and a photograph that had been moved three inches. It sounded small when he said it out loud. It sounded like nothing. But the Marines didn't react like it was nothing.

"Classic intimidation," Wes said. He was standing by the window, arms crossed, his face set in the hard expression of a man who'd seen this kind of thing before and knew exactly what it meant. "They don't steal anything. They don't break anything. They just let you know they were there. It's a calling card. We've been made, they know where Knox lives, and they know who matters to him."

"The Reapers," Tommy said. It wasn't a question.

"Has to be," Reece said. "First the note on Archie's car. Now this. They're escalating."

"We should go to the police," Knox said.

"And tell them what?" Wes asked. "That someone moved a picture frame? Salcedo's building a case against Archie. She's not going to redirect her investigation because your girlfriend's photograph got turned forty-five degrees. She'll write it up and file it under 'insufficient evidence of criminal activity' and move on."

"Then what do we do?" Knox asked.

"We keep working," Reece said. "And Knox, you and Delaney stay here for a while. This house has better locks, better sight lines, and four Marines. Your apartment has a deadbolt and a hope."

Delaney arrived twenty minutes later. She walked through the front door with a bag of groceries she'd picked up on the way — because Delaney Park was the kind of woman who brought food to a crisis — and looked around the living room at the four men standing in various postures of controlled tension.

"Someone want to tell me what's happening?" Delaney asked. She set the groceries on the kitchen counter and turned to face Knox. Her voice was steady, but her eyes were doing the thing they did when she was scared — going wide and still, the eyes of a woman holding herself together by deciding not to blink.

Knox told her. The unlocked door. The photograph. The note on Archie's car. The Reapers. Dante Voss. All of it — not just today, but everything. The motorcycle he'd seen outside Lorraine's apartment. The eight months of silence. The secret he'd carried and the guilt that was crushing him.

Delaney listened without interrupting. When he finished, she stood very still for a long time. The kitchen was quiet. The groceries sat on the counter, unpacked. The Marines had retreated to the living room to give them space, but the house was small enough that privacy was a courtesy, not a reality.

"Eight months," Delaney said. Her voice was calm. The calm before the verdict. "You've known about this for eight months."

"Yes," Knox said.

"And you didn't tell your father," Delaney said. "And you didn't tell your brother. And you didn't tell me."

"I was trying to protect everyone," Knox said.

"You were trying to protect yourself," Delaney said. "From the conversation. From the fallout. From having to choose between your sister and the truth." She took a breath.

"Knox, someone was in our home today. They touched my things. They wanted us to know they could get to us. To me."

"I know," Knox said. "I'm sorry."

"Sorry isn't what I need right now," Delaney said. She stepped closer to him. Her eyes were wet but her jaw was set, and Knox recognized the expression — it was the expression Delaney wore when she was about to say something that would change the shape of a room. "I need to know if I can marry a man who keeps secrets that put the people he loves in danger. I need to know if you're going to tell the police what you know — all of it — so that this stops."

"Delaney —" Knox started.

"If you won't tell the truth to protect your father's memory," Delaney said, "will you tell it to protect me?"

The question filled the kitchen the way water fills a glass — completely, leaving no room for anything else. Knox looked at the woman he loved, standing in his dead father's kitchen with grocery bags on the counter and fear in her eyes, and he understood for the first time that the compromise he'd been making — the peacemaker's bargain, the middle ground, the silence that held everyone together — had stopped working. The silence wasn't holding anything together anymore. It was tearing everything apart.

"I'll tell them," Knox said. "Everything. Tomorrow."

"Not tomorrow," Delaney said. "Soon. But not just the police. Tell Marcus Hale first. Let him decide how to use it."

Knox looked at her. She looked back. The kindergarten teacher who spent her days teaching five-year-olds to share and take turns was standing in front of him with a strategic mind that would have made Reece Calloway proud.

"When did you become a lawyer?" Knox asked.

"When someone broke into our home," Delaney said.

Knox reached for her. She let him. They stood in the kitchen holding each other, and the groceries sat on the counter getting warm, and the porch light burned through the window, and somewhere in the living room, four men who'd survived a war together were quietly making plans to survive this one.

CHAPTER 13: "The Name"

Reece had been working since Knox described the man and the motorcycle, and by Friday afternoon the kitchen table at Cyril's house looked like a field intelligence office — laptop open, printouts in neat stacks, a legal pad covered in Reece's tight, angular handwriting.

Knox hadn't known the rider's name. He'd given them a description — big, dark hair, skull-and-wings tattoo on the right side of his neck, Reapers patches on the saddlebags of a black Harley Road King. Reece had done the rest, cross-referencing the description with known Reapers associates in public arrest records until one name matched every detail.

Dante Voss.

Archie sat across from Reece with a cup of coffee he'd stopped drinking an hour ago. Tommy was on the road. Wes was on the couch reviewing the Kern County criminal code. Knox had gone back to school — Delaney had insisted, saying that sitting in his dead father's house watching other men work was going to break him faster than teaching would. She was right. She was usually right.

"Dante Michael Voss," Reece said. He turned the laptop so Archie could see the screen. "Age thirty-eight. Born in Riverside, California. Two prior convictions — aggravated assault, 2016, eighteen months served. Possession with intent to distribute, 2019, charges reduced to simple possession in a plea deal, six months served. Known associate of the Reapers Motorcycle Club, Bakersfield chapter. Booking photos from the 2019 arrest show the skull-and-wings tattoo on the right side of the neck. It's the same man Knox described."

"Known associate," Archie said. "Not a full member?"

"The distinction matters legally, not operationally," Reece said. "Full-patch members are the inner circle. Associates do the work — the distribution, the enforcement, the day-to-day business. Voss operates at the associate level, which means he's running the local pipeline but answering to someone above him. Someone connected to the Central American supply chain that Bella's contact described."

"Where does he live?" Archie asked.

"2741 East Brundage Lane," Reece said. "It's registered in his name — no shell company, no LLC. He's not hiding his residence. He's hiding his business."

"The warehouse," Archie said.

"The warehouse," Reece said. He pulled up a property record. "Registered to an LLC called Golden Valley Agricultural Services. Voss is the registered agent. Golden Valley shares a PO box in Lamont and a formation attorney in Fresno with two other LLCs — Central Harvest Group and

Valley Sun Transport. All three formed within six months of each other. None of them file tax returns. The properties they lease are in the agricultural corridor — surrounded by legitimate farming operations, which makes the truck traffic look normal."

"Money laundering," Archie said.

"Almost certainly," Reece said. "Drug money goes in through the shell companies, comes out looking like agricultural revenue. Classic Central Valley operation. The volumes are similar enough that nobody asks questions unless they know what to look for."

"And nobody's looking," Archie said.

"Nobody with a badge," Reece said. "Which brings us to the interesting part."

Reece pulled up his phone and dialed Tommy on speaker. Tommy answered on the first ring, the sound of his truck engine rumbling in the background.

"Tommy, tell Archie about the new face," Reece said.

"I've been logging traffic at the warehouse for nine days," Tommy said. "The regulars are Reapers — big guys, loud bikes, they come and go on a schedule that matches distribution runs. But three days ago, a new player showed up. Gray Honda Civic, California plates. He doesn't fit the pattern. The bikers are loud. This guy is quiet. He parks behind the building where you can't see the car from the road. Comes early morning or late night. Carries a duffel bag in, carries it out. Medium build, mid-forties, dark hair, dark complexion."

"You get the plates?" Archie asked.

"I did," Tommy said. "Ran them through a contact. The car is registered to a Victor Padilla, address in Delano. Here's where it gets interesting — the registration is six months old, purchased with cash. And when I ran the name, Victor Padilla has a Social Security number, a California driver's license, and absolutely nothing before 2023. No credit history. No employment records. No prior addresses. No tax filings. The man didn't exist eighteen months ago."

"Purchased identity," Reece said. "The SSN is bought. The license is either bought or obtained with fraudulent documents. The entire profile is a shell — built to give someone a name and a paper trail just deep enough to rent an apartment and register a car."

"So who is he really?" Archie asked.

"That's what we need to find out," Reece said. "But here's what we know — he's operating out of Voss's warehouse with a false identity, and he showed up in Bakersfield within the timeframe of Cyril's murder. That's not coincidence."

"Wes," Archie said, turning toward the living room. "What does this give us?"

Wes set down his phone and leaned forward. "It gives us a theory," Wes said. "Voss is the organizer. He had motive — the estate money, through Lorraine. He had access — Lorraine gave him the alarm code and the key location, whether she understood what she was doing or not. But Voss didn't do it himself. A man with two priors doesn't walk into a house and commit murder when he's got people who do that kind of work for him. He sends someone. Someone with no local ties, no record, no real identity. Someone who shows up, does the job, and disappears."

"Padilla," Archie said.

"Maybe," Wes said. "We don't have proof. But the profile fits. A ghost with a duffel bag and a purchased name working out of a warehouse owned by the man your sister was involved with. That's not nothing."

"It's not enough, either," Reece said. "We need the connection between Padilla and the night Cyril died. Phone records. A witness. Physical evidence. Something that puts him at the house or links him to Voss in a way the police can't ignore."

"Then we keep watching," Archie said. "Tommy, can you get closer?"

"I can try," Tommy said. "But the warehouse has eyes. If I push too hard, they'll make me."

"Stay at your current distance," Reece said. "Log everything. Plates, times, faces. If Padilla has a pattern, we'll find it. And patterns lead to mistakes."

"Copy," Tommy said. The line went dead.

Marcus Hale arrived Saturday morning with a coffee from a drive-through and the expression of a man who'd been awake since before the sun.

Archie walked him through everything — Reece's dossier on Voss, the shell companies, Tommy's surveillance logs, Bella's Central Valley intel, and the ghost named Victor Padilla. Hale sat at the kitchen table with his legal pad and listened for forty-five minutes without writing a word. When Archie finished, Hale picked up his pen and tapped it against the pad three times.

"This is good work," Hale said. "It's organized and it gives us something I didn't have a week ago — a suspect. Dante Voss. Connected to Lorraine through Knox's observations. Connected to the Reapers through public records. Connected to a warehouse where a man with a purchased identity is coming and going at odd hours. That's a narrative I can use."

"So we take it to Salcedo," Archie said.

"I take it to Salcedo," Hale said. "You stay here. You stay quiet. You let me present it."

"Will she act on it?" Archie asked.

Hale set down his pen. "I want everyone in this room to prepare for the possibility that she hears all of this and doesn't move," Hale said.

"Why?" Archie asked.

"Because she's got a case against you," Hale said. "Circumstantial, but coherent. And now I walk in with a story about a motorcycle club and a mystery man at a warehouse and ask her to pivot. She's going to ask one question — where's the evidence that connects any of this to Cyril's murder? Not to Lorraine. Not to the warehouse. To the murder itself."

"We're building that connection," Reece said.

"Build faster," Hale said. "The preliminary hearing is in three weeks."

Hale left with the dossier, the surveillance logs, and a copy of Bella's notes. Archie stood in the driveway and watched him drive away. The GPS monitor on his ankle pressed against his skin. His fate was in someone else's hands, and there was nothing he could do but wait.

He went back inside. He sat at Cyril's desk. He opened the top drawer to look for a pen and found instead a stack of envelopes — utility bills, bank statements, junk mail. The ordinary paperwork of an ordinary life. He closed the drawer. He wasn't ready to go through all of it yet.

Hale called Saturday evening. Archie put him on speaker. The kitchen was full — Reece, Tommy, Wes, Knox, Bella. All of them waiting.

"I met with Salcedo for two hours," Hale said. "She listened. She took notes. She asked good questions. She looked at the dossier and the surveillance logs."

"And?" Archie asked.

"She said every defendant in the history of murder has an alternative suspect theory," Hale said. "She said your Marine friends are running around Bakersfield playing detective, and I'm asking her to redirect her investigation based on a description and some corporate filings. She said the shell companies could belong to anyone. She said the surveillance logs were compiled by civilians with no law enforcement authority. And she said the man in the Honda Civic is an unknown with no established connection to the victim."

The kitchen was quiet. The clock on the wall ticked — the old clock, white face, black numbers, the second hand sweeping its endless circle.

"She's not going to help us," Archie said.

"She's not going to help us yet," Hale said. "There's a difference. Salcedo is cautious. She got burned chasing an alternative theory that collapsed at trial. Her supervisor put a note in her file. She's not going to stick her neck out without hard evidence — the kind that doesn't come from your friends."

"So what does she need?" Archie asked.

"A direct link between Voss and the murder," Hale said. "Phone records. Physical evidence. A witness who puts Voss or one of his people at the house the night Cyril died. Something the DA can take to court and say this changes everything."

"Then we find it," Archie said.

"Find it fast," Hale said. "Three weeks."

The line went dead. Archie looked around the kitchen. Six faces looking back at him. Six people who'd put pieces of their lives on hold — careers, marriages, safety — to stand in this room and fight for something they believed in.

"The warehouse is the key," Tommy said. "Padilla is the key. Whatever he's carrying in that duffel bag, whoever he really is — that's where the answer is."

"Then we watch him," Archie said. "We watch him until he makes a mistake."

"Everyone makes a mistake," Wes said. "Even

professionals. You just have to be patient enough to catch it."

"And fast enough," Reece said. "Three weeks."

Three weeks. Twenty-one days to find the evidence that would clear Archie's name or watch the system convict him for a crime he didn't commit. The threads were connecting — Voss, Padilla, the warehouse, the shell companies, Lorraine. But the thread that mattered most — the one that ran from that warehouse to Cyril's living room — was still out there, waiting to be found.

They would find it. They had to.

CHAPTER 14: "Recon"

Tommy Fuentes had been sitting in his truck on a dirt road east of Bakersfield for six hours, and the thing that was bothering him had nothing to do with Dante Voss or Victor Padilla or the warehouse two hundred yards ahead of him behind a row of almond trees.

It was the workers.

He'd been watching them all morning through binoculars — men and women moving between the packing house and the field rows, carrying crates, loading trucks, doing the work that kept the Central Valley fed and the rest of the country comfortable. They moved the way farm workers always moved — steady, efficient, heads down. But there was something else in their posture. A tightness. A watchfulness. The way a person carries their body when they know someone is watching them and the someone is not friendly.

Tommy had grown up with these people. His parents had worked the fields outside Bakersfield for thirty years — grapes, almonds, cotton, whatever was in season. His mother had picked table grapes in 110-degree heat while pregnant with his older sister. His father had driven a harvest truck until his back gave out at fifty-two. Tommy had escaped the fields through the Marine Corps, the way some kids escape through college or sports or sheer luck. But the fields were still in him — the dust, the heat, the knowledge that the people who fed America were often the people America forgot.

Now he was watching those same people being used as cover for a drug pipeline, and the anger that rose in his chest was different from the cold, professional focus he'd carried through two tours overseas. This was personal. This was his valley. His people. His parents' world, twisted into something his parents would never have recognized.

He logged the morning's activity in the notebook on the passenger seat. Two panel vans had arrived at 7:00 AM — the same unmarked vans he'd seen before. Four men unloaded crates into the warehouse. The crates were stenciled with the name of a produce distributor that Reece had already flagged as a shell company subsidiary. The workers in the adjacent field kept their eyes on the ground.

At 9:15 AM, the gray Honda Civic appeared.

Tommy raised the binoculars. Victor Padilla — or whatever his real name was — pulled around to the back of the warehouse and parked in his usual spot, behind the building, out of sight from the road. He got out carrying the duffel bag. Same routine. Same bag. Same careful, measured movements of a man who'd been trained to be invisible.

But today, Padilla did something different.

Instead of going inside the warehouse, he walked to one of the panel vans and spoke with the driver. The conversation lasted less than a minute. Padilla handed the driver something — small, flat, could have been an envelope or a phone. The driver nodded. Padilla went inside the warehouse. The driver got back in the van and left.

Tommy wrote it down. Time, description, direction of travel. He got the van's plates as it passed his position on the dirt road. Different plates from the ones he'd logged before. A rotation. They were swapping plates on the vans, which meant they knew enough about surveillance to make tracking difficult.

These weren't amateurs. The Reapers might be outlaw bikers, but whoever was running the supply chain above Voss had operational discipline. The purchased identity. The plate rotation. The scheduled arrivals. This was organized, funded, and protected.

Tommy called Reece at noon.

"New plates on the vans," Tommy said. "They're rotating them. And Padilla made contact with a driver this morning — handed off something small. Envelope or phone."

"Could be payment," Reece said. "Could be instructions. Either way, it means Padilla isn't just storage. He's coordinating."

"There's something else," Tommy said. He paused. Through the binoculars, he could see two women walking from the packing house to a portable toilet at the edge of the field. One of them looked over her shoulder three times in thirty seconds. "The workers are scared, Reece. Not nervous — scared. The way people get when the threat isn't hypothetical."

"Bella's contact said the same thing," Reece said. "Two workers disappeared last year. One showed up in Fresno with broken ribs."

"I know these people," Tommy said. "I grew up with these people. My mother could be one of those women walking across that field. And Voss is using them like furniture."

"Stay focused," Reece said. "I know it's personal. But we're here for Archie."

"I am focused," Tommy said. "But when this is over, someone needs to answer for what's happening in that corridor. Not just for Cyril. For all of it."

"One mission at a time," Reece said.

"Copy," Tommy said. But his jaw was tight when he said it, and the notebook on the passenger seat had a dent in the cover where he'd gripped it too hard.

At 3:00 PM, Padilla left the warehouse. Tommy

followed.

He kept three car lengths back on the county road, then five on the highway. The gray Civic headed north on Highway 99 toward Delano. Tommy expected Padilla to exit at the address on his registration — the month-to-month rental Reece had flagged. He didn't. He passed the exit and kept driving.

Ten minutes later, Padilla pulled off the highway at a truck stop outside McFarland. He drove past the gas pumps and the fast food restaurants and parked at the far end of the lot, next to a two-story motel called the Valley Rest Inn. The kind of place that rented rooms by the night or the week and didn't ask questions about either.

Tommy parked at the gas pumps, two hundred yards away, and watched through the binoculars.

Padilla got out of the Civic, duffel bag in hand, and walked to the motel office. He was inside for three minutes. He came out with a room key — not a card, a physical key, the old-fashioned kind — and walked to room 14 on the ground floor. He unlocked the door, went inside, and closed it behind him.

Tommy waited fifteen minutes. Padilla didn't come out.

He drove to the motel office and parked. Inside, a

woman in her sixties sat behind a counter watching a game show on a small television. She looked up when Tommy walked in.

"Help you?" the woman asked.

"Just looking for a friend," Tommy said. He smiled. The easy, wide smile of a man who'd spent his life in the Valley and knew how to talk to people who worked behind counters. "Big guy, dark hair, just checked in. Drives a gray Honda. I think we got our wires crossed on which room."

"Mr. Rios?" the woman said. "Room 14. He's been here off and on for a couple weeks. Quiet man. Pays cash."

"That's him," Tommy said. "Rios. Thanks."

He walked back to his truck and called Reece.

"Padilla checked into a motel outside McFarland," Tommy said. "The Valley Rest Inn. But he didn't use the name Padilla. He's registered as Rios."

"A second alias," Reece said. "A rented apartment in Delano under one name, a motel room in McFarland under another. He's maintaining multiple locations."

"Operational security," Tommy said. "He doesn't sleep where he works. He doesn't use the same name twice. This guy is not a local biker, Reece. He's something else."

"Something worse," Reece said.

"Something professional," Tommy said.

Tommy reported everything at Cyril's kitchen table that evening. Archie, Reece, Wes, Bella, Knox, and Delaney — all of them listening. The plate rotation. The handoff with the van driver. The motel. The second alias.

"Two names," Wes said. He was sitting forward now, elbows on his knees, the tremor in his hands barely visible. The work was steadying him — giving his mind something to hold onto besides the wreckage of his personal life. "Padilla for the apartment and the car. Rios for the motel. Neither one is real. This man is a ghost with a job, and when the job is done, he disappears."

"What kind of job?" Knox asked.

"The kind you don't put on a resume," Wes said. He looked at Archie. "I need to say something, and nobody in this room is going to like it."

"Say it," Archie said.

"We're approaching the line," Wes said. "Tommy followed a man to a motel. He went inside and got information from the desk clerk by pretending to be someone he wasn't. That's not illegal — there's no law against being friendly. But it's close. If the prosecution finds out we've been conducting mobile surveillance and extracting information under false pretenses, they'll argue we contaminated the evidence chain. Everything we've gathered becomes questionable."

"So what do you suggest?" Archie asked.

"I suggest we're careful about what comes next," Wes said. "We log. We observe. We document. But we don't cross the line into territory that a prosecutor can use to throw out everything we've built. Marcus Hale told us — nothing illegal. Nothing that looks like obstruction. We're not cops. We're not licensed investigators. We're four guys who love our brother and want to keep him out of prison. The law doesn't give us a badge for that."

"Wes is right," Reece said. "From this point forward, we tighten up. Tommy, no more motel visits. No more friendly conversations with desk clerks. Binoculars and notebooks. That's it."

"Understood," Tommy said. He didn't like it — Archie could see that. Tommy was a ground man, built for action, and being told to sit in a truck and watch was like telling a dog to sit while a squirrel ran past. But he was a Marine, and Marines follow orders even when the orders chafe.

"We give what we have to Hale," Archie said. "The second alias. The motel. The plate rotation. It builds the picture. It doesn't prove the murder, but it proves that Voss's operation is sophisticated enough to hire a professional with multiple identities. That's not a small-time motorcycle club. That's organized crime."

"Salcedo will say the same thing she said before," Wes said. "Interesting, but not connected to Cyril."

"Then we keep building until it connects," Archie said.

The meeting broke up at 10:00 PM. Knox and Delaney went to the guest room — they'd been staying at Cyril's house since the break-in, and nobody had discussed when they'd go back to their apartment. The answer was obvious. They wouldn't go back until this was over.

Reece stayed at the kitchen table, working. Tommy drove home — his own apartment across town, a place he'd lived for six years and defended with the same territorial loyalty he'd once applied to forward operating bases. Wes went to the back porch with a glass of water instead of bourbon. Archie noticed. He didn't say anything. Some victories are small and quiet and don't need an audience.

Bella had gone back to her motel two hours earlier. She hadn't mentioned the silver sedan again, and Archie hadn't asked. He sensed she was carrying something she wasn't ready to share, and he was learning — slowly, painfully — that controlling the people he loved was not the same as protecting them.

At midnight, Archie was in the living room reviewing

Reece's printouts when he heard it.

A crash. Glass breaking. Sharp and sudden, the sound cutting through the quiet house like a gunshot.

He was on his feet before the sound finished. Marine reflex — move first, assess second. The crash came from the front of the house. The living room window — the big one that faced the street.

A brick lay on the carpet, surrounded by broken glass. The window had a hole the size of a softball. Cold air poured through it, carrying the smell of the street — exhaust, dust, the faint petroleum edge of Bakersfield at night.

Reece was in the hallway in three seconds. Wes came through the back door in five. Knox appeared at the guest room doorway with Delaney behind him, her face white.

Archie picked up the brick. Something was attached to it with a rubber band — a small metal object, tarnished silver, about the size of a quarter. He turned it over in the porch light.

A skull. Tiny, detailed, with wings spreading from the temples. The Reapers insignia. A calling card.

"They've been here," Archie said.

Wes took the skull from Archie's hand and held it up to the light. His jaw tightened. The tremor in his hands was gone — replaced by something steadier and more dangerous.

"This isn't a warning," Wes said. "The note on your car was a warning. The break-in at Knox's place was a warning. This is a promise. They're telling us the next one won't be a brick."

"We should call the police," Knox said.

"And tell them what?" Wes said. "That someone threw a brick through the window of the house where a murder suspect is living while out on bail? Salcedo will file it under harassment and move on. Or worse — she'll argue that Archie staged it to build sympathy."

"So we do nothing?" Knox asked.

"We do everything," Reece said. He picked up the brick with a kitchen towel and set it on the counter next to the metal skull. "We photograph it. We bag it. We give it to Hale. And we accept that the people we're investigating now know exactly where we are and what we're doing."

Tommy arrived ten minutes later. Archie had called him, and Tommy had driven across town in eight minutes flat. He walked through the front door, looked at the broken window and the brick and the skull on the counter, and his face settled into an expression Archie recognized from the old days. Not anger. Not fear. Readiness. "Now they know what's coming," Tommy said.

"Nobody does anything reckless," Reece said. "We stay disciplined. We stay on mission. We're close to something — that's why they're escalating. If we were wasting our time, they wouldn't bother with bricks."

Archie looked at the broken window. The night air moved through the hole, cold and steady. Somewhere out there — on a dark street, on a motorcycle, in a warehouse east of town — the men who had killed his father were getting nervous. Nervous people make mistakes. And mistakes leave evidence.

"Board up the window tonight," Archie said. "We keep working in the morning."

Reece found plywood in Cyril's garage. Tommy nailed it in place. Wes swept the glass. Knox held the flashlight. Delaney made coffee.

By 1:00 AM, the window was covered, the brick and skull were sealed in plastic bags on the kitchen counter, and the house was quiet again. But nobody slept. The porch light burned through the November darkness, and inside, five men and two women sat in a dead man's house and understood for the first time that the fight they'd started was a fight the other side intended to finish.

CHAPTER 15: "Pressure"

The burner phone was small, black, and cheap — the kind you could buy at any gas station for thirty dollars and throw in a ditch when you were done with it. Dante tossed it to Lorraine the way you'd toss a dog a treat, and she caught it with both hands because her reflexes were shot and because catching things with one hand required a level of coordination that methamphetamine had taken from her weeks ago.

"From now on, you use that," Dante said. "Not your regular phone. Not your brother's number. Not anyone who can be traced back to me. You call me on this phone and only this phone. When we're done, you break it and throw it away."

They were in Dante's living room on East Brundage Lane. It was Tuesday night, and the house was quieter than usual — no Buckle, no Pike, no other Reapers coming and going with the casual territorial confidence of men who treated every room like their own. Just Dante, in his leather recliner, the television off, the lockbox on the card table replaced by a laptop and a stack of papers that Lorraine had never seen before.

Dante was stressed. Lorraine could see it in the way he moved — faster than usual, his gestures sharper, his jaw working even when he wasn't talking. In the fourteen months she'd known him, she'd never seen Dante stressed. Angry, yes. Cold, often. Calculating, always. But not stressed. Stress was a vulnerability, and Dante Voss did not show vulnerability the way other men did. He showed it by becoming more dangerous.

"What's going on?" Lorraine asked.

"The estate," Dante said. "Your father's estate. It's tied up."

"Of course it's tied up," Lorraine said. "Archie's been arrested. He's the executor. Nothing moves until the legal situation is resolved."

"That's the problem," Dante said. "I've got people waiting on money. Suppliers. The kind of people who don't send invoices and don't accept excuses. Your father's estate was supposed to be settled by now. Your third was supposed to be in hand. And instead, your brother is sitting in your daddy's house with three Marines and a lawyer, and the whole thing is frozen."

"I can't control that," Lorraine said.

"You can push it," Dante said. "Call the lawyer. The estate lawyer. Tell him you need an advance on your share. Tell him you've got debts, you've got bills, you need the money now. Executors can authorize partial distributions before the estate is fully settled. Your brother may be the executor, but you're a beneficiary. You have rights."

"Archie will block it," Lorraine said. "He controls everything. He always has."

"Then go around him," Dante said. "File a petition with the court. Get your own lawyer. Make noise. The more pressure on the estate, the faster it moves."

Lorraine looked at the burner phone in her hands. It was warm from being in Dante's pocket. She turned it over and stared at the blank screen and felt the weight of what she was holding — not the phone, but the leash attached to it. Every call she made on this phone would be a call Dante controlled. Every conversation would be a conversation that existed in a shadow world where nothing was recorded and nothing could be traced and the only person who knew the truth was the man sitting across from her telling her to push harder.

"There's something else," Dante said. His voice dropped. Not to a whisper — Dante didn't whisper. To a register that was lower and flatter and carried the specific gravity of a man about to say something he'd been thinking about for a while.

"What?" Lorraine asked.

"Your brother's defense," Dante said. "His lawyer is poking around. Asking questions about the Reapers. Asking about the warehouse. Someone gave him a name — my name — and he took it to that detective. Salcedo."

Lorraine felt the blood leave her face. "How do you know that?" Lorraine asked.

"I know everything that happens in this town," Dante said. "Salcedo didn't bite. Not yet. But if Archie's lawyer keeps pushing, and if those Marine friends of his keep sniffing around the corridor, eventually someone's going to connect a dot that shouldn't be connected."

"What do you want me to do?" Lorraine asked.

"I want you to help me make sure the dots stay disconnected," Dante said. He leaned forward. "There are things that could surface. Evidence. Testimony. Things that point away from Archie and toward — other explanations. If those things surface, the case against Archie falls apart. And if the case falls apart, the questions start. Real questions. The kind that end with people in handcuffs."

"People like me," Lorraine said.

"People like both of us," Dante said. "So here's what I'm thinking. We give the police something. Something that makes Archie look worse. Something that seals the case."

"Like what?" Lorraine asked.

"A witness," Dante said. "Someone who saw Archie near your father's house that night. Someone credible. I've got people who can do that."

"You want to fabricate a witness," Lorraine said.

"I want to solve a problem," Dante said.

Lorraine stared at him. The recliner. The laptop. The papers on the card table. The man who'd looked at her in a bar fourteen months ago with interest and attention and something that felt like respect, and who was now sitting in front of her proposing to frame her brother for murder.

"No," Lorraine said.

The word came out before she'd fully decided to say it, propelled by something that lived deeper than the meth and the fear and the fourteen months of compromise. It came from the same place that had made her say "don't touch him" when Dante threatened Archie. The place where the sister she used to be still lived, locked in a room she'd stopped visiting, banging on a door she'd stopped opening.

"No?" Dante said. He said it the way you'd say a word in a foreign language — testing its shape, measuring its weight, deciding whether it was worth responding to.

"I planted the seeds," Lorraine said. "I told Salcedo about the money arguments. I told her Archie had a temper. I did that. But fabricating a witness — putting someone on the stand who lies under oath to put my brother in prison for something he didn't do — that's a line I haven't crossed."

"You've crossed plenty of lines," Dante said.

"Not that one," Lorraine said.

Dante looked at her for a long time. The silence in the room was the kind of silence that has a temperature — cold, pressurized, the silence between a question and a consequence. Lorraine held his gaze because looking away would mean something she couldn't afford. In Dante's world, looking away was the same as saying yes. Looking away was permission.

"Fine," Dante said. He leaned back in the recliner. "For now. But the clock is ticking, Lorraine. My suppliers don't care about your family drama. They care about money. And if the money doesn't come through, the problem stops being legal and starts being physical. For both of us."

He picked up the laptop and turned his attention to whatever was on the screen, dismissing her the way he always dismissed her — completely, instantly, as if she'd stopped existing the moment she stopped being useful.

Lorraine drove home with the burner phone on the passenger seat and the windows down, letting the cold November air hit her face, trying to feel something other than the sick, gnawing dread that had taken up permanent residence in her stomach.

She was using more. She knew she was using more. The bags Dante gave her were lasting two days instead of three. She was sleeping in two-hour intervals, waking up with her heart hammering and her sheets soaked and the image of Cyril's face floating behind her eyelids like a photograph projected on a wall she couldn't look away from. She was eating less. Her jeans were loose at the waist. The mirror in the bathroom — the one she'd stopped looking at weeks ago — would have shown her a woman who was disappearing, one gram at a time, into the same substance that had been erasing her for years.

At home, she locked the door and turned on the television. The local news was running a segment she'd seen three times already but couldn't stop watching. The DA — a man named Craig Jessup, who Lorraine had never heard of before her father's murder and now saw everywhere — was standing behind a podium at a press conference, flanked by two assistant prosecutors and a woman from the victim's advocacy office.

"The Butterworth case is a straightforward domestic murder motivated by greed," Jessup said. He spoke with the polished confidence of a man who'd rehearsed every word and believed all of them. "The defendant, Archibald

Butterworth, had the motive, the means, and the opportunity to murder his father for financial gain. We are confident in our case and we will pursue justice for Cyril Butterworth and his family."

Lorraine watched her brother's face appear on the screen — the mugshot from his arrest, the one where he looked exactly like what the prosecution wanted him to look like: calm, controlled, unfeeling. The face of a man who could kill his father and walk into a police station without breaking a sweat.

She knew that face. She'd grown up with that face. It wasn't the face of a killer. It was the face of a man who'd learned in the Marines that showing emotion was a liability, and who carried that lesson into every room he entered for the rest of his life. Archie didn't look like a killer. He looked like a man who didn't know how to look like anything else.

The segment cut to a reporter outside Kessler-Braun Capital. "The defendant's employer has confirmed that Butterworth has been placed on indefinite leave pending the outcome of the investigation," the reporter said. "Sources within the firm describe him as a high-performing trader who kept to himself and rarely discussed his personal life."

Lorraine turned off the television. The apartment was quiet. The burner phone sat on the nightstand next to her regular phone, the two devices side by side like the two versions of her life — the one the world could see and the one that existed in the dark.

She thought about what Dante had asked her to do. Fabricate a witness. Frame Archie. Seal the case. Close the door on the truth and lock it from the outside. It would be easy. A phone call. A name. Someone who shows up at the police station and says, "I saw Archie Butterworth at his father's house that night." Not a dark SUV — an eyewitness. A face. A positive identification that no jury could ignore. The lie would fit perfectly into the case Salcedo was already building. It would be the last nail, and Archie would spend twenty-five years in a cell for a crime he didn't commit.

She'd said no. She'd meant it. But the no was fragile — built on a foundation of guilt and meth and the fading memory of a sister who used to love her brother, and Lorraine knew better than anyone how quickly foundations crumbled when the pressure was enough.

The guilt was leaking through. Not in large, dramatic ways — not in confessions or breakdowns or the kind of collapse that movies made it look like. In small ways. A flinch when she heard Cyril's name on the news. A moment in the shower when she pressed her forehead against the tile and said "I'm sorry" to no one. A dream where Cyril was standing at the kitchen sink, washing dishes, and she was watching him from across the street in the dark, and he turned and looked at her through the window and said, "I left the light on for you."

She woke up from that dream at 3:00 AM and sat on the mattress in the dark, shaking. Not from withdrawal. From the weight of what she'd done and the growing certainty that the weight would never get lighter, no matter how many grams she put in her body or how many lies she told the police or how many burner phones Dante handed her.

She picked up the burner phone. She turned it over in her hands. She thought about calling Knox. Not on this phone — on her real phone. Just to hear his voice. Just to hear someone say her name without wanting something from her.

She didn't call.

She put the phone down. She reached for the plastic bag on the nightstand. She used. The meth hit fast, the way it always did — a chemical sunrise that burned away the shadows and the dreams and the memory of a porch light that was still on, somewhere across town, in a house where her father had lived and died and loved her more than she deserved.

The guilt retreated. The thinking stopped. And Lorraine Butterworth sat in the dark and let the drug do the only thing it had ever been good at — making the truth feel like someone else's problem.

CHAPTER 16: "The Notebook"

Archie had been putting it off for weeks.

The executor's duties didn't wait for grief or murder charges or the slowly tightening noose of a criminal justice system that had decided he was guilty. There were accounts to close, bills to pay, insurance claims to file, and a house full of forty years of accumulated life that needed to be sorted, cataloged, and dealt with. The lawyer handling the estate — a probate attorney named Sandra Webb, separate from Hale — had been patient, but patience had limits. The estate couldn't move forward until Archie went through Cyril's personal effects.

So on a Wednesday morning, three weeks after his father's death, Archie finally sat down at Cyril's desk and opened the drawers. He'd been avoiding it. The top drawers were practical — bills and office supplies, the business of a life that needed managing. The bottom drawers were personal, and personal meant pain. But Sandra Webb had called twice that week asking for documents, and Archie couldn't put it off any longer.

The first drawer held what he'd already seen — utility bills, bank statements, junk mail. The second held office supplies — pens, tape, a stapler, a box of paper clips that had been there so long the box had yellowed at the edges. The third drawer held files — tax returns going back a decade, the deed to the house, Helen's death certificate in a manila envelope with her name written on it in Cyril's handwriting.

Archie handled each item carefully, the way you handle things that belong to the dead — with the awareness that every object is a fragment of a life that no longer exists, and the weight of that awareness pressing down on your hands like something physical.

The bottom drawer was deeper than the others. Inside, beneath a stack of old Bakersfield Californian newspapers that Cyril had saved for reasons only Cyril knew, Archie found a notebook.

It was a black composition book, college-ruled, the kind you could buy at any drugstore for two dollars. It was worn at the edges, the cover soft from years of handling. Archie picked it up and opened it to the first page.

A date. A dollar amount. A sentence.

March 12, 2010 — $500 — "Lorraine says rent is late again. I believe her."

Archie turned the page.

September 3, 2011 — $800 — "Lorraine needs textbooks for community college. Proud of her for trying."

He turned another page.

January 18, 2013 — $1,200 — "Lorraine dropped out. Says she needs a fresh start. I give her the money and I pray."

Archie sat at the desk and read every entry. There were dozens of them, spanning fourteen years, each one the same — a date, a dollar amount, and a sentence or two written in Cyril's careful, slanted handwriting. The handwriting of a man who kept records because he couldn't keep his daughter.

July 4, 2015 — $2,000 — "Lorraine says she owes someone. Won't say who. I don't ask. I should ask."

November 22, 2016 — $1,500 — "Lorraine missed Thanksgiving. Said she was sick. I drove by her apartment. The lights were off. I sat in the car for an hour."

August 4, 2018 — $1,200 — "Lorraine needs car repair. I don't believe her but I give it anyway."

March 30, 2020 — $3,000 — "Lorraine called from the county jail. Possession charge. I paid the bail. Archie says I'm enabling her. He's probably right. I can't stop."

June 15, 2022 — $500 — "Lorraine came for dinner. She looked thin. She ate everything on her plate and asked for seconds. I made her a plate to take home. She hugged me at the door. First time in months."

February 2, 2024 — $2,500 — "Lorraine says she's in trouble. Real trouble. I give her the money. I don't tell

Archie or Knox. They'd be right to be angry."

And then the last entry. The one Archie had to read three times before the words stopped blurring.

October 19, 2024 — $0 — "Lorraine asked for $20,000. I said no. First time I've ever said no. She was angry. God help me."

The last thing Cyril Butterworth ever wrote.

Archie closed the notebook. He set it on the desk. He pressed both hands flat on the wood surface and leaned forward, his head bowed, his eyes shut. The grief hit him — not the clean, sudden kind, but the slow, deep kind that starts in your chest and spreads outward like a stain, coloring everything it touches. Fourteen years. Every dollar documented. Every excuse recorded. Every prayer written down in the handwriting of a man who loved his daughter so completely that he documented his own destruction one entry at a time.

He sat there for a long time. Then he picked up the notebook and carried it to the kitchen, where Reece was working at the table.

"I found something," Archie said. He set the notebook in front of Reece. "In Dad's desk. Bottom drawer, under a stack of old newspapers. He kept a record. Every dollar he gave Lorraine. Fourteen years."

Reece opened the notebook and read. His face didn't change — Reece's face rarely changed — but his eyes moved across the entries with the focus of a man who understood that he was looking at something that could change the case.

"The last entry is October 19," Reece said. "The day Lorraine asked for twenty thousand and Cyril said no."

"Two weeks before he was murdered," Archie said.

"This is the motive," Reece said. "Not yours. Hers. Fourteen years of financial dependency, and the one time the money stopped, Cyril ended up dead. Hale needs to see this today."

Archie called Hale and told him about the notebook. Hale said he'd come by that afternoon. In the meantime, Archie walked through the rest of the house, room by room, making notes for the probate attorney. The bedroom. The guest rooms. The garage. The hallway closet where Cyril kept his tools.

He reached the front door and stopped.

The doorframe, just above the doorbell, had a small rectangular outline — a mounting bracket, screwed into the wood, with two loose wires hanging from behind it. Something had been attached there. Recently. The screw holes were clean, the wood around them undamaged.

"Knox," Archie called. Knox was in the kitchen. He came to the hallway. "Did Dad install a doorbell camera?" Archie asked, pointing at the bracket.

Knox looked at it. "Yeah," Knox said. "A few weeks before — before everything. I was here for dinner and he was up on a stepladder screwing it in. I asked him why. Dad never locked his doors, never worried about any of that. He said he just wanted to know who was coming to the house. He didn't explain it, but he had this look — the look he got when he was worried about Lorraine but didn't want to say her name. I helped him connect it to his phone and didn't push it."

"It's gone," Archie said. "The bracket's here but the camera isn't."

"The police must have taken it," Knox said.

Archie called Hale back. "Marcus, did the police recover a doorbell camera from the front of my father's house?" Archie asked.

"Hold on," Hale said. Archie could hear papers shuffling. "The crime scene report mentions a doorbell camera. It says the device was recovered as evidence, but the footage was corrupted. The hard drive was damaged — that's the police conclusion. No usable footage was extracted."

"Corrupted," Archie said. "Or deleted."

"That's a significant distinction," Hale said. "If the footage was deliberately deleted, that means someone with access to the camera's system erased it after the murder. Your father couldn't have done it — he was dead. The question is who else had access."

"Knox helped Dad connect it to his phone," Archie said. "The camera links to a phone app. Footage streams to a cloud account or saves to the device's internal storage. If someone had Dad's phone and knew his passcode, they could delete the footage from the app."

"Or someone who knew the system could access it remotely," Reece said. He'd been listening from the kitchen doorway. "If Lorraine knew Cyril's phone passcode, or if whoever entered the house that night took the phone and deleted the footage before leaving."

"Cyril's phone was recovered at the scene," Hale said. "It's in evidence. I'll file a motion to have the camera's hard drive examined by an independent forensic tech. If the footage was deleted rather than corrupted, the tech may be able to recover it — or at least prove that someone deliberately erased it."

"If the footage shows someone at the door that night," Archie said, "someone who isn't me —"

"Then we have something Salcedo can't ignore," Hale said. "I'll file the motion today."

Archie hung up. He looked at the notebook and the empty mounting bracket and felt the two discoveries pulling the case in a direction nobody had been looking. A father's private record of heartbreak and a missing piece of technology that might have captured his killer's face. Both had been waiting — one in a desk drawer, one on a doorframe — for someone to notice.

Archie's phone rang at 4:15 PM. Tommy's name on the screen.

"I've been made," Tommy said.

The words hit Archie like ice water. "What happened?" Archie asked.

"Two Reapers spotted my truck," Tommy said. "I was in my usual position on the farm road, quarter mile from the warehouse. A pickup pulled up behind me — two guys, both wearing Reapers cuts. One of them got out and walked toward my door. I pulled out before he got close, but he got a good look at my plates. They know my truck. They know my face."

"Where are you now?" Archie asked.

"Heading south on the county road," Tommy said. "They're not following. But they don't need to. They know who I am. I've been running the same route for two weeks. They've probably had eyes on me for days."

Archie looked at Reece. Reece was already standing, his laptop closed, his bag over his shoulder. Wes was pulling on his jacket.

"Come to the house," Archie said. "Don't go home. Come straight here."

"I'm not running from these guys, Archie," Tommy said.

"Nobody's running," Archie said. "We're regrouping. Get here."

Tommy arrived in twenty minutes. He walked through the door with his jaw set and his eyes hard and the posture of a man who'd been doing surveillance in combat zones since he was twenty years old and didn't appreciate being flushed out by motorcycle club muscle.

"They'll go back to the warehouse," Tommy said. "They'll tell Voss. And Voss will either pull his operation or fortify it. Either way, we lose the surveillance position."

"Or he does something stupid," Wes said. "Men like Voss don't run from problems. They solve them. If he thinks we've been watching his warehouse, he'll want to know what we've seen and who we've told."

"Which means he might come to us," Reece said.

"Or send someone," Wes said.

Archie's phone rang again. An unknown number. He answered.

"Who is this?" Archie asked.

"Your friend in the tow truck should mind his own business," the voice said. Male. Calm. Not Dante — someone else. "Next time, we won't let him drive away."

The line went dead.

The room was silent. Archie, Reece, Tommy, Wes, Knox, and Delaney — all of them staring at Archie's phone.

"They've got my number," Archie said.

"They've had your number," Wes said. "The note on your car. The brick through the window. They've been tracking us since we got here. The phone call just means they're done being subtle."

"We should call the police," Knox said.

"And tell them what?" Wes said. "Salcedo will file it next to the brick and the break-in."

"We call Hale," Archie said. "And we stay put tonight. Nobody goes near that warehouse."

But Tommy's surveillance gear was still out there — his camera mount and log book, hidden in the brush on the farm road. Detailed records of everyone who'd come and gone from the warehouse for two weeks. Plates. Faces.

Times. Evidence they needed, and evidence that put Tommy at risk if the Reapers found it.

"I need to get my gear," Tommy said. "It's on the farm road, in the brush where I set up my position. If they find it, they find everything."

"At night," Reece said. "Minimal exposure. We don't go near the warehouse. We go to Tommy's position, grab the gear, and leave."

"And if they're waiting?" Wes asked.

"Then we deal with it," Reece said.

Wes looked at Reece. Reece looked at Wes. The kind of look that didn't need translation — the look of two Marines who'd walked into uncertain situations before and knew exactly what "deal with it" meant.

"When?" Archie asked.

"Tonight," Reece said. "0200."

They went at 2:00 AM. Reece, Tommy, and Wes. Archie stayed behind — the GPS monitor on his ankle made him a liability in the field. If his location data showed him anywhere near the warehouse, the DA would revoke his bail before sunrise. He stood in the driveway and watched the three Marines drive away in Tommy's truck, and the helplessness he felt was worse than anything the handcuffs had done.

Knox stood beside him. Neither of them spoke. Bella was inside with Delaney. The house was dark except for the porch light, which burned the way it always burned.

The call came at 2:47 AM.

Reece's voice. Tight. Controlled. But underneath the control, the unmistakable sound of adrenaline.

"We've got a problem," Reece said.

Gunfire. Archie could hear it through the phone — sharp, staccato, the distinct crack of pistol rounds and the heavier boom of a shotgun. Not close to the phone. But close enough.

"Tommy's hit," Reece said. "Left shoulder. He's behind his truck. Three shooters — Reapers associates, not Voss. Pistols and shotguns. We're on the farm road, two hundred yards east of the warehouse."

"I'm calling 911," Archie said.

"Already done," Reece said. "ETA fifteen minutes. We need to hold."

The line stayed open. Archie stood in the driveway with the phone pressed to his ear and listened to the firefight — the sounds compressed and distorted by the phone's microphone, but unmistakable. He'd heard those sounds before, in a different country, in a different life. The crack of rounds. The pause of reloading. The shout of a voice he recognized as Wes.

Later — after the ambulances and the police and the statements that would take all night — Tommy would tell him what happened.

Three Reapers associates had been waiting on the farm road. Not at Tommy's surveillance position — farther north, near the tree line, parked with their lights off. They'd opened fire when Tommy's truck pulled onto the road. Tommy took a round in the left shoulder before he got behind the engine block.

Reece flanked left through the almond trees, using the rows for cover the way they'd used building walls in combat. He drew fire from two of the shooters, giving Tommy time to get low. A ricochet fragment caught Reece across the forearm — a gash, bloody but shallow.

And Wes.

Wes was supposed to stay with the truck. Wes was supposed to provide covering fire from a defensive position. That was the plan. But Tommy was bleeding, pinned behind the wheel well, and the shotgun shooter was advancing — moving between the trees, pumping rounds into the truck's body, getting closer with every shot.

Wes crossed open ground.

Twenty yards of bare dirt road with no cover and a shotgun pointed in his direction. His hands were shaking — they'd been shaking for months, the tremor that he hid with bourbon and willpower and the stubborn refusal to acknowledge that something inside him was broken. But the training took over. The muscle memory that the Marine Corps had burned into his nervous system overrode the damage that everything since had done to it. He moved low and fast, the way they'd trained at Camp Pendleton, and the shotgun blast that should have taken him in the chest caught him across the ribs — a pellet graze, painful, bloody, but not fatal.

He reached Tommy. He grabbed him by the vest and pulled him behind the truck's rear axle. Tommy was conscious, his left arm useless, his face gray. Wes pressed his hand over the wound and held it there, his own blood mixing with Tommy's on the dirt road.

"Stay with me, brother," Wes said. "Stay with me."

Tommy looked up at Wes — the bloodshot eyes, the shaking hands now steady with purpose, the face of a man who'd been falling apart for months and had just found the one thing that could put him back together.

"You're laughing," Tommy said.

And Wes was. Not crazy. Not manic. The laugh of a man who was alive — truly, completely alive — for the first time in longer than he could remember. The mission had burned through the fog. The tremor was gone. The hands that couldn't hold a coffee cup without shaking were holding a wounded Marine against his chest with the grip of a man who would not let go.

Reece finished it. He flanked the third shooter through the tree line and came up behind him. The man surrendered. The other two were wounded — one from Reece's pistol, one from Tommy's one-handed return fire from behind the truck. No fatalities. The farm road fell silent.

When the police arrived, they found three wounded Marines and three wounded Reapers associates, and a farm road that looked like a piece of a war zone transplanted into the almond orchards of Kern County.

They also found something else.

In the rush to set the ambush, the Reapers associates had left the warehouse unlocked. The first officer on the scene, securing the perimeter, walked the property and looked through the open warehouse door. In plain view, on a table just inside — visible from outside, which made it admissible under the plain-view doctrine — were two items.

A prepaid cell phone. And a photograph.

The phone's call log showed a pattern — calls to and from a burner number during the week of Cyril's murder.

The same burner number that had called another phone, which had called another phone, in a chain that started somewhere and ended at Cyril's front door.

The photograph showed two men standing in front of the warehouse. One was Dante Voss. The other was Victor Padilla.

The officer logged them, photographed them, and secured them as evidence.

At 4:30 AM, Archie's phone rang. Reece's voice, tired and tight, but with something underneath it that Archie hadn't heard in weeks.

Hope.

"Tommy's in surgery," Reece said. "Shoulder. He'll make it. Wes took a graze across the ribs — stitches and bruises. I've got a cut on my arm that needs closing. We're at Kern Medical."

"And the warehouse?" Archie asked.

"The responding officers found a phone and a photograph," Reece said. "On a table inside the warehouse, visible through the open door. The phone has calls that match the murder timeline. The photograph shows Voss with Padilla. The police have both."

Archie leaned against the kitchen counter. The notebook sat on the table. And now, in an evidence room at the Bakersfield Police Department, a phone and a photograph were telling a story that had nothing to do with Archibald Butterworth.

"It's not over," Reece said. "But the ground just shifted."

"Get some rest," Archie said.

"Archie," Reece said. "Wes saved Tommy's life tonight. Crossed open ground under fire with his hands shaking and a shotgun pointed at his chest. He pulled Tommy out and held the wound until the medics came."

"That sounds like Wes," Archie said.

"It sounded like the old Wes," Reece said. "The one we thought was gone."

Archie hung up. He stood in the kitchen and looked at the clock on the wall. The second hand swept its circle. Outside, the sky was still dark, but somewhere past the oil fields and the almond orchards, the first gray line of dawn was forming on the horizon.

The notebook. The doorbell camera hard drive in police evidence. The phone. The photograph. The pieces were falling into place, one by one, and for the first time, they were falling in Archie's direction.

CHAPTER 17: "Fallout"

The firefight on the farm road made the morning news before Archie finished his first cup of coffee.

He stood in Cyril's kitchen at 6:00 AM with the television on and watched a reporter stand in front of the yellow tape that now stretched across the county road east of town. Behind her, the almond orchard looked peaceful in the early light — rows of bare trees, stripped for winter, standing in the kind of quiet order that made it hard to believe three men had been shot there five hours ago.

"Three men associated with a local motorcycle club are in custody this morning after a shooting on a rural road east of Bakersfield," the reporter said. "Three other men — described by police as private citizens — were injured in the exchange and are being treated at Kern Medical Center. Sources tell us the shooting occurred near a warehouse property that has been under investigation by the Kern County Sheriff's Department in connection with narcotics trafficking."

Under investigation. Archie looked at the television and felt the words settle into place. The warehouse wasn't just Tommy's surveillance target anymore. It was now a crime scene. The sheriff's department had secured it. Whatever was inside — the prepaid phone, the photograph, and anything else the Reapers had been too careless or too arrogant to hide — was now in law enforcement hands.

His phone rang. Hale.

"Are you watching the news?" Hale asked.

"I'm watching it," Archie said.

"We need to talk," Hale said. "In person. I'll be there in an hour."

Hale arrived at 7:15 with two coffees and the expression of a man who'd been awake all night and had come out the other side with something he didn't have when the night started.

"The shooting changes everything," Hale said. He sat at the kitchen table — Reece's usual spot, but Reece was at Kern Medical getting stitches. "Here's what I know. The three Reapers associates are in custody. One of them is talking — not about Cyril, not yet, but about the warehouse operation. Meth distribution. The shell companies. Voss's role. The sheriff's department is building a narcotics case, and the warehouse is the centerpiece."

"And the phone?" Archie asked. "The photograph?"

"Both in evidence," Hale said. "The responding officers logged them at the scene. The phone's call history shows activity during the week of your father's murder — calls to and from burner numbers in a chain that starts at the warehouse and ends somewhere in Bakersfield. The photograph shows Voss with a man matching the description of the individual your friend Tommy identified as Victor Padilla."

"So Salcedo has it," Archie said.

"Salcedo has a problem," Hale said. "She's been building a case against you for three weeks. Now there's a shooting at a warehouse connected to the Reapers, a phone with calls matching the murder timeline, and a photograph of the Reapers' local operator standing next to a man with a purchased identity. She can't ignore it. Not anymore. Not with the media covering the shooting and the sheriff's department opening a narcotics investigation on the same property."

"What about Lieutenant Garza?" Archie asked. "He's been pushing her to close the case."

"Garza's going to push harder now," Hale said. "Not to close the case — to distance himself from it. If it comes out that the Bakersfield PD was focused on the wrong suspect while the real killer was operating out of a warehouse ten miles away, that's Garza's career. He'll want to get ahead of the story. And the only way to get ahead of it is to let Salcedo follow the evidence wherever it goes."

"Even if it goes away from me," Archie said.

"Especially if it goes away from you," Hale said. He pulled the notebook from his briefcase — Cyril's notebook, sealed in a clear evidence bag. "Now let's talk about this."

"What are you going to do with it?" Archie asked.

"I'm presenting it to the court at the preliminary hearing," Hale said. "Along with the motion for forensic examination of the doorbell camera. The notebook establishes Lorraine's financial motive — fourteen years of dependency, escalating amounts, and the final entry on October 19 when the money stopped. Combined with the warehouse evidence, it creates an alternative narrative that the prosecution cannot dismiss."

"Salcedo dismissed everything I gave her before," Archie said.

"Salcedo dismissed your Marine friends' surveillance logs," Hale said. "She can't dismiss a shooting that put three people in the hospital and a phone the police recovered from a crime scene. The evidence isn't coming from us anymore, Archie. It's coming from her own colleagues in the sheriff's department. That's a different conversation."

"Will it be enough to drop the charges?" Archie asked.

Hale paused. He set down his coffee and looked at Archie with the measured honesty that was the thing Archie valued most about his lawyer — the refusal to say what his client wanted to hear when the truth was something else.

"I don't know," Hale said. "The notebook is powerful. The warehouse evidence is powerful. But the prosecution still has their case — the cell tower gap, the financial motive they've built around the estate, the witnesses who said you talked about your father's money. Craig Jessup isn't going to drop murder one because the defense produced a notebook and a shooting happened near a warehouse. He'll argue the notebook proves family dysfunction, not Lorraine's guilt. He'll argue the warehouse is a separate criminal enterprise with no proven connection to Cyril's death."

"Then what do we need?" Archie asked.

"The doorbell camera," Hale said. "If the forensic tech can recover that footage, and if it shows someone other than you at your father's door that night, the case collapses. Without it, we're in a fight. A fight I think we can win, but a fight."

"When will the tech have results?" Archie asked.

"I filed the motion yesterday," Hale said. "The judge will rule this week. If approved, the examination takes three to five days. We're cutting it close to the preliminary hearing, but we'll make it."

Hale left with the notebook. Archie stood in the

kitchen and looked at the empty spot on the table where it had been. Fourteen years of his father's handwriting, sealed in plastic, on its way to a courtroom where strangers would read Cyril's private prayers and use them as evidence in a case that should never have been built.

Archie drove to Kern Medical Center at noon. The GPS monitor allowed travel within Kern County, and Hale had confirmed that hospital visits wouldn't raise flags with the DA's office.

Tommy was in a room on the third floor — left arm in a sling, IV in his right hand, the hospital gown making him look smaller than he was. His face was gray but his eyes were alert, and when Archie walked in, Tommy smiled the way he always smiled — wide, open, the smile of a man who found something to be glad about in every room he entered.

"You look terrible," Archie said.

"You should see the other guys," Tommy said.

"I heard they look worse," Archie said.

"One of them does," Tommy said. "The other two are fine. Flesh wounds. They'll be out in a day." Tommy shifted in the bed, wincing as his shoulder reminded him it had a hole in it. "The doctors say six weeks for full recovery. I told them four. They said I was being optimistic. I told them I was being a Marine."

Archie pulled a chair next to the bed and sat down. "Tommy, I'm sorry," Archie said. "This is my fight. You shouldn't be here."

"Don't do that," Tommy said. His smile faded, replaced by something harder and more serious. "Don't apologize for my choices. I came here because your father was a good man who didn't deserve what happened to him. I came here because you're my brother. And I came here because the people running that warehouse are poisoning my valley — the fields my parents worked, the communities I grew up in. This isn't just your fight, Archie. It's mine too."

"Your parents know?" Archie asked.

"My mother called at five this morning," Tommy said. "She'd seen the news. She cried for ten minutes and then she told me she was proud of me and to stop getting shot. My father got on the phone and said, 'Mijo, you need to learn to duck.' That's my old man."

Archie laughed. A real laugh, the kind that hurt because it came from a place that was still raw.

"How's Wes?" Tommy asked.

"Twelve stitches across the ribs," Archie said. "He's at the house. Delaney's making him eat soup. He keeps trying to get off the couch and she keeps pushing him back down. I think he's met his match."

"He saved my life," Tommy said. His voice changed when he said it — quieter, stripped of the humor, carrying the weight of a debt that couldn't be repaid with words. "He crossed open ground, Archie. Twenty yards with a shotgun pointed at him. His hands were shaking the whole time. But he came."

"That's Wes," Archie said.

"That's who Wes used to be," Tommy said. "Before everything broke. Last night, for about three minutes, he was that guy again. And I think he needed those three minutes more than I needed the rescue."

Archie sat with Tommy for an hour. They talked about the case — the notebook, the doorbell camera, the warehouse evidence. They talked about Bakersfield — the changes since they were kids, the way the valley had grown in some places and hollowed out in others. They talked about Cyril, and Tommy told a story Archie had never heard — about the barbecue three years ago when Tommy had helped Cyril with the grill and Cyril had spent twenty minutes asking Tommy about his tow truck business, genuinely interested, asking questions nobody else had ever asked.

"He asked me if I was happy," Tommy said. "Just like that. We're standing at the grill and he says, 'Tommy, are you happy?' I said yes. He said, 'Good. That's all that matters.' Your old man understood something most people never figure out, Archie. He knew that the only question worth asking is whether the people you love are okay."

Archie left the hospital at 1:30 PM. He sat in the rental car in the parking lot and pressed his forehead against the steering wheel and let the grief come. Not a wave this time — a river. Steady, deep, carrying everything with it. The notebook entries. The porch light. Tommy in a hospital bed because he'd come to help. Wes crossing open ground with shaking hands. Knox crumbling under the weight of his silence. Bella giving up her career. Delaney making soup for a wounded Marine she'd met two weeks ago.

All of it flowing from a single source — a man named Cyril Butterworth who left the porch light on every night and loved his children so much that the love itself became the weapon that destroyed him.

Archie sat in the car for ten minutes. Then he wiped his face, started the engine, and drove back to Columbus Street. There was work to do. There was always work to do. And the preliminary hearing was coming, and the notebook was on its way to a courtroom, and somewhere in an evidence room, a doorbell camera's hard drive was waiting to tell the truth about the night Cyril Butterworth died.

The tide was turning. Slowly, painfully, at a cost measured in blood and stitches and sleepless nights. But it was turning.

CHAPTER 18: "The Offer"

Marcus Hale sat at Cyril's kitchen table on a Friday morning with a manila folder in front of him and a look on his face that Archie had never seen before. It wasn't defeat. It wasn't worry. It was the look of a man holding something he didn't want to hand over.

"The DA's office called me yesterday afternoon," Hale said. "Craig Jessup wants to meet."

"About what?" Archie asked.

"A plea deal," Hale said.

The words landed in the kitchen like a dropped glass — sharp, sudden, wrong. Archie was standing at the counter with a cup of coffee. He set it down.

"Tell me," Archie said.

Hale opened the folder. "Voluntary manslaughter," Hale said. "Reduced from murder one. The offer is eight to twelve years, with the possibility of parole after six. You plead guilty. You allocute — that means you stand in front of a judge and say you did it. You go to prison. In exchange, the DA takes the death penalty and life without parole off the table."

"I didn't kill my father," Archie said.

"I know," Hale said. "But I have an obligation to

present every offer the prosecution makes, and I have an obligation to explain the landscape so you can make an informed decision. That's what I'm doing."

"Then explain the landscape," Archie said.

Hale closed the folder and leaned back in his chair. "The warehouse evidence helps us," Hale said. "The phone, the photograph, the narcotics investigation — all of it gives us an alternative narrative. The notebook is powerful. The doorbell camera motion is pending. But here's the truth, Archie. As of today, none of that evidence directly links anyone other than you to your father's murder. The phone has burner numbers in a chain. The photograph shows Voss with Padilla. But there's no call to Cyril's number. No DNA at the scene. No fingerprints. No witness who puts Padilla or anyone else at the house that night."

"The camera might change that," Archie said.

"The camera might change everything," Hale said. "Or it might show nothing. The police said the footage was corrupted. The forensic tech might recover it. Or he might confirm what the police already concluded — that the hard drive is damaged and there's nothing to recover. We won't know until the results come back, and the results won't come back until after the preliminary hearing."

"When is the hearing?" Archie asked.

"Eight days," Hale said.

"And if we go to the hearing without the camera footage?" Archie asked.

"Then we present what we have," Hale said. "The notebook. The warehouse evidence. Knox's testimony about the biker at Lorraine's apartment. Bella's Central Valley contacts. Tommy's surveillance logs. Reece's dossier on Voss and the shell companies. It's a strong alternative narrative. But it's circumstantial. The prosecution's case is also circumstantial. Two circumstantial cases in front of a judge, and the judge has to decide whether there's enough to go to trial."

"What are the odds?" Archie asked.

"I don't deal in odds," Hale said. "I deal in arguments. My argument is strong. Jessup's argument is weakening. But a preliminary hearing isn't a trial — the standard is probable cause, not beyond a reasonable doubt. Jessup doesn't have to prove you did it. He just has to show there's enough evidence for a reasonable person to believe you might have."

"And a former Marine with no alibi and a sister who says there were money tensions might have," Archie said.

"That's what Jessup will argue," Hale said.

The kitchen was quiet. The clock ticked. Through the window, the porch light was off — daytime, no need for it.

But Archie could still see the bulb, waiting for dark, waiting to do the one thing Cyril had asked it to do.

"What happens if I take the deal?" Archie asked. He didn't ask because he was considering it. He asked because he needed to hear the shape of the thing he was rejecting.

"You plead guilty to voluntary manslaughter," Hale said. "You serve eight to twelve years. With good behavior and parole, you could be out in six. You'd be forty-one. You'd have a felony record. You'd never work in finance again. You'd never hold a professional license. And the record would say that Archibald Butterworth killed his father."

"And the real killer walks," Archie said.

"And the real killer walks," Hale said.

"And Lorraine gets away with it," Archie said.

"Lorraine's involvement is still inference," Hale said. "We believe she gave Voss the information he needed. We can't prove it yet."

"And Dante Voss keeps running meth through the valley," Archie said.

"The narcotics case is separate," Hale said. "The sheriff's department will pursue it regardless of what happens with your case. But yes — if you take the plea, the investigation into your father's murder stops. The case is closed. Voss is never questioned about Cyril. Padilla disappears into whatever identity he's using next. And the notebook goes into a file that nobody ever opens again."

Archie looked at the folder on the table. Manila. Ordinary. The kind of folder that held tax returns and insurance forms and the unremarkable paperwork of unremarkable lives. This one held six years of his future and the permanent erasure of his father's truth.

"No," Archie said.

"You're sure," Hale said.

"I'm sure," Archie said. "I didn't kill my father. I'm not going to stand in front of a judge and say I did. Not for six years. Not for six months. Not for six minutes. If the system wants to convict me, it's going to have to do it with a trial and a jury and every piece of evidence laid out in the open where the truth has a chance."

Hale nodded. He didn't smile — Hale wasn't a man who smiled at decisions that carried this much weight. But something in his posture shifted, a loosening, as if a tension he'd been carrying since he walked through the door had finally released.

"I'll inform Jessup this afternoon," Hale said. "He won't be surprised. This offer was a pressure move — he knows the warehouse evidence weakened his case, and he's trying to lock in a conviction before it weakens further. Your refusal tells him you're not afraid of trial. That changes the dynamic."

"How?" Archie asked.

"Because a man who's guilty takes the deal," Hale said. "A man who's innocent fights. Jessup knows that. The judge will know it too."

Bella was in the living room when Hale left. She'd been listening from the couch — not hiding, not eavesdropping, just present in the way she'd been present since she arrived in Bakersfield. Available. Alert. Ready for whatever came next.

"You heard," Archie said.

"I heard," Bella said. She was sitting with her legs tucked under her, a legal pad on her lap, a pen she wasn't using in her right hand. Her face was composed but her eyes were doing the thing they did when she was processing something too big for a single expression — moving, searching, calculating.

"Say what you're thinking," Archie said.

"I'm thinking you made the right decision," Bella said. "And I'm thinking that the right decision might put you in prison for the rest of your life if the camera doesn't come through."

"I know," Archie said.

"I'm thinking that six years is a long time," Bella said. "And I'm thinking that forty-one is young enough to start over. And I'm thinking that I would have supported you either way — if you'd taken the deal or if you'd done exactly what you did. Because this isn't my choice. It's yours."

"But," Archie said.

"But nothing," Bella said. "I said what I'm thinking. All of it. No buts."

She looked at him across the living room — the woman who'd left her career, her case, her firm, and her apartment in San Francisco to sit on a dead man's couch in Bakersfield and watch the man she loved gamble his freedom on a doorbell camera that might show nothing.

"Come here," Archie said.

She set down the legal pad. She crossed the room. He held her, and for a moment the case and the hearing and the plea deal and the camera all receded, and there was just this — two people holding each other in a house that still smelled like Cyril's coffee, with the clock ticking on the wall and the porch light waiting for dark.

"We're going to be okay," Archie said.

"You don't know that," Bella said.

"No," Archie said. "But I believe it."

"That's not the same thing," Bella said.

"It's close enough," Archie said.

Knox came by that evening after school. Delaney was with him — she'd been driving him to and from Cyril's house every day since the break-in, the two of them traveling in a unit that felt less like a couple and more like a small, determined army.

Archie told them about the plea deal. He told them he'd refused it. He laid out the terms the way Hale had laid them out — voluntary manslaughter, eight to twelve years, parole after six, a felony record, and the permanent inscription in the public record that Archibald Butterworth had killed his father.

Knox listened. His face didn't move. His hands were flat on the kitchen table, the way they'd been flat the day he told Archie about Dante Voss — the posture of a man trying to keep himself from shaking apart.

When Archie finished, Knox stood up from the table. He walked to the window. He stood there for a long moment, looking out at the street where he'd ridden his bike as a kid, where Cyril had taught him to throw a football, where the porch light had burned every night for as long as he could remember.

"If you'd taken that deal," Knox said, "it would have been my fault."

"No," Archie said. "It wouldn't."

"Yes, it would," Knox said. He turned from the window. His eyes were red. His voice was steady but thin, held together by the kind of control that comes from being on the verge of breaking and choosing not to. "I knew about the motorcycle. I knew about the Reapers. I kept my mouth shut for eight months because I was afraid of the conversation. And because I kept my mouth shut, Dad died and you got arrested and the police spent three weeks building a case against the wrong person. If you'd taken that plea — if you'd gone to prison for something you didn't do — I would have put you there. My silence would have put you there."

"Knox —" Archie started.

"Let me finish," Knox said. "I can't change what I did. I can't go back and tell Dad about Lorraine. I can't go back and tell you about the motorcycle. But I can tell the truth now. At the hearing. On the stand. Under oath. Everything I know, everything I saw, everything I should have said a year ago. I'll say it in front of a judge and a courtroom and God and whoever else is listening. That's the least I can do."

"It's not the least," Archie said. "It's everything."

Knox looked at his brother. Archie looked back. The distance between them — the distance that had always existed, the gap between the achiever and the peacemaker, the Marine and the teacher, the man who charged ahead and the man who held the middle — felt smaller than it ever had.

Delaney stood in the doorway, watching. She didn't say anything. She didn't need to. The look on her face said it all — pride and grief and the fierce, quiet love of a woman who'd watched the man she was going to marry find his spine in the worst month of his life.

"The hearing is in eight days," Archie said. "Hale is preparing the case. The notebook, the warehouse evidence, the doorbell camera if the results come back in time. Knox, Hale will want to prep you for testimony."

"I'll be ready," Knox said.

"And Lorraine?" Delaney asked. It was the first time she'd spoken, and the name landed in the kitchen like a stone in still water.

"Lorraine is Hale's problem," Archie said. "And Salcedo's. Not ours."

"She's always going to be ours," Knox said. "She's our sister."

The word hung in the air — sister — carrying fourteen years of notebook entries and a lifetime of love that had been weaponized and wasted and turned into the instrument of a good man's death. Lorraine was their sister. She would always be their sister. And the truth about what she'd done was coming, whether any of them were ready for it or not.

Archie looked at the clock. Eight days. The second hand swept its circle, steady and indifferent, counting down to a hearing that would either set him free or send him to trial for a crime committed by the people his father had loved most.

"Eight days," Archie said.

"We'll be ready," Knox said.

"All of us," Delaney said.

The kitchen was quiet. The clock ticked. Outside, the sun was setting over the valley, and the porch light clicked on the way it did every evening — automatic now, set on a timer Knox had installed because leaving it to chance felt like breaking a promise.

CHAPTER 19: "Cracks"

Lorraine saw the warehouse on the news and felt the floor of her life give way.

She was sitting on her mattress at 6:00 AM, the television on because she hadn't slept and the silence was worse than any noise the screen could make. The local morning broadcast led with the story — aerial footage of the farm road, police tape across the county road, the warehouse with its doors open and officers moving in and out like ants dismantling a hill.

"Authorities have confirmed that a property east of Bakersfield linked to narcotics trafficking was secured early this morning following an exchange of gunfire between three members of an outlaw motorcycle club and three private citizens," the anchor said. "Three suspects are in custody. Sources say the property is connected to the Reapers Motorcycle Club, a known criminal organization operating in Kern County."

Lorraine stared at the screen. The warehouse. Dante's warehouse. The building where she'd sat on a leather couch and watched him count money. The building where Buckle and Pike came and went. The building that held whatever was in the back room she'd been told never to ask about.

It was on the news. It was surrounded by police. And three of Dante's people were in handcuffs.

She picked up the burner phone and called Dante. It rang six times. He didn't answer. She called again. Same result. A third time. Nothing.

She sat on the mattress and felt the tremor start — not in her hands, which were already shaking from the meth, but somewhere deeper, in the center of her chest, where the architecture of lies she'd built over the past three weeks was developing fractures she couldn't patch.

The regular phone buzzed. A text from Knox: "Are you okay? Please call me."

She stared at the message for a long time. Knox. Sweet, quiet Knox, who'd been calling her every few days since Cyril's death, leaving voicemails she listened to but never returned. His voice in those messages was always the same — careful, gentle, the voice of a man trying to hold a door open for someone who kept walking past it.

She typed a reply: "I'm fine. Just tired." She stared at the words on the screen. Two lies in four words. She sent it anyway.

At 9:00 AM, the burner phone rang. Dante.

"Where are you?" Dante asked. His voice was different — tighter, faster, the words clipped short like he was biting them off. She'd never heard him sound like this. Dante Voss, the man who spoke in flat, businesslike sentences, the man who counted money with steady hands and dismissed people with a glance — that man was gone. The man on the phone was angry in a way that had edges.

"Home," Lorraine said.

"Stay there," Dante said. "Don't go anywhere. Don't talk to anyone. Don't answer your regular phone."

"I saw the news," Lorraine said. "The warehouse —"

"I know what happened at the warehouse," Dante said. "Your brother's Marine friends happened at the warehouse. They've been watching it for weeks. They got into a firefight with three of my guys and now the sheriff's department is crawling all over my operation. Do you understand what that means?"

"I understand," Lorraine said. But she wasn't sure she did. The scope of what was unraveling was larger than anything she'd been able to hold in her mind since the night Dante called and said "it's done."

"It means I'm exposed," Dante said. "The warehouse is gone. The vans are impounded. Three of my people are in lockup and one of them is talking — not about your father, not yet, but about the operation. If he keeps talking, the chain goes up. And the chain leads to me."

"What are you going to do?" Lorraine asked.

"I'm going to handle it," Dante said. "But the timeline just got shorter. The estate, Lorraine. Your father's money. I need it now. Not next month. Not when the lawyers finish their paperwork. Now."

"I can't make the estate move faster," Lorraine said. "Archie is the executor. Everything goes through him."

"Then go around him," Dante said. "I told you before — file a petition. Get a lawyer. Force a partial distribution. I don't care how you do it. I need money in hand within two weeks or the people above me are going to start solving problems their way. And their way doesn't involve lawyers."

"Dante, I can't —" Lorraine started.

"You can," Dante said. "Because the alternative is worse. For both of us. Do you understand me?"

"Yes," Lorraine said. The word came out flat, empty, the sound of a woman agreeing to something because disagreeing was no longer an option she could afford.

The line went dead.

Lorraine spent the rest of the morning on the couch, the television muted, the two phones on the cushion beside her — one cracked, one cheap, both connecting her to a world she wanted to leave and couldn't.

She thought about the estate. Half a million dollars,

split three ways. Her third was roughly a hundred and sixty-seven thousand. Half of that went to Dante — that was the deal. Eighty-three thousand for her. Eighty-three thousand dollars for a lifetime of loss and a father's murder and the complete destruction of everything Cyril Butterworth had built.

She thought about what eighty-three thousand dollars would buy. A year of rent. A car that didn't break down. Enough meth to kill herself slowly over two or three years, which was the trajectory she was on whether the money came or not.

She thought about what it wouldn't buy. A father who answered the phone when she called. A brother who looked at her without disappointment. A life she could stand to live in without chemical assistance.

The guilt was getting worse. It had been manageable in the first week — a dull ache, buried under layers of meth and denial and the survival instinct that had kept Lorraine functional through fifteen years of dysfunction. But the layers were thinning. The meth was losing its power to erase. The denial was cracking. And underneath, the guilt was expanding, filling the spaces the drugs used to occupy, pressing against the walls of her mind like water behind a dam.

She dreamed about Cyril every night now. Not the

same dream — different versions of the same scene. Cyril at the kitchen sink. Cyril in the driveway. Cyril on the phone saying "I love you, sweetheart" in the voice he used only for her, the voice that was different from the one he used with Archie or Knox, softer and more careful, the voice of a man handling something precious and fragile.

In the dreams, he always turned and looked at her. And in the dreams, his face was never angry. It was never accusatory. It was never anything but what it had always been — patient, tired, full of a love that didn't know how to quit.

She woke from those dreams gasping, her chest tight, her eyes burning, and reached for the bag on the nightstand the way a drowning person reaches for anything that floats.

At 2:00 PM, she turned the volume back on. The noon news was rerunning the warehouse story with updated information. The anchor mentioned the Butterworth murder case — a connection she'd been dreading.

"Sources close to the investigation say that evidence recovered from the warehouse property may have connections to the murder of Cyril Butterworth, the Kern County facilities manager found dead in his home last month," the anchor said. "Butterworth's son, Archibald Butterworth, is currently awaiting a preliminary hearing on murder charges. His attorney, Marcus Hale, declined to comment, but sources say the defense is expected to present an alternative theory involving the Reapers Motorcycle Club."

Alternative theory. The words hit Lorraine like a slap. They weren't just investigating the warehouse for drugs. They were connecting it to her father's murder. The phone. The photograph. Whatever else the police had found inside those walls — it was all pointing in a direction that led away from Archie and toward the truth.

Toward her.

She changed the channel. Another station was running a different angle — a reporter outside the Kern County courthouse, talking about the upcoming preliminary hearing.

"In a related development, sources say the prosecution offered the defendant a plea deal earlier this week — voluntary manslaughter with a reduced sentence. The defendant reportedly refused the offer, signaling his intention to fight the charges at trial."

Archie refused the deal.

Lorraine sat on the couch and felt something shift inside her — a tectonic movement, slow and deep, the kind of shift that rearranges everything above it. Archie had been offered a way out. Six years instead of life. A guilty plea, a reduced sentence, a path that was terrible but survivable. And he'd said no.

He'd said no because he didn't do it.

The simplicity of that fact — the clean, unavoidable truth of it — cut through the meth and the denial and the carefully constructed fiction of Lorraine's survival with the precision of a blade. Archie didn't do it. Archie was innocent. And Archie would rather risk life in prison than stand in front of a judge and say he killed the father he loved.

That was who Archie was. That was who Archie had always been — the man who didn't bend, didn't compromise, didn't take the easy road when the easy road was a lie. Lorraine had spent years resenting him for it. She'd called it arrogance. She'd called it coldness. She'd told herself that Archie's discipline was just another word for selfishness, that his refusal to indulge her was proof that he didn't care.

But a man who didn't care would have taken the deal. A man who didn't care would have pleaded guilty to manslaughter and done his six years and come out the other side and moved on with his life. Archie refused because the truth mattered to him more than his freedom. And the truth was that he didn't kill Cyril Butterworth.

Lorraine did.

Not with her hands. Not with a weapon. But with her

mouth and her rage and the alarm code and the key location and every piece of information she'd handed to Dante Voss in a moment of fury that she would spend the rest of her life trying to undo.

She picked up her regular phone. She pulled up Knox's number. Her thumb hovered over the call button. One press. One conversation. She could tell Knox everything — Dante, the alarm code, the night she sat in the car outside Cyril's house, the call at 11:15 PM when Dante said "it's done." She could tell him and Knox would tell Archie and Archie would tell Hale and the truth would come out and the case would collapse and Archie would go free.

And Lorraine would go to prison.

Not for six years. Not for manslaughter. For conspiracy to commit murder. For the rest of her life. She would die in a cell, in an orange jumpsuit, with the notebook entries and the porch light and her father's voice playing on a loop in her memory until the memory itself finally went dark.

Her thumb trembled over the button.

She didn't press it.

She put the phone down. She picked up the burner phone instead and turned it over in her hands, feeling the weight of the cheap plastic, the weight of the choice she was making by not making a choice. Silence was a choice.

Inaction was a choice. Every minute she didn't call Knox was a minute she was choosing herself over Archie, choosing survival over truth, choosing the same path she'd been choosing for fifteen years — the path that led away from pain and toward the only kind of comfort she knew how to find.

She reached for the bag on the nightstand. It was almost empty. One hit left. Maybe two if she stretched it. She'd need more soon, and getting more meant calling Dante, and calling Dante meant being useful, and being useful meant doing whatever he told her to do next.

The cycle had no exit. Or it had one exit, and the exit was the truth, and the truth was a door she couldn't walk through because walking through it meant losing everything she had left — which was almost nothing, but almost nothing was still more than the absolute nothing that waited on the other side.

She used. The last of the bag. The meth hit her bloodstream and the thinking slowed and the guilt retreated and the image of Archie refusing the plea deal — standing in his dead father's kitchen and saying no to six years because the truth mattered more than his freedom — faded into the chemical haze that was the only home Lorraine Butterworth had left.

But it didn't fade all the way. Not this time.

Something was different. The drug wasn't working the

way it used to. The erasure wasn't complete. Underneath the high, in a place the meth couldn't quite reach, the guilt was still there — patient, steady, growing. Like a porch light that someone had left on, burning in the dark, waiting for her to come home.

CHAPTER 20: "The Hearing"

The courtroom smelled like wood polish and tension, and Archie Butterworth sat at the defense table in a suit he hadn't worn in five weeks and tried to remember the last time his future had been decided by someone else.

The Marines, he thought. Boot camp. The moment when a drill instructor held your fate in his hands and you stood at attention and waited. But even then, the outcome depended on what you did — how fast you ran, how straight you shot, how much punishment you could absorb without breaking. This was different. This was sitting in a chair while two lawyers argued about whether he'd killed his father, and the only thing required of him was silence.

Department 12 of the Kern County Superior Court was fuller than Archie expected. The gallery held reporters, courthouse regulars, and a handful of Cyril's former colleagues from the county facilities department — men and women in their fifties and sixties who'd worked alongside his father for decades and had come to watch the system process his death. Knox and Delaney sat in the second row, Knox in the sport coat he'd worn to the bail hearing, Delaney holding his hand. Bella sat behind them, alone, her back straight, a legal pad on her lap.

Wes was in the back row. His ribs were taped under

his shirt, and he moved carefully when he sat down, but he was there. Reece sat beside him, his forearm bandaged, his laptop bag on the floor between his feet. Tommy was still in the hospital — the doctors had refused to discharge him, and Tommy had threatened to walk out until his mother called and told him she'd personally drive to Bakersfield and drag him back to bed if he left that room.

Lorraine was not there.

Marcus Hale sat beside Archie at the defense table, his briefcase open, his legal pad covered in notes, his tie slightly crooked in the way it always was — the small imperfection that made juries trust him. Across the aisle, Craig Jessup sat at the prosecution table with two assistant DAs and a file that had grown thicker since the last time Archie had seen it. Jessup looked confident. He always looked confident. It was his best weapon and his biggest liability.

Judge Patricia Moreno entered at 9:00 AM. The bailiff called the room to order. Moreno settled into her chair, adjusted her reading glasses, and looked at the two tables with the expression of a woman who had presided over enough hearings to know that the truth usually lived somewhere between the two stories she was about to hear.

"This is a preliminary hearing in the matter of the People versus Archibald Butterworth," Moreno said. "The purpose of this hearing is to determine whether there is sufficient probable cause to bind the defendant over for trial on the charge of murder in the first degree. Mr. Jessup, you may proceed."

Jessup built his case the way a bricklayer builds a wall — one piece at a time, steady, methodical, each piece placed to support the next.

He called Detective Salcedo first. She took the stand in a navy blazer and white blouse, her badge visible, her posture as controlled as it had been in every interaction Archie had witnessed. She laid out the facts of the investigation — the crime scene, the cause of death, the lack of forced entry, the disarmed alarm, the family's access to the house.

"No forced entry," Jessup repeated, standing near the witness box. "The alarm was disarmed. The victim appears to have opened the door to someone he knew or wasn't afraid of. Is that consistent with your findings, Detective?"

"Yes," Salcedo said.

"And the defendant had the alarm code and knowledge of the spare key," Jessup said.

"All three of the victim's children had the alarm code," Salcedo said. "And the spare key's location was known to the family."

Jessup moved to the cell tower data. Salcedo confirmed that Archie's phone records showed coverage overlap between his condo and SFO during the window of the murder. She confirmed there was a gap — no digital activity from Archie's devices between 8:00 PM and 11:47 PM on the night Cyril died.

Then the witnesses. Jessup introduced the statements from Graham Whitfield and Derek Yoon — the former business partner and the college friend, both of whom had described Archie as cold, transactional, and focused on his father's money. Hale objected to their relevance. Moreno allowed them as background but noted they were not eyewitness testimony.

Jessup finished with the financial motive — the estate, the three-way split, the hundred and sixty-seven thousand dollars.

"The defendant is a wealthy man," Jessup said in his summary. "But wealth does not preclude greed. The defendant had the means, the motive, the opportunity, and the access. He was home alone with no verifiable alibi. He flew to Bakersfield within hours of the murder. And two witnesses describe a man with a pattern of viewing relationships — including his relationship with his father — through the lens of money."

It was clean. It was coherent. And it was built entirely on inference, which Hale intended to demolish.

"Mr. Hale," Moreno said. "Your response."

Hale stood slowly. He buttoned his jacket. He picked up a clear evidence bag from the defense table and held it up so the courtroom could see it.

"Your Honor, this is a notebook," Hale said. "A black composition book, college-ruled, purchased at a drugstore for approximately two dollars. It was found by the defendant in the bottom drawer of his father's desk, beneath a stack of old newspapers, during his duties as executor of the estate."

He set the notebook on the ledge in front of the judge. "This notebook contains fourteen years of entries," Hale said. "Each entry records a date, a dollar amount, and a brief note — written in Cyril Butterworth's handwriting. Each entry documents a payment made by Cyril Butterworth to his daughter, Lorraine Butterworth. The payments span from March 2010 to October 2024. The amounts range from two hundred dollars to three thousand dollars. The total exceeds one hundred thousand dollars."

A murmur rippled through the gallery. Moreno tapped her gavel once, lightly, and the sound died.

"The final entry," Hale said, "is dated October 19, 2024 — seventeen days before Cyril Butterworth was murdered. The amount is zero. The note reads: 'Lorraine asked for $20,000. I said no. First time I've ever said no. She was angry. God help me.'"

Hale let the words sit in the courtroom for five

seconds. Five seconds of silence in which every person in the gallery heard the voice of a dead man asking for help from a God who didn't answer.

"The prosecution's theory is that Archibald Butterworth killed his father for a hundred and sixty-seven thousand dollars," Hale said. "The defendant's net worth exceeds two million dollars. He makes more in a single quarter than the entire estate is worth. The financial motive the prosecution has constructed is, with respect, absurd."

"Objection," Jessup said. "Counsel is editorializing."

"Sustained," Moreno said. "Stick to the facts, Mr. Hale."

"The facts, Your Honor," Hale said. "The facts are that Lorraine Butterworth received over a hundred thousand dollars from her father over fourteen years. The facts are that she asked for twenty thousand dollars seventeen days before his murder. The facts are that he refused. The facts are that she was, by her father's own words, angry."

Hale called Knox to the stand.

Knox walked to the witness box with the posture of a man carrying something heavy and setting it down in public for the first time. He was sworn in. He sat down. He looked at Hale.

"Mr. Butterworth," Hale said. "Please describe for the

court what you observed at your sister's apartment building beginning in March of this year."

Knox described it. The Harley Road King. The Reapers patches. The man with dark hair and a skull-and-wings tattoo on his neck. Four sightings over eight months — the apartment, the gas station, the apartment again, the bar on Edison Highway. He described each one clearly, specifically, without embellishment.

"Did you know the identity of this man at the time?" Hale asked.

"No," Knox said. "I didn't know his name. I only knew what I saw — a man with Reapers patches on his motorcycle spending time at my sister's apartment."

"Did you report these observations to the police?" Hale asked.

"No," Knox said. His voice tightened. "I should have. I didn't. I was trying to protect my family."

"When did you eventually share this information?" Hale asked.

"After my brother's arrest," Knox said. "I told Archie. His friend, Reece Calloway, identified the man through public arrest records as Dante Voss — a known associate of the Reapers Motorcycle Club with prior convictions for assault and drug possession."

Jessup objected. "Hearsay," Jessup said. "The witness is testifying to the conclusions of a third party who is not a law enforcement officer."

"Your Honor," Hale said, "the identification of Dante Voss is corroborated by public arrest records which I am prepared to enter as exhibits. The witness is describing the sequence of events, not offering expert testimony."

"I'll allow it," Moreno said. "But tread carefully, Mr. Hale."

Hale moved to the warehouse. He presented Tommy's surveillance logs — dates, times, plate numbers, descriptions. He presented Reece's dossier on the shell companies. He presented the arrest report from Lorraine's 2020 possession charge, which listed an unnamed male companion matching Voss's description.

Then he got to the firefight.

"On the night in question," Hale said, "three associates of the Reapers Motorcycle Club ambushed three private citizens on a farm road near the warehouse. In the aftermath, responding officers discovered two items in plain view inside the warehouse — a prepaid cell phone whose call log shows activity matching the timeline of Cyril Butterworth's murder, and a photograph of Dante Voss standing with a man identified as Victor Padilla, an individual operating under a purchased identity."

Jessup was on his feet. "Objection, Your Honor. The items recovered from the warehouse are part of an ongoing narcotics investigation by the Kern County Sheriff's Department. The defense is attempting to introduce evidence from a separate case."

"The evidence is directly relevant to the murder of Cyril Butterworth," Hale said. "A phone with calls matching the murder timeline found at a property operated by the man connected to the victim's daughter is not a separate case. It is this case."

"I'll hear it," Moreno said. "Objection overruled."

Hale turned back to the courtroom. "Your Honor, the prosecution asks you to believe that Archibald Butterworth — a decorated Marine veteran, a successful professional with no criminal record, a man whose net worth dwarfs his father's estate — murdered his father for money. The defense asks you to consider an alternative supported by evidence. A daughter with a fourteen-year history of financial dependency. A motorcycle club enforcer connected to that daughter. A warehouse containing a phone and a photograph linking that enforcer to an unidentified man with a false identity. And a father who wrote 'God help me' seventeen days before someone he trusted walked through his front door and killed him."

Hale sat down.

Moreno called a recess at 11:30 AM. Archie sat at the defense table while the courtroom emptied around him. Hale leaned over.

"How are you?" Hale asked.

"Waiting," Archie said.

"The judge will rule after lunch," Hale said. "She's seen enough. The question is whether she thinks the prosecution's case meets probable cause despite the alternative narrative."

"Does it?" Archie asked.

"Honestly?" Hale said. "It could go either way. The notebook and the warehouse evidence raised serious questions. Knox was credible. But Jessup's case isn't baseless — the cell tower gap and the financial motive are real, and the judge has to weigh whether a reasonable person could believe you did it, not whether you actually did."

"The camera," Archie said. "Any word?"

Hale checked his phone. "The forensic tech's report was due this morning," Hale said. "I haven't received it."

They broke for lunch. Archie didn't eat. He sat in a conference room with Hale and stared at the wall and waited for a phone to ring. Knox and Delaney were in the hallway. Bella was making calls — to whom, Archie didn't know. Wes and Reece sat in the lobby, two wounded Marines in a courthouse, looking like exactly what they were — men who'd bled for something they believed in.

At 12:45 PM, Hale's phone buzzed. He looked at the screen. His face changed.

"The forensic tech," Hale said. He opened the email and read. His eyes moved across the screen for thirty seconds. Then he looked up at Archie, and the expression on his face was something Archie had never seen from Marcus Hale.

"The footage wasn't corrupted," Hale said. "It was deleted. The tech recovered it."

"What does it show?" Archie asked.

"A man," Hale said. "Approaching the front door at 9:23 PM on the night of the murder. Medium build, dark hair, dark complexion. He enters a code on the alarm panel, uses a key, and goes inside. He's inside for eighteen minutes. He comes out at 9:41 PM. His face is partially visible."

"Is it Padilla?" Archie asked.

"The tech can't make that determination from the footage alone," Hale said. "But the physical description matches. And the timestamp — 9:23 PM — falls within the medical examiner's estimated window for the murder."

"It's not me," Archie said.

"It's not you," Hale said. "The man on the footage is

shorter, heavier, and enters through the front door using a key and the alarm code. At 9:23 PM, your cell phone was pinging a tower in San Francisco. The prosecution's own evidence puts you two hundred miles away."

Archie sat in the conference room and felt the weight that had been sitting on his chest for five weeks lift — not completely, not yet, but enough to breathe. Enough to feel the air in his lungs instead of the pressure.

"Get it to the judge," Archie said.

"I'm filing an emergency motion right now," Hale said. His fingers were already moving on his phone. "We go back in at 1:30. The judge will have the report and the footage before she rules."

At 1:30 PM, the courtroom reconvened. Moreno was at the bench. Jessup was at his table, his face tight — he'd been notified of Hale's emergency filing during the break, and the confidence that had carried him through the morning was gone, replaced by the rigid composure of a man watching his case develop a crack he couldn't repair.

"Mr. Hale," Moreno said. "I've received your emergency filing. You wish to introduce additional evidence."

"Yes, Your Honor," Hale said. He stood with a folder in his hand. "During the recess, the defense received the results of a forensic examination of a doorbell camera recovered from the victim's residence. The examination was conducted pursuant to this court's order. The forensic tech has determined that the footage stored on the camera's hard drive was not corrupted, as initially reported by the investigating officers. It was deliberately deleted."

The courtroom stirred. Moreno tapped her gavel.

"The tech recovered the deleted footage," Hale continued. "It shows an individual approaching the victim's front door at 9:23 PM on the night of the murder. The individual enters the alarm code, uses a key to unlock the door, and enters the residence. He exits eighteen minutes later, at 9:41 PM. The individual is not the defendant. The physical description does not match the defendant. And at the time the footage was recorded, the prosecution's own cell tower data places the defendant in San Francisco."

Moreno looked at Jessup. "Mr. Jessup?" Moreno asked.

Jessup stood. His voice was controlled but strained. "Your Honor, the defense is introducing evidence that has not been available for the prosecution to examine. We have not had an opportunity to verify the forensic tech's findings or review the footage. We request a continuance to evaluate this evidence."

"Mr. Jessup," Moreno said. "The defense filed a motion for this examination two weeks ago. The prosecution was notified. The court ordered the examination. The results are here. You'll have an opportunity to challenge the findings at trial — if there is a trial." She paused. "Is there anything else?"

"No, Your Honor," Jessup said. He sat down.

Moreno removed her reading glasses. She looked at the prosecution table. She looked at the defense table. She looked at Archie.

"The court has reviewed the evidence presented by both parties," Moreno said. "The prosecution has presented a circumstantial case based on financial motive, opportunity, and the absence of a verified alibi. The defense has presented an alternative narrative supported by documentary evidence, witness testimony, and physical evidence recovered from a related crime scene. Additionally, the defense has introduced forensic evidence showing that the doorbell camera footage from the victim's residence was deliberately deleted, and that the recovered footage depicts an unidentified individual — not the defendant — entering the victim's home during the estimated time of the murder."

She set her glasses on the bench.

"The standard at a preliminary hearing is probable cause," Moreno said. "The court must determine whether a reasonable person would believe the defendant committed the charged offense. Given the totality of the evidence — including the recovered doorbell footage, the notebook documenting the victim's financial relationship with another family member, and the evidence linking associates of the Reapers Motorcycle Club to the victim's residence — the court finds that the prosecution has not met its burden."

Moreno looked at Jessup. "The charge of murder in the first degree is dismissed," Moreno said. "The defendant is released from all conditions of bail, including GPS monitoring. This court is adjourned."

The gavel came down.

The courtroom erupted. Reporters stood. Cameras that weren't supposed to be there flashed. Knox grabbed Delaney and held her. Bella pressed both hands to her face and closed her eyes.

Archie sat at the defense table and didn't move. Hale put a hand on his shoulder.

"It's over," Hale said.

"No," Archie said. "It's not over. The charge is dismissed. But my father's killer is still out there. And my sister helped put him at the door."

He stood. He shook Hale's hand. He walked into the gallery, where Knox was waiting with tears on his face and

Delaney was holding him and Bella was standing with her arms at her sides and her war face finally, finally cracking.

Archie hugged Knox first. Then Delaney. Then Bella — a long embrace, her face pressed against his chest, her body shaking with the release of five weeks of controlled terror.

Wes and Reece were at the back of the courtroom. Archie walked to them. He shook Reece's hand. He looked at Wes.

"Thank you," Archie said.

"Don't thank me," Wes said. "Thank the doorbell camera."

"I'm thanking you," Archie said. "All of you. Tommy included. When he's out of that hospital bed, I'm thanking him too."

"He'll hate that," Wes said.

"I know," Archie said.

They walked out of the courtroom together — the brothers, the fiancée, the girlfriend, and the two wounded Marines. The hallway was bright with fluorescent light and buzzing with reporters, and Archie walked through it without stopping, without speaking, without looking at the cameras or the microphones or the faces of strangers who wanted a piece of a story that belonged to his family and no one else.

Outside, the Bakersfield sun was high and warm. Archie stood on the courthouse steps and felt it on his face — the same sun that had been shining every day since Cyril died, indifferent and constant, the sun that didn't care about murder charges or preliminary hearings or the porch light on Columbus Street.

The GPS monitor was still on his ankle. It would be removed within the hour. He could feel its weight — the last five weeks compressed into a plastic band strapped to his skin.

Soon it would be gone. But the weight of everything else — the notebook, the camera, the sister who wasn't in the courtroom, the father who would never know his son had been cleared — that weight would stay.

The fight wasn't over. It was changing shape.

CHAPTER 21: "Lorraine's Choice"

The television told Lorraine everything she needed to know about how her life was ending.

She was on the couch, the blinds drawn, the apartment dark except for the blue glow of the screen. She'd been watching the news since noon, flipping between channels, each one carrying the same story from a different angle, the way they did when something big happened in a town the size of Bakersfield.

"In a dramatic turn of events at the Kern County Superior Court this afternoon, Judge Patricia Moreno dismissed the first-degree murder charge against Archibald Butterworth in the death of his father, Cyril Butterworth," the anchor said. "The defense presented previously undiscovered evidence, including a notebook kept by the victim documenting fourteen years of financial payments to his daughter, and recovered doorbell camera footage showing an unidentified individual entering the victim's home on the night of the murder."

The screen cut to the courthouse steps. Archie walked out with Knox and Delaney and Bella, and behind them, two men Lorraine didn't recognize — one with a bandaged forearm, one moving carefully like his ribs hurt. They walked past the reporters without stopping. Archie's face was composed, controlled, the same face he'd worn his entire life. He walked past the reporters without breaking stride, and even on a television screen, Lorraine could see that her brother looked like a man who'd just set down something heavy.

He was free.

Lorraine stared at the screen and felt two things at the same time — relief and terror. Relief because her brother was not going to prison for something he didn't do. Terror because if Archie was free, then the investigation had nowhere to go but toward the truth. And the truth was a road that ended at her front door.

The anchor continued. "Sources say the defense presented a notebook found in the victim's desk, containing entries spanning fourteen years. Each entry documented a payment from Cyril Butterworth to his daughter, Lorraine Butterworth. The final entry, dated October 19, 2024 — seventeen days before the murder — records a request for twenty thousand dollars that the victim denied."

The notebook. Her father's notebook. Lorraine hadn't known it existed. She hadn't known that Cyril had been writing down every dollar, every date, every prayer, in a composition book hidden in the bottom of his desk. She tried to picture it — her father at his desk, pen in hand, documenting the slow hemorrhage of his savings with the same careful handwriting he used for birthday cards and grocery lists. The image was so specific, so detailed, so perfectly Cyril that it cut through the meth and the numbness and hit something raw.

He'd kept a record. Not to use against her. Not to build a case or prove a point. But because that's who Cyril was — a man who documented things, who believed in keeping track, who needed the act of writing to make sense of a world that had stopped making sense the day his youngest daughter chose methamphetamine over everything he'd offered her.

"The defense also introduced recovered footage from a doorbell camera at the victim's residence," the anchor said. "Forensic examination revealed that the footage had been deliberately deleted, not corrupted as initially reported by investigators. The recovered footage shows an individual — not the defendant — entering the home at 9:23 PM on the night of the murder using the alarm code and a key."

Using the alarm code and a key. Helen's birthday. The code Lorraine had given Dante on a leather couch in a cinder-block building on South Union Avenue while rage and meth and fifteen years of shame burned through her like a fire she couldn't put out.

The key under the mat by the back door. The key Cyril had kept there for twenty years because he trusted the world even when the world didn't deserve it.

She'd given Dante both. And Dante had given them to whoever he'd sent to her father's house. And now that person — that ghost with a duffel bag and a purchased name — was on a doorbell camera that her father had installed because, for the first time in his life, he was afraid of who might come to his door.

Lorraine turned off the television. The apartment went dark. She sat in the silence and felt the walls closing in — not metaphorically, not poetically, but physically, the room shrinking around her, the air getting thicker, the space between the couch and the door and the window and the ceiling contracting like a box being folded shut.

The burner phone rang.

She picked it up. "Dante," she said.

"You watching the news?" Dante asked. His voice was different from the last time they'd spoken — not angry, not tight. Flat. The voice of a man who'd moved past anger into something colder.

"I'm watching," Lorraine said.

"Then you know," Dante said. "Your brother walked. The notebook. The camera. The warehouse. It's all out there now. The police have the phone. They have the photograph. They've got three of my guys in lockup. And now they've got camera footage of someone walking into your daddy's house with the alarm code you gave me."

"Dante, I —" Lorraine started.

"Shut up," Dante said. "Listen. The police are going to come for me. Maybe tomorrow. Maybe next week. But they're coming. When they do, they're going to ask about you. They're going to ask how I knew the alarm code. They're going to ask about the key. They're going to put together a case, and the case is going to have your name in it."

"What do you want me to do?" Lorraine asked.

"Disappear," Dante said. "I've got a place in Nevada. Safe house. You go there, you stay quiet, and you wait until this blows over. I'll send you the address."

"Blows over?" Lorraine said. "My father is dead, Dante. There's a camera showing someone entering his house. There's a notebook with my name on every page. This doesn't blow over."

"Everything blows over if you're patient enough," Dante said. "The question is whether you're smart enough to be patient or stupid enough to talk."

"I'm not running," Lorraine said. The words came out before she'd decided to say them — the same way "don't touch him" had come out when Dante threatened Archie, the same way "no" had come out when he'd proposed fabricating a witness. From the place where the sister still lived. The place that was smaller now, and quieter, but not gone.

"Then you're stupid," Dante said. "And stupid gets people killed."

"Is that a threat?" Lorraine asked.

"It's a fact," Dante said. "I don't threaten, Lorraine. I inform. And I'm informing you that if you talk to the police — if you say my name, if you say anything about the alarm code or the key or anything that happened between us — I will make sure you regret it. Not in court. Not through lawyers. The other way."

The line went dead.

Lorraine set the burner phone on the couch cushion. She looked at it. The cheap black plastic. The blank screen. The leash that Dante had put around her neck and that she'd been too broken to pull off.

She picked up the phone and threw it against the wall. It hit the plaster and broke into three pieces — the battery popping out, the screen cracking, the casing splitting down the middle. The pieces fell to the carpet and lay there, small and dead and harmless.

She sat in the dark for a long time.

The memories came in no particular order, the way they did when the meth was wearing off and her mind couldn't sort them properly.

Lorraine at seven, sitting on Cyril's lap in the rocking chair on the front porch, listening to him read from a book of fairy tales. His voice was deep and steady, and he did different voices for the different characters — a high voice for the princess, a grumbling voice for the troll, a brave voice for the hero. She laughed so hard she got the hiccups, and he held her until they stopped.

Lorraine at fourteen, crying in the kitchen because a boy at school had called her ugly. Cyril got down on one knee and looked her in the eye and said, "Little star, the people who try to make you feel small are the ones who are afraid of how bright you are."

Lorraine at twenty-three, calling from a pay phone at 2:00 AM because her car had broken down on Highway 99 and she had no money and no one else to call. Cyril drove forty-five minutes in his bathrobe. He didn't ask why she was on the highway at 2:00 AM. He didn't ask about the smell in the car or the bruise on her arm. He put gas in the tank and followed her home and called the next morning to make sure she was okay.

Lorraine at thirty-one, standing in Dante Voss's living room, telling a man with a skull on his neck that the alarm code was 0712 and the key was under the mat.

The memories collapsed into each other like a

building falling floor by floor, each one taking the next one down, until all that was left was rubble and the sound of her father's voice saying "I love you, sweetheart" in a kitchen that would never smell like his coffee again.

She was crying. She hadn't cried since the night Dante called and said "it's done." Five weeks of chemical numbness, five weeks of performance, five weeks of the hardest acting she'd ever done — harder than any audition she'd failed, harder than any lie she'd told Cyril — and now the dam was breaking and there was nothing left to hold it back.

She cried on the couch in the dark apartment with the broken burner phone on the carpet and the regular phone on the cushion beside her and the two versions of her life — the one that was ending and the one that hadn't started yet — pressing against each other like tectonic plates.

She didn't know how long she cried. When it stopped, the apartment was still dark and the silence was still heavy and the phone was still on the cushion. She picked it up. The cracked screen glowed.

Three options.

She could run. Nevada. Dante's safe house. A room in a state she'd never been to, waiting for something to blow over that would never blow over, getting high in a stranger's house until the money ran out or the police found her or the meth finished what it had been working on for years.

She could stay silent. Stay in the apartment. Don't answer calls. Don't watch the news. Wait for the knock on the door that was coming whether she opened it or not. Let the system do what it did — the arrest, the charges, the trial, the conviction. Let Marcus Hale and Craig Jessup and Detective Salcedo sort through the wreckage while she sat in a cell and said nothing and carried the truth like a stone in her chest until the stone was all that was left of her.

Or she could talk.

She could call Knox. She could call Archie. She could walk into the Bakersfield Police Department the way she'd walked in three weeks ago — but this time without the performance, without the rehearsed alibi, without the carefully placed seeds about Archie's temper and the family's money tensions. This time she could walk in and sit down and look Detective Salcedo in the eye and say the words she'd been running from since the night her father died.

I did this. Not with my hands. But with my mouth. I gave him the code. I gave him the key. I gave him the map to my father's front door.

The words were there. Right there. Sitting in her chest like a breath she'd been holding for five weeks. All she had to do was let them out.

She looked at the phone. She looked at Knox's

number. She looked at the message she'd sent that morning — "I'm fine. Just tired." Two lies in four words.

She thought about Archie on the courthouse steps. Free. Walking in the sunlight. The weight gone from his shoulders. She thought about Knox in the courtroom, testifying, finally telling the truth about the motorcycle and the Reapers patches, carrying his guilt to the witness stand and setting it down in public.

They'd both told the truth. They'd both paid a price for it. And they were both still standing.

Lorraine looked at her hands. Thin. Shaking. The hands of a woman who'd been disappearing for years and had nearly succeeded. These hands had held her father's face when she was seven. These hands had taken his money when she was twenty-five. These hands had caught a bag of crystal meth tossed by the man who would use the information she gave him to murder the only person who'd never stopped loving her.

She put the phone down.

She picked it up.

She put it down again.

The porch light on Columbus Street burned in her memory — steady, constant, faithful. Cyril had left it on every night. Knox had put it on a timer after Cyril died, because leaving it to chance felt like breaking a promise.

The light was still on. It was always on. Waiting for her to come home.

Lorraine picked up the phone. She dialed Knox's number. It rang once. Twice. Three times.

"Lorraine?" Knox's voice. Surprised. Careful. The voice of a man who'd been calling his sister for weeks and had stopped expecting her to call back.

"Knox," Lorraine said. "I need to talk to you. I need to tell you something. Can you come to my apartment?"

"Right now?" Knox asked.

"Right now," Lorraine said. "Please. It's important."

A pause. "I'll be there in twenty minutes," Knox said.

"Knox," Lorraine said. "I'm sorry. For everything. I'm so sorry."

Another pause. Longer.

"I'll be there," Knox said.

The line went dead. Lorraine sat on the couch with the phone in her hands and waited. The apartment was dark. The broken burner phone lay on the carpet in three pieces. Outside, the Bakersfield night was quiet and warm and indifferent.

She didn't use. For the first time in weeks, she didn't reach for the bag on the nightstand. There was nothing left in it anyway. But even if there had been, she wouldn't have reached. Not tonight. Tonight she needed to feel everything — the grief, the guilt, the terror of what she was about to do.

She was going to tell the truth. The whole truth. Every piece of it.

And the truth was going to destroy her. But it was also going to set her brother free — fully, completely, permanently. Not just from the charges, but from the doubt. From the whispers. From the stain that a dismissed case still leaves on a man's name.

She owed him that. She owed Cyril that. She owed the porch light that.

Lorraine Butterworth sat in the dark and waited for her brother, and for the first time in fifteen years, she wasn't running from the truth.

She was walking toward it.

CHAPTER 22: "The Confession"

Knox stood outside Lorraine's apartment door on South Chester Avenue and tried to remember the last time his sister had asked him for anything that wasn't money.

He couldn't.

The hallway smelled like carpet cleaner and cigarette smoke, the universal scent of apartment buildings that charged below market rate and didn't ask questions. The overhead light flickered — a bulb that needed replacing, the kind of small maintenance issue that Cyril would have noticed and fixed within an hour. Knox stood under it and felt the flicker in his chest, a pulse of dread that matched the rhythm of the dying bulb.

Delaney had driven him. She was in the car, parked under the streetlight, engine running. He'd told her to wait. She'd said, "I'll wait. But if you're not out in an hour, I'm coming up." He believed her. Delaney Park did not make idle statements.

He knocked.

The door opened immediately, as if Lorraine had been standing on the other side of it waiting for the sound. She looked worse than the last time he'd seen her — thinner, paler, the hollows under her cheekbones deeper, her eyes red and swollen in a way that had nothing to do with drugs and everything to do with crying. She was wearing a sweatshirt that was too big for her and sweatpants and no shoes, and her hair was unwashed, and she looked like a woman who had stopped maintaining the basic architecture of being alive.

"Come in," Lorraine said.

Knox stepped inside. The apartment was dark — blinds drawn, one lamp on, the television off. The air was thick with cigarette smoke and the stale, sweet smell that Knox had learned to associate with his sister's worst periods. The mattress was visible through the bedroom doorway, sheets tangled, nightstand cluttered with an ashtray and an empty plastic bag and a lighter. On the living room carpet, near the wall, three pieces of a broken phone lay scattered like the remains of something that had been thrown.

Lorraine sat on the couch. Knox sat in the only chair — a folding chair at a card table that served as her dining area. They faced each other across four feet of space that felt like four miles.

"Thank you for coming," Lorraine said.

"You sounded different on the phone," Knox said. "Different from — different from how you've sounded."

"I am different," Lorraine said. "Or I'm trying to be. For the next hour, at least."

She wasn't performing. Knox could see that immediately. Every other time he'd been with Lorraine in the past five weeks — the voicemails she didn't return, the text that said "I'm fine. Just tired" — had carried the flat, controlled quality of a woman managing a script. This was not that. This was raw. Her hands were shaking. Her voice was unsteady. Her eyes kept moving to the broken phone on the carpet and then back to Knox, as if the phone was a marker on a timeline she was trying to follow.

"Knox, I need to tell you something," Lorraine said. "And once I start, I can't stop. If I stop, I won't be able to start again. So please — just let me talk."

"Okay," Knox said.

Lorraine took a breath. It was the breath of a woman about to jump from a height she couldn't see the bottom of.

"I killed Dad," Lorraine said.

The words hit Knox like a physical blow — not a punch, but a fall, the sensation of the ground disappearing beneath his feet and the air rushing up around him. He gripped the edges of the folding chair and stared at his sister.

"Not with my hands," Lorraine said. "I didn't — I wasn't in the house. I didn't touch him. But I killed him. I'm the reason he's dead."

"Lorraine —" Knox started.

"Please," Lorraine said. "Let me talk."

Knox closed his mouth. His heart was hammering. His hands were white on the chair.

Lorraine told him.

She told him about October 19 — the phone call with Cyril, the twenty thousand dollars, the rage when he said no. She told him about driving to Cyril's house that night and sitting in the dark under the jacaranda tree, watching her father wash dishes through the kitchen window. She told him about sitting in the car under the jacaranda tree, watching Cyril wash dishes through the kitchen window. She told him she'd thought about going inside — she knew the code, she knew about the key, she could have walked right in and screamed at him for saying no. But she didn't. She drove away. She drove to Dante's house instead.

She told him about Dante's house. The leather couch. The boxing match on the television. The way Dante had asked questions — specific questions, quiet questions, the questions of a man who was listening for information, not conversation. How much is the house worth? What about savings? The alarm code? The key? When is he home alone?

"I answered every question," Lorraine said. Her voice was steady now — not because the emotion had passed, but because she'd moved through it into the numb clarity that exists on the other side of collapse. "I told him the code. I told him about the key. I told him about the money. I told him Dad lived alone. I gave him everything he needed, Knox. Everything."

Knox said nothing. His jaw was clenched so tight his teeth ached.

Lorraine told him about the night of the murder. November 5. She'd been at Dante's house, in the bathroom, high. The phone call at 11:15 PM. Dante's voice saying "it's done." The instructions — you were at a friend's house, you don't know anything, when the money comes through we split it fifty-fifty.

She told him about the alibi she'd built. Carla. The friend without a last name. The rehearsed story she'd practiced for nine hours before walking into the police station. She told him about planting the seeds against Archie — the money arguments, the temper, the parting comment to Salcedo on her way out the door.

She told him about the burner phone. About Dante pressuring her to push for the estate money. About the fabricated witness he'd proposed and she'd refused. About the phone call tonight — Dante telling her to run to Nevada, the threat, the flat voice of a man who'd moved past anger into something worse.

She pointed at the broken phone on the carpet. "That's the burner," Lorraine said. "I threw it against the wall. It's done. He's done. I'm done."

The apartment was quiet. The lamp cast its yellow light across the room, catching the smoke still hanging in the air, turning it gold. Knox sat in the folding chair and looked at his sister — the girl who'd laughed on their father's lap, the teenager who'd cried in the kitchen, the woman who'd handed a killer the keys to their father's house — and tried to find a single coherent thought in the wreckage of what she'd just told him.

"Did you know?" Knox asked. His voice came out hoarse, scraped raw. "When you told Dante about the code and the key — did you know what he was going to do?"

"No," Lorraine said. "And yes. I didn't know the way you know something you've decided. I knew the way you know something you're pretending not to see. Dante asked specific questions. He asked about the alarm. He asked about the key. He asked when Dad was alone. Those aren't the questions of a man who wants to have a conversation. I knew what they meant. And I answered them anyway."

"Why?" Knox asked.

"Because I was angry," Lorraine said. "Because Dad said no for the first time in my life and I couldn't handle it. Because the meth makes everything louder — the anger, the shame, the feeling that everyone has given up on you and the one person who hasn't just closed the door. I was out of my mind, Knox. But that's not an excuse. Being out of your mind doesn't erase what your mouth says."

Knox stood up from the chair. He walked to the window. He stood with his back to Lorraine and pressed his forehead against the glass and felt the cold of it against his skin. Outside, the streetlight illuminated Delaney's car. She was in there, waiting. Patient and steady and unbroken. The life he was building with her — the teaching, the wedding, the paper leaves on the coffee table — felt like it belonged to someone else. Someone who hadn't just heard his sister confess to being the reason their father was dead.

"Knox," Lorraine said. "Say something."

He turned from the window. His face was wet. He hadn't realized he was crying.

"You need to go to the police," Knox said. "Tonight. Right now."

"I know," Lorraine said.

"You need to tell Salcedo everything you just told me," Knox said. "The code. The key. Dante. The phone call. The alibi. Everything."

"I know," Lorraine said.

"And you know what happens after that," Knox said. It wasn't a question.

"Prison," Lorraine said. "For a long time. Maybe

forever."

"Yes," Knox said. The word came out harder than he intended — not cruel, but final, the sound of a door closing on a possibility he would have given anything to keep open. "Lorraine, you — I want to help you. I've always wanted to help you. But you helped kill our father. I can't make that smaller than it is."

"I'm not asking you to make it smaller," Lorraine said. "I'm asking you to take me to the police station. I can't do it alone. I've been alone for five weeks and alone is what got me here."

Knox looked at his sister. She looked back. Her eyes were clear — not sober, not clean, but clear in a way he hadn't seen in years. The eyes of a woman who had finally stopped running and was standing still long enough to see where she was.

"I need to call Archie," Knox said.

"I know," Lorraine said. "Call him."

Knox pulled out his phone and dialed. Archie answered on the second ring.

"Knox," Archie said. "What's going on?"

"I'm at Lorraine's apartment," Knox said. "She wants to talk. She wants to tell the truth. All of it."

Silence. Three seconds.

"What truth?" Archie asked.

"She gave Dante Voss the alarm code," Knox said. "And the key. And the information about Dad's money. She did it the night Dad said no to the twenty thousand. Dante had Dad killed. She's known since that night."

The silence on the other end was longer this time. Five seconds. Six. Seven. Knox could hear Archie breathing — controlled, measured, the breath of a man processing something enormous and refusing to let it knock him off balance.

"Put her on," Archie said.

Knox handed the phone to Lorraine. She took it with both hands.

"Archie," Lorraine said.

"Is it true?" Archie asked.

"Yes," Lorraine said. "All of it."

"You let me get arrested," Archie said. His voice was flat. Not angry — not yet. Flat in the way of a man who was holding the anger in a place where it couldn't get out. "You planted evidence against me. You told Salcedo I argued with Dad about money. You told her I had a temper. You sat in that police station and aimed the investigation at me while you knew — you knew — that you'd given Dante Voss the alarm code to our father's house."

"Yes," Lorraine said.

"Five weeks," Archie said. "Five weeks I wore a GPS monitor. Five weeks my life stopped. Knox's life stopped. Bella gave up her career. Three Marines bled for me. Tommy took a bullet. And you sat in that apartment and let it happen."

"Yes," Lorraine said.

Silence again. Lorraine held the phone and waited. She could hear Archie breathing on the other end, and she thought about all the phone calls they'd had over the years — the awkward conversations, the long silences, the careful distance he kept between his world and hers. This was the last phone call they would ever have as the people they used to be. Whatever came after this — the police, the charges, the trial — would change them both in ways that couldn't be undone.

"Go to the police," Archie said. "Tonight. Knox will take you. Tell them everything."

"Archie —" Lorraine started.

"Don't," Archie said. "Don't apologize. Don't explain. Don't tell me you're sorry. Go to the police and tell the truth. That's the only thing you can do for Dad now."

The line went dead.

Lorraine handed the phone back to Knox. Her hands

were steady. The shaking had stopped — not because the fear was gone, but because the decision had been made and the decision was bigger than the fear.

"Let's go," Lorraine said.

"Are you sure?" Knox asked.

"No," Lorraine said. "But I'm going anyway."

Knox looked at his sister. The girl on the bicycle. The teenager crying in the kitchen. The woman in the sweatshirt with the hollowed cheeks and the red eyes and the broken phone on the carpet. She was all of those people. She was none of those people. She was someone new — someone who had done the worst thing she would ever do and was about to walk into a building and say so out loud.

"Okay," Knox said. "Let's go."

They walked out of the apartment together. Down the hallway, under the flickering light. Down the stairs, into the parking lot. Delaney was in the car, engine running. She saw them coming and her face changed — not surprise, not confusion, but the quick, steady recognition of a woman who understood that the situation had shifted and her job was to adjust.

Knox opened the back door. Lorraine got in. Knox got in the front.

"We're going to the police station," Knox said.

Delaney looked in the rearview mirror at Lorraine. Lorraine looked back. No words passed between them — just a look, brief and honest, the look of two women who understood that what was about to happen was necessary and terrible and right.

"Okay," Delaney said.

She put the car in drive and pulled out of the parking lot. The streetlight passed over them and was gone. The road to the Bakersfield Police Department was eleven minutes long, and Lorraine rode it in silence, watching the city pass through the window — the same streets she'd driven a thousand times, the same lights, the same buildings, the same valley that had held her whole life and was about to hold the end of it.

The porch light on Columbus Street was behind her now. But she could still feel it. Burning. Waiting. The way it always had.

She was going home. The long way. The only way left.

CHAPTER 23: "The Truth"

The Bakersfield Police Department looked different at night. The fluorescent lights were the same, the industrial carpet was the same, the beige walls and the vending machines and the institutional hum were all the same. But at 10:30 PM on a Friday night, the building had a different population — the drunk drivers and the domestic disputes and the small-time dealers who kept the night shift busy. Knox sat in a plastic chair in the lobby and watched them come and go and thought about how strange it was that the worst night of his sister's life was an ordinary night for everyone else in the building.

Delaney sat beside him. She hadn't said much since they'd left Lorraine's apartment. She'd driven the eleven minutes to the station in silence, her hands steady on the wheel, her eyes on the road, the kindergarten teacher operating with the focused calm of a woman who understood that the best thing she could do right now was be present and quiet and ready.

Lorraine had walked through the front door and asked for Detective Salcedo. The officer at the desk had made a phone call. Fifteen minutes later, Salcedo had come down the hallway — not in a blazer this time, but in jeans and a pullover, called in from home on a Friday night. She'd looked at Lorraine, then at Knox, then back at Lorraine.

"Ms. Butterworth," Salcedo had said. "What can I do for you?"

"I need to make a statement," Lorraine had said. "About my father's murder. I need to tell you the truth."

Salcedo's expression hadn't changed. The controlled mask, the neutral eyes — the same face she'd worn in every interaction Knox had ever witnessed. But something shifted behind it — a flicker, fast and brief, the recognition of a moment she'd been trained to expect but never fully prepared for.

"Before you say anything," Salcedo had said, "I need to advise you of your rights. You have the right to remain silent. Anything you say can and will be used against you in a court of law. You have the right to an attorney. If you cannot afford an attorney, one will be provided for you. Do you understand these rights?"

"I understand," Lorraine had said.

"Do you wish to have an attorney present?" Salcedo had asked.

Lorraine had looked at Knox. He'd wanted to say yes — wanted to grab her arm and say, wait, don't do this without a lawyer, don't walk into that room alone. But the look on her face stopped him. It was the clearest he'd seen her in years — not sober, not clean, but clear. The eyes of a woman who had made a decision and was not going to be talked out of it.

"No," Lorraine had said. "I don't want a lawyer. I want to tell the truth."

Salcedo had led her down the hallway. The door to the interview room had closed. Knox had watched it close, and the sound of it — the click of the latch, the soft thud of the frame settling — was the loneliest sound he'd ever heard.

That was forty-five minutes ago.

Knox sat in the plastic chair and stared at the floor. The tiles were gray, scuffed, the kind of institutional flooring that existed in every government building he'd ever been inside — schools, courthouses, police stations. He'd spent his career walking on floors like this. Tonight, the floor felt like it was the only solid thing in the world.

Delaney reached over and took his hand. She didn't say anything. She just held it. Her hand was warm and small and steady, and Knox held on to it the way a man holds on to a rope in deep water.

"She's doing the right thing," Delaney said.

"I know," Knox said.

"It doesn't feel like the right thing," Delaney said.

"No," Knox said. "It doesn't."

He thought about what was happening behind that door. Lorraine sitting in the same chair where Archie had sat, where Knox had sat, where Lorraine herself had sat five weeks ago and planted seeds against her own brother. The same table. The same recorder. The same Detective Salcedo, with her notebook and her pen and her face that didn't move.

But this time, the story would be different. This time, Lorraine wasn't performing. She wasn't rehearsing. She wasn't calculating the next sentence two moves ahead like a chess player. She was sitting in a chair and telling a woman with a badge the worst thing she'd ever done, and the words were coming out in the order they happened — not the order that protected her, but the order that was true.

Knox had heard the confession once. He didn't need to hear it again. The words were burned into his memory — the alarm code, the key, Dante's questions, the phone call at 11:15 PM. He could hear Lorraine's voice in his head, flat and steady, describing the architecture of her father's murder with the precision of a woman who had been living inside that architecture for five weeks and knew every wall, every door, every crack.

He thought about Cyril. Not the dead version — the living one. Cyril at the kitchen table with his crossword puzzle. Cyril in the driveway with a garden hose. Cyril on the phone at 9:47 PM saying "I just wanted to hear your voice" to a son who didn't know it was the last time.

What would Cyril say if he could see this? His daughter in a police station, confessing. His youngest son in the lobby, waiting. His eldest son at home, free but damaged, carrying a wound that no acquittal could heal.

Knox thought Cyril would say the same thing he always said. The same thing he wrote in the notebook, entry after entry, year after year, check after check. I love you. I can't stop. God help me.

Even now. Even after everything. Cyril would still love her. That was the tragedy of it — not just that Lorraine had destroyed the man who loved her most, but that the love itself was indestructible. It would outlive Cyril. It would outlive the trial and the sentence and whatever came after. It would sit in a notebook in an evidence room, written in careful handwriting, until the paper rotted and the ink faded and the last person who remembered Cyril Butterworth was gone.

Knox squeezed Delaney's hand. She squeezed back.

At 11:45 PM, the door to the hallway opened. Salcedo walked into the lobby. She looked at Knox.

"Mr. Butterworth," Salcedo said. "Can I speak with you?"

Knox stood. Delaney stayed seated — she understood,

without being told, that this was a conversation for Knox alone.

Salcedo led him to a small office off the main hallway — not the interview room, a different room, with a desk and two chairs and a window that looked out on the parking lot. She closed the door and sat down. Knox sat across from her.

Salcedo looked tired. Not the professional fatigue of a detective working a long shift, but the deeper tiredness of a woman who had just heard something that rearranged everything she thought she knew.

"Your sister gave a full statement," Salcedo said. "Detailed. Consistent. She described providing Dante Voss with the alarm code, the location of the spare key, information about your father's finances, and his schedule. She described a phone call on the night of the murder in which Voss told her it was done. She described building a false alibi and deliberately misleading this department during her initial statement."

Knox said nothing. There was nothing to say that the facts didn't already cover.

"She also described Voss's instructions regarding the estate," Salcedo said. "A fifty-fifty split of her inheritance. She described a burner phone Voss gave her for communication, which she says she destroyed this evening. And she described Voss's proposal to fabricate a witness placing your brother at the scene, which she says she refused."

"She told me the same thing," Knox said. "That's why I brought her here."

Salcedo looked at him for a long moment. Her expression was still controlled — the mask was still in place. But underneath it, Knox could see something he'd never seen from Rina Salcedo before. Not regret, exactly. Something closer to reckoning.

"Mr. Butterworth, I owe your brother an apology," Salcedo said. "I built a case against him based on circumstantial evidence and institutional pressure from my supervisor to close quickly. When your attorney presented the alternative narrative — Voss, the warehouse, the shell companies — I dismissed it. I was cautious. I had reasons to be cautious. But caution isn't an excuse for failing to follow evidence that was in front of me."

"You were doing your job," Knox said. He said it because it was true, not because it made him feel better.

"I was doing part of my job," Salcedo said. "The part that builds cases. The part that follows evidence wherever it leads — I failed at that. Your brother spent five weeks under a murder charge because I was more afraid of making a mistake than I was of making the wrong arrest."

Knox didn't know what to say to that. He'd spent five weeks watching Salcedo from the other side — the detective who wouldn't listen, who kept building against Archie, who dismissed the Marines' evidence as civilian noise. He'd resented her. He'd been angry. And now she was sitting across from him admitting she'd been wrong, and the anger had nowhere to go.

"What happens to Lorraine?" Knox asked.

"She'll be arrested tonight," Salcedo said. "Conspiracy to commit murder. Accessory before the fact. Obstruction of justice for the false statement. The DA will file formal charges within seventy-two hours."

"What's the sentence for conspiracy to commit murder?" Knox asked.

"In California, it carries the same penalty as the underlying offense," Salcedo said. "First-degree murder. Twenty-five years to life."

The number filled the room like a sound — not loud, but heavy, the kind of sound that displaces air and leaves a vacuum behind it. Twenty-five years to life. Lorraine was thirty-one. She would be fifty-six at the earliest. The wedding Knox was planning for March, the children he hoped to have, the family dinners and the holidays and the ordinary milestones of an ordinary life — Lorraine would miss all of it. She would be behind a wall, in a jumpsuit, and Knox would visit her in a room with plastic chairs and vending machines and a clock on the wall that counted time the way prison counts it — slowly, mercilessly, one minute at a time.

"And Dante Voss?" Knox asked.

"We'll arrest him tonight," Salcedo said. "Your sister's statement, combined with the warehouse evidence and the doorbell camera footage, gives us more than enough for a warrant. We'll also be seeking charges against the individual identified as Victor Padilla — the man on the doorbell footage. His real identity is still unknown, but your sister's statement confirms that Voss arranged the murder and used a third party to carry it out."

"Will she testify against Voss?" Knox asked.

"If she's willing, her testimony would be the centerpiece of the prosecution's case against him," Salcedo said. "The DA may offer her a reduced sentence in exchange for cooperation. That's not my decision — that's between the DA, her attorney, and the court."

"She doesn't have an attorney," Knox said. "She waived her right."

"For the statement, yes," Salcedo said. "But she'll need one for what comes next. I'd recommend she get one soon."

Knox nodded. He stood up. He looked at Salcedo.

"Detective," Knox said. "My father left the porch light on every night. For Lorraine. In case she came home. She's not coming home. But the light is still on."

Salcedo looked at him. The mask held. But her eyes — for one second, less than a second — were the eyes of a woman who understood what that porch light meant, and what it cost, and why it mattered.

"I'm sorry about your father," Salcedo said. "I mean that."

"I know you do," Knox said.

He walked back to the lobby. Delaney stood when she saw him. He took her hand.

"She's being arrested," Knox said. "Conspiracy to commit murder. They're going after Voss tonight."

Delaney closed her eyes. When she opened them, they were wet, but her voice was steady. "Can we see her?" Delaney asked.

"I don't think so," Knox said. "Not tonight."

They stood in the lobby of the Bakersfield Police Department at midnight, holding hands, while somewhere down the hallway, behind a door Knox couldn't see, his sister was being photographed and fingerprinted and processed into a system that would hold her for a very long time.

At 12:15 AM, Salcedo walked through the lobby one more time. She stopped at the front door and looked at Knox.

"We're executing the warrant on Voss now," Salcedo said. "I thought you'd want to know."

"Thank you," Knox said.

Salcedo left. The lobby was quiet. The night shift officer behind the desk was reading a newspaper. The fluorescent lights hummed. The vending machine offered its twelve varieties of disappointment.

Knox called Archie.

"It's done," Knox said. And then, hearing the echo of those words — the same words Dante had used on the phone to Lorraine on the night their father died — he corrected himself. "She gave her statement. She's been arrested. They're going after Voss tonight."

"Okay," Archie said. His voice was quiet. Not angry. Not relieved. Quiet in the way of a man who had been carrying something for five weeks and had set it down and was now standing in the empty space where the weight used to be, not sure what to do with his hands.

"Are you okay?" Knox asked.

"No," Archie said. "Are you?"

"No," Knox said.

"Then we're the same," Archie said. "Come home."

Knox hung up. He looked at Delaney. She looked back.

"Let's go home," Knox said.

They walked out of the police station and into the Bakersfield night. The air was cold and clean and the stars were visible above the city lights and the parking lot was empty except for Delaney's car and two police cruisers pulling out of the lot, heading east, heading toward Dante Voss.

Knox got in the car. Delaney started the engine. They drove to Columbus Street in silence, and when they pulled into the driveway, the porch light was on. It was always on.

CHAPTER 24: "Justice"

The call came at 3:17 AM.

Archie was sitting at Cyril's kitchen table, not sleeping, not trying to sleep, just sitting in the dark with a glass of water and the silence of a house that had held too much grief for one family. Knox and Delaney were in the guest room. Bella was asleep on the couch, curled under a blanket she'd pulled from the hall closet, her legal pad on the floor beside her. Reece had gone to a motel for the night, his arm freshly stitched and his body running on the fumes of two weeks of sustained effort. Wes was on the back porch, awake, sitting in Cyril's rocker, staring at the yard.

Archie's phone lit up. Hale.

"They got him," Hale said. "Salcedo arrested Dante Voss at 2:45 AM at his residence on East Brundage Lane. He was packing a bag when they came through the door. Truck was running in the driveway. He was about thirty minutes from disappearing."

"Was he alone?" Archie asked.

"Two other Reapers were in the house," Hale said. "Both arrested. Salcedo also executed a search warrant on the property. They found cash — a significant amount, she didn't give me numbers — firearms, and additional burner phones. The phones are being processed."

"And Padilla?" Archie asked.

"That's the other piece," Hale said. "Salcedo sent officers to the motel in McFarland — the Valley Rest Inn, where your friend Tommy tracked him. Room 14. The room was empty. The bed had been slept in. The duffel bag was gone. Padilla — or Rios, or whatever his real name is — cleared out."

"He's running," Archie said.

"He's running," Hale said. "But Salcedo's put out a BOLO — be on the lookout — statewide. California Highway Patrol, county sheriffs, border crossings. The gray Honda Civic is flagged. And the doorbell camera footage gives them a partial face. It's not enough for a positive ID, but it's enough to match against if they find him."

"If they find him," Archie said.

"They'll find him," Hale said. "Men with purchased identities have a shelf life. The identity that got him into Bakersfield won't get him out of California. He'll need a new one, and new identities take time and contacts. Salcedo is working with the FBI on the identity chain — the Social Security number, the license, the paper trail. Whoever built Victor Padilla built him from somewhere, and that somewhere has records."

Archie leaned back in the chair. The kitchen was dark

except for the light above the stove — the small light Cyril had always left on at night, along with the porch light, because Cyril believed a house should never be completely dark.

"Marcus," Archie said. "What happens to Lorraine?"

"She's in custody," Hale said. "She'll be arraigned within seventy-two hours. The charges are conspiracy to commit murder, accessory before the fact, and obstruction of justice. The conspiracy charge alone carries twenty-five to life."

"Will the DA offer a deal?" Archie asked.

"Almost certainly," Hale said. "Lorraine's testimony is the key to the case against Voss. Without her, the prosecution has circumstantial evidence — the phone, the photograph, the shell companies, the doorbell footage. With her, they have a cooperating witness who can describe the entire chain from motive to execution. The DA will want that testimony. The price will be a reduced sentence."

"How reduced?" Archie asked.

"That depends on the DA and the judge," Hale said. "If she cooperates fully, testifies against Voss, and pleads guilty to the conspiracy charge, she could be looking at fifteen years instead of twenty-five. Maybe twelve with good behavior. It's still a long time, Archie."

"I know," Archie said.

"There's one more thing," Hale said. "Salcedo asked me to pass along a message. She said — and I'm quoting — 'Tell your client I'm sorry. I should have listened sooner.'"

Archie held the phone and said nothing for a moment. Five weeks ago, Rina Salcedo had sat across from him in an interview room and measured his composure and his calm and filed him away as a suspect. She'd built a case against him while the real killers operated ten miles away. She'd dismissed the Marines' evidence. She'd dismissed Hale's alternative narrative. And now she was sending an apology through his lawyer at three in the morning.

"Tell her I heard her," Archie said. "And tell her to find Padilla."

"I will," Hale said. "Get some sleep, Archie."

"Goodnight, Marcus," Archie said.

He hung up. He sat in the dark kitchen and listened to the house. The refrigerator hummed. The clock ticked. Bella's breathing was soft and steady from the living room. Outside, a dog barked somewhere down the block — the same dog that had been barking every night since Archie had arrived, a constant in a world that had lost most of its constants.

He walked to the back porch. Wes was in the rocker, a

glass of water on the railing. Not bourbon. Water. Archie noticed.

"They got Voss," Archie said. He sat down in the chair beside Wes. "Packing a bag when they came through the door."

"Running," Wes said. "They always run."

"Padilla's gone," Archie said. "Cleared out of the motel. Statewide BOLO."

"He'll surface," Wes said. "Ghosts can't stay invisible forever. They need money, food, transportation. The identity that got him here is burned. He'll have to build a new one, and building takes time. Time is what he doesn't have."

They sat in silence for a while. The yard was dark. The sprinklers hadn't run in weeks. The grass was brown at the edges, the way it had been since Archie arrived — a small neglect that Cyril would have never allowed, and that nobody had thought to fix because fixing the grass felt like an insult to the grief.

"How are your ribs?" Archie asked.

"Sore," Wes said. "Delaney keeps making me soup. I told her I'm fine. She told me to shut up and eat the soup. I eat the soup."

"Smart man," Archie said.

"I'm learning," Wes said. He rocked the chair slowly.

The creak of the wood was the only sound besides the dog and the distant hum of the city. "Archie, when this is over — when Padilla's caught and Voss is locked up and the case is closed — I'm going to go home."

"To Fresno?" Archie asked.

"To the VA," Wes said. "Not the pamphlet guy. A real program. Inpatient. Thirty days, maybe sixty. The kind where they take your phone and your car keys and you sit in a room and talk about the things you've been drinking to forget."

"What changed?" Archie asked.

"That night on the farm road," Wes said. "When Tommy was down and the shotgun was coming and I crossed that ground. My hands were shaking the whole time. They've been shaking for months. But when I got to Tommy — when I put my hands on his shoulder and pressed down and held him — the shaking stopped. Not because the fear was gone. Because I had something to hold on to."

Wes looked at his hands. They were resting on his knees, still, steady in the porch light.

"I need something to hold on to that isn't a wounded Marine," Wes said. "I need to figure out what that is. I can't do it alone. And I can't do it with bourbon."

"I'm proud of you, Wes," Archie said.

"Don't get sentimental," Wes said. "I'm not fixed. I'm just admitting I'm broken. That's step one. Steps two through twelve are the hard part."

"You crossed twenty yards of open ground under shotgun fire," Archie said. "I think you can handle twelve steps."

Wes almost smiled. Almost. The closest thing to a smile Archie had seen from him since the night he'd arrived in Bakersfield with bloodshot eyes and shaking hands and a willingness to bleed for a brother who'd called.

In the morning, the news carried the story.

Archie stood in the kitchen with Knox and Bella and Delaney and watched the broadcast. The anchor was in front of the Kern County jail, where Dante Voss was being held without bail.

"Dante Michael Voss, age thirty-eight, was arrested early this morning in connection with the murder of Cyril Butterworth," the anchor said. "Voss is a known associate of the Reapers Motorcycle Club. Sources say a cooperating witness — a member of the Butterworth family — provided a detailed statement linking Voss to the crime. In addition, Lorraine Butterworth, thirty-one, was arrested last night and charged with conspiracy to commit murder and obstruction of justice."

A photograph of Lorraine appeared on the screen —
not a mugshot, but an older photo, maybe from social media,
showing a younger version of Lorraine with fuller cheeks and
brighter eyes, before the meth had done its work. She was
smiling in the photograph. The kind of smile that belonged
to a different person in a different life.

Knox turned away from the television. Delaney put
her hand on his back.

"Authorities are also seeking a man identified as
Victor Padilla in connection with the case," the anchor
continued. "Padilla is believed to be operating under a false
identity and is considered a person of interest in the murder.
He is described as a male in his mid-forties, medium build,
dark hair. Anyone with information is asked to contact the
Kern County Sheriff's Department."

Archie turned off the television. The kitchen was
quiet.

"I need to see her," Archie said.

The room shifted. Knox looked up. Bella set down her
coffee cup. Delaney's hand stayed on Knox's back.

"Are you sure?" Bella asked.

"No," Archie said. "But I'm going."

"Why?" Knox asked. The question wasn't a challenge.
It was a genuine question from a man who couldn't

understand why his brother would want to sit across from the woman who'd put him in handcuffs and aimed a murder charge at his head.

"Because Dad would," Archie said.

Nobody argued with that. Nobody could.

The Kern County jail visiting room was exactly what Archie expected — plastic chairs, a table bolted to the floor, a window of reinforced glass, and a phone on each side. The room smelled like disinfectant and vending machine coffee. A guard stood by the door, bored, scrolling through something on his phone.

Lorraine came through the door on the other side of the glass. She was wearing an orange jumpsuit. Her hands were cuffed in front of her. Her hair was pulled back. Her face was bare — no makeup, no performance, no mask. She looked smaller than Archie remembered. Not thinner — smaller. As if the confession had compressed her, reduced her to something essential and exposed.

She sat down. She picked up the phone. Archie picked up his.

For a long moment, neither of them spoke. The glass between them was thick enough to stop a bullet and thin enough to see every line on her face. Archie looked at his sister and saw all of her at once — the girl on the bicycle, the teenager in the auditorium, the woman at Dante's house with the alarm code on her lips. All of them present. All of them real.

"I didn't come here to forgive you," Archie said. "I don't know if I can. Not yet. Maybe not ever."

"I know," Lorraine said.

"I came because Dad would have come," Archie said. "If he were alive, he'd be sitting in this chair right now. He'd pick up this phone. He'd look at you through this glass and he'd say something that made no sense to anyone but him. Something about love, or porch lights, or the fact that you're still his daughter no matter what."

Lorraine's eyes filled. She didn't wipe them. She let the tears fall, and they tracked down her cheeks and dropped onto the orange jumpsuit and left dark spots on the fabric.

"I can't say those things," Archie said. "I'm not Dad. I'm the son who almost went to prison because of what you did. I'm the brother who wore a GPS monitor for five weeks and watched his friends bleed. I'm angry, Lorraine. I'm going to be angry for a long time."

"You should be," Lorraine said.

"But I'm also here," Archie said. "And I'm going to make sure you have a lawyer. A good one. Not because you deserve it — I haven't decided if you deserve it. Because Dad would want me to. And because whatever you did, you walked into that police station last night and told the truth. That counts for something. Not everything. But something."

Lorraine pressed her hand against the glass. Five fingers, spread wide, the hand of a woman reaching for something she knew she couldn't touch.

Archie didn't press his hand to the glass. He wasn't there yet. He didn't know if he'd ever be there. But he didn't look away.

"Get a lawyer," Archie said. "Cooperate with the DA. Testify against Voss. Tell them everything. And when this is over — when the trial is done and the sentence is handed down and you're sitting in a cell somewhere — I want you to think about Dad. Not the version you hurt. The version who loved you. The one who wrote your name in a notebook for fourteen years because he couldn't stop hoping you'd come home."

"I think about him every day," Lorraine said.

"Good," Archie said. "Don't stop."

He hung up the phone. He stood. He looked at Lorraine through the glass one more time — his sister, his father's daughter, the woman who'd destroyed everything and confessed to everything and was sitting in a plastic chair in an orange jumpsuit with tears on her face and nothing left to hide behind.

He turned and walked out of the visiting room. The guard held the door. The hallway was long and bright and smelled like floor wax. Archie walked through it with the stride of a man who was free — legally, physically, permanently free — and carried with him the weight of a family that would never be whole again.

Outside, the Bakersfield sun was warm. Bella was waiting in the car. She didn't ask how it went. She looked at his face and understood.

"Home?" Bella asked.

"Home," Archie said.

She drove him to Columbus Street. The porch light was off — daytime, no need. But it would come on at dark. Knox had set the timer. The light would burn, the way it always burned, for a daughter who was no longer coming home and a father who would never know the truth had finally been told.

CHAPTER 25: "The Reckoning"

Tommy Fuentes walked out of Kern Medical Center on a Tuesday morning with his left arm in a sling, a bottle of pain medication he swore he wouldn't need, and a discharge summary that used the word "remarkable" three times in describing his recovery.

Archie was waiting in the parking lot. Tommy came through the automatic doors and squinted in the sunlight like a man emerging from a cave, which, in a sense, he was — eleven days in a hospital room with beige walls and a television that only got four channels and a nurse named Gloria who called him "mijo" and refused to let him leave until his white blood cell count met her personal standards.

"Freedom," Tommy said. He stood on the sidewalk and breathed in the Bakersfield air — diesel, dust, the faint petroleum edge — and smiled the wide, open smile that was as much a part of him as the sling on his arm. "Gloria threatened to follow me home and check my dressing. I think she meant it."

"She gave me her number," Archie said. "She told me to call if you do anything stupid."

"Define stupid," Tommy said.

"She said I'd know it when I saw it," Archie said.

They drove to Columbus Street. The house was full — or what passed for full in the strange, temporary community that had formed inside Cyril Butterworth's walls over the past five weeks. Knox and Delaney were in the kitchen. Bella was at the table with her laptop, drafting a motion for a case she'd picked back up two days ago — the Hernandez deportation hearing, rescheduled, David Castellano having called to say the firm wanted her back whenever she was ready. Reece was at Cyril's desk, closing down the intelligence operation he'd built from a kitchen table and a laptop, organizing files that would eventually be turned over to Hale for the prosecution's case against Voss.

Wes was on the back porch. He was always on the back porch. But the bottle on the railing was gone, replaced by a coffee mug, and the tremor in his hands was still there but quieter, like a signal fading as the source moved farther away.

Tommy walked through the front door and the house changed. Not physically — the rooms were the same, the furniture was the same, the porch light was still set on Knox's timer. But Tommy's presence filled spaces that had been empty, the way a familiar voice fills a quiet room. Delaney hugged him carefully, mindful of the sling. Knox shook his hand. Bella smiled — a real smile, the first one Archie had seen from her in days. Reece stood up from the desk and gripped Tommy's good hand and said nothing, because nothing needed saying.

Wes came in from the porch. He looked at Tommy. Tommy looked at Wes. The last time they'd been face to face, Wes had been pressing his hands against Tommy's shoulder on a dirt road while his own blood soaked through his shirt.

"You look better than you should," Wes said.

"You look worse than you should," Tommy said.

"I always look like this," Wes said.

"I know," Tommy said. "That's what worries me."

They embraced — carefully, because Tommy's shoulder and Wes's ribs were both still healing, but firmly, the embrace of two men who had bled together and didn't need to explain what that meant.

That afternoon, they gathered in the living room. All of them — Archie, Knox, Delaney, Bella, Reece, Tommy, Wes. Seven people in a dead man's house, sitting on furniture that had been rearranged to cover the place where Cyril had died, drinking coffee from mugs Cyril had collected over forty years of county service.

It wasn't a meeting. It wasn't a debrief. It was something else — something without a name, the way the most important moments in life often are. A gathering. A reckoning. A quiet acknowledgment that the thing they'd been doing for five weeks was finished, and the people they'd been when it started were not the people sitting in this room.

"I want to say something," Archie said. He was standing by the window, the way he'd stood on the first morning when the Marines arrived — the same window that now had plywood where the brick had gone through, the glass not yet replaced because nobody had gotten around to it. "I want to say it while everyone's here."

The room was quiet. Seven faces turned toward him.

"Five weeks ago, my father was murdered," Archie said. "I was arrested for it. I wore a GPS monitor. I lost my job. I sat in this house and watched the system build a case against me for something I didn't do. And every single person in this room gave up something to be here."

He looked at Reece. "You left your business. You got stitched up on a farm road. You built an intelligence operation from a kitchen table that a federal agency would be proud of."

He looked at Tommy. "You took a bullet. You spent eleven days in a hospital. You watched your valley being poisoned by the people we were investigating, and you stayed on mission even when the mission got personal."

He looked at Wes. "You crossed twenty yards of open ground under shotgun fire. You saved Tommy's life. And you made a decision about your own life that took more courage than anything that happened on that farm road."

He looked at Bella. "You gave up a case. You risked your career. You pulled threads in the Central Valley that nobody else could have pulled. You were followed, threatened, and you didn't stop."

He looked at Knox. "You told the truth. It took you too long — you know that, I know that — but when you told it, you told all of it. And you took the stand and said it under oath. That took spine."

He looked at Delaney. "You made soup. You cut paper leaves. You held Knox together when he was falling apart. And you drove my sister to the police station on the night she confessed. You didn't have to do any of that. You did it because you're the kind of person who shows up."

The room was still. Nobody moved. Nobody spoke.

"My father left the porch light on every night," Archie said. "For Lorraine. For all of us. Because that's who he was — a man who believed that if you left the light on long enough, the people you loved would find their way home. I don't know if he was right. I don't know if Lorraine will ever find her way home. But I know that the people in this room are the reason the light is still on. And I will never forget that."

Tommy broke the silence. "You're buying dinner," Tommy said. "Somewhere expensive. I got shot for you."

The room laughed. Not a big laugh — a small one, the kind that releases pressure without pretending the pressure was never there. Archie almost smiled.

"I'm buying dinner," Archie said.

The goodbyes happened over the next two days, one at a time, the way goodbyes do when people have been living in close quarters and need to separate slowly.

Reece left first. He packed his laptop, his files, and the legal pad that had served as the backbone of the investigation. He shook Archie's hand at the front door, and the handshake lasted longer than either of them intended.

"If you ever need anything," Reece said.

"I know where to find you," Archie said.

"Sacramento," Reece said. "Same office. Same number. Same khakis."

"You do iron your khakis," Archie said.

"I have never confirmed or denied that," Reece said.

He got in his car and drove north. Archie watched from the porch until the car turned the corner and was gone.

Tommy left the next morning. His mother had called three times demanding he come home. His father had called once, which meant the situation was serious — Tommy's father didn't call unless he had something to say, and what he had to say was usually two sentences long and impossible to argue with.

"My old man told me to come home and eat his enchiladas," Tommy said. "That's a direct order I can't refuse."

"Your arm," Archie said.

"My arm works fine," Tommy said. He demonstrated by carefully lifting it six inches from the sling and wincing. "See? Fine."

"That looked painful," Archie said.

"Everything worth doing is painful," Tommy said. "That's what the Corps taught me. That and how to iron a shirt, which Reece has apparently perfected and I have not."

They stood in the driveway. Tommy looked at the house — the white paint, the brown trim, the porch light that would click on in a few hours.

"Your pops was a good man, Archie," Tommy said. "The best kind. The kind that doesn't make the news until something terrible happens to them. I'm glad we fought for him."

"So am I," Archie said.

Tommy got in his truck — a borrowed truck, since his

own had bullet holes in the body panels and was sitting in a police impound lot as evidence. He backed out of the driveway one-handed, which was reckless and exactly what Archie expected, and drove east toward the house where his mother was making enchiladas and his father was waiting to say something two sentences long.

Wes left last.

He came to the kitchen on Wednesday morning with his bag packed and his face carrying an expression Archie had never seen from him — not the wry exhaustion, not the tremor-hiding composure, not the sharp-edged humor that deflected everything he didn't want to feel. Something new. Something that looked, if Archie was reading it right, like the beginning of honesty.

"I called the VA this morning," Wes said. "Inpatient program in Palo Alto. Thirty days. I check in Friday."

"Good," Archie said.

"I'm scared," Wes said. He said it the way he'd said "I'm fine" for the past three years — quickly, without fanfare, as if the words were small and ordinary. But these words were neither.

"I know," Archie said.

"Crossing that ground on the farm road — I wasn't scared," Wes said. "Shotgun, no cover, Tommy bleeding. I wasn't scared. But sitting in a room and talking about why I drink? That terrifies me."

"The farm road was three seconds," Archie said. "The VA is thirty days. Different kind of courage."

"The harder kind," Wes said.

"The harder kind," Archie said.

They stood in the kitchen. The clock ticked. The coffee maker gurgled. The house was quieter now — the Marines gone or going, the intelligence operation dismantled, the card table cleared, the laptops closed. The house was returning to what it had been before — a dead man's home, quiet and patient, waiting for someone to decide what came next.

"Thank you, Wes," Archie said.

"Don't thank me," Wes said. "I came because you called. That's what we do."

"I'm thanking you anyway," Archie said.

Wes picked up his bag. He walked to the front door. He stopped on the porch and looked back.

"Leave the light on," Wes said.

"Always," Archie said.

Wes walked to his car. He got in. He sat for a moment, his hands on the wheel — the hands that had shaken for months and held a wounded Marine on a dirt road and were now steady enough to drive to Palo Alto and check into a program that would ask him to do the one thing he'd been avoiding for years.

Feel everything. Without the bourbon. Without the mission. Without the noise.

He started the engine and drove away. Archie stood on the porch and watched until the car was gone.

The street was quiet. The neighborhood was still. The porch light was off — daytime — but the bulb was there, waiting, the way it always waited, for the dark to come and the light to do its work.

CHAPTER 26: "Padilla"

Ten days after Dante Voss's arrest, the man who killed Cyril Butterworth was caught at a gas station in Needles, California, forty miles from the Arizona border.

Archie got the call from Hale at 7:00 PM on a Thursday evening. He was sitting on the back porch in Cyril's rocker — the one with the frayed cushion Helen had picked out — watching the sun drop behind the valley. The sky was orange and purple and streaked with thin clouds, the kind of sunset Cyril would have called "God showing off." Bella was inside making pasta. Knox and Delaney had gone home to their apartment for the first time since the break-in, the locks changed, a security system installed, the photograph of Pismo Beach back on the left side of the nightstand where it belonged.

"They got him," Hale said.

Archie didn't ask who. There was only one person left to get.

"Tell me," Archie said.

"California Highway Patrol pulled over a gray Honda Civic on Interstate 40 outside Needles," Hale said. "Routine traffic stop — broken taillight. The driver produced a California license in the name of Miguel Rios. The officer ran the name through the system and got a hit on the BOLO. The driver was detained and transported to the San Bernardino County Sheriff's Department. FBI agents arrived within two hours."

"Rios," Archie said. "The motel name."

"He burned the Padilla identity but kept Rios," Hale said. "That was his mistake. Tommy found the Rios alias at the Valley Rest Inn. It was in the BOLO. If he'd built a third name, he might have made it across the border."

"Who is he?" Archie asked.

"His real name is Esteban Molina," Hale said. "Age forty-four. Born in Sinaloa, Mexico. He entered the United States on a tourist visa in 2019 and never left. No criminal record under his real name — not in the U.S., not in Mexico. At least not one that shows up in standard databases. But the FBI has been in contact with Mexican federal authorities, and the picture is getting clearer."

"What picture?" Archie asked.

"Molina is connected to a cartel supply network that operates through the Central Valley," Hale said. "He's not a boss. He's not a lieutenant. He's what they call a 'facilitator' — a man who moves between operations, handles problems, and disappears. The purchased identities, the motel rooms, the careful movement patterns — that's his profile. He goes where he's needed, does what needs doing, and moves on."

"A professional," Archie said.

"A professional," Hale said. "The FBI believes Voss contracted Molina through the supply chain — the same chain that feeds meth into the Reapers' distribution network. Voss needed someone outside his local circle to handle the job. Someone who couldn't be traced back to the club. Molina fit the profile."

Archie sat in the rocker and listened to the creak of the wood beneath him. Esteban Molina. The man who had walked up to his father's front door at 9:23 PM on November 5, entered the alarm code Lorraine had given Dante, used the key from under the mat, and gone inside. Eighteen minutes later, he'd walked out. Cyril was dead on the living room floor. Molina had driven away in a gray Honda Civic and gone back to his motel room and slept, or didn't sleep, or did whatever a man does after he kills a sixty-five-year-old facilities manager who left the porch light on for his daughter.

"Has he confessed?" Archie asked.

"No," Hale said. "He's not talking. He lawyered up immediately — a federal public defender out of San Bernardino. He knows the system. He's been through it before, even if the record doesn't show it."

"Will the doorbell footage be enough?" Archie asked.

"The footage, combined with Lorraine's testimony and the phone records from the warehouse, gives the prosecution a strong case," Hale said. "Lorraine can testify that she gave Voss the alarm code and the key location. The phone records establish communication between Voss and a burner number linked to Molina during the week of the murder. The doorbell footage shows a man matching Molina's physical description entering the house. And now they have Molina himself — his fingerprints, his DNA. If there's any physical trace of him inside that house, the crime lab will find it."

"They didn't find anything the first time," Archie said.

"The first time, they weren't looking for Esteban Molina," Hale said. "They were looking for you. A second sweep of the house won't help — too many people have been living there since the murder. But they don't need the house. They have Molina in custody now. His fingerprints and DNA are on file. If the crime lab preserved anything from the original sweep — latent prints, trace evidence that didn't match anyone in the family — they can run it against Molina's profile. Sometimes the evidence was there all along. It just needed the right name to match it to."

Archie rocked the chair. The sunset was fading, the orange bleeding into gray, the first stars appearing above the rooftops. He thought about his father in the living room that night — probably in his chair, maybe doing the crossword, maybe watching television. The alarm disarmed. The key turning in the lock. The front door opening. And a stranger walking in like he belonged there, because he had the code and the key and the information that a daughter had given to a man with a skull on his neck.

Had Cyril heard the door? Had he looked up from his chair and seen a face he didn't recognize? Had there been a moment — even a second — when Cyril understood what was happening? Or had Molina been fast enough, professional enough, that Cyril never saw it coming?

Archie would never know. Molina wasn't talking. And Cyril was dead. The eighteen minutes between 9:23 and 9:41 PM on November 5, 2024, would remain a closed room — a space that belonged only to the killer and the killed, and that no amount of evidence or testimony could fully illuminate.

"Archie," Hale said. "There's one more thing."

"What?" Archie asked.

"The DA has formally offered Lorraine a plea agreement," Hale said. "In exchange for her full cooperation and testimony against both Voss and Molina, the conspiracy charge will be reduced. She'll plead guilty to voluntary manslaughter and accessory after the fact. The recommended sentence is twelve to fifteen years, with the possibility of parole after ten."

"Ten years," Archie said.

"It's a significant reduction from twenty-five to life," Hale said. "Her attorney — the one you hired after her arraignment — is recommending she take it. The DA needs her testimony. Without it, the case against Voss is strong but not airtight. With it, Voss goes away for life and Molina goes away for life. Lorraine's cooperation is the linchpin."

"She'll take it," Archie said. He didn't say it as a guess. He said it as a fact — the same way he'd say a market would correct or a trade would close. He knew his sister. He knew the woman who'd walked into a police station and confessed without a lawyer. That woman would take the deal. Not because it was easy, but because it was the only path that led toward something other than darkness.

"I think she will too," Hale said.

"Is there anything else I need to do?" Archie asked.

"No," Hale said. The investigation is out of our hands now, Hale said. "Salcedo and the FBI will build the case. The DA will prosecute. You don't have to fight anymore."

"I'm not sure I know how to stop," Archie said.

"You'll figure it out," Hale said. "You've got good people around you."

The line went dead. Archie set the phone on the armrest of the rocker. The sky was dark now, the stars scattered across it like punctuation in a sentence he couldn't quite read. The porch light clicked on — Knox's timer, set for sunset, faithful and automatic — and the yellow circle fell across the steps the way it had every night since Cyril had first screwed in the bulb.

Bella came to the back door. "Pasta's ready," Bella said. She looked at his face and stopped. "What happened?"

"They caught him," Archie said. "The man who killed my father. His name is Esteban Molina. He was forty miles from the Arizona border."

Bella stood in the doorway. The kitchen light was behind her, warm and golden, and Archie could smell garlic and olive oil and the specific comfort of a meal cooked by someone who loved you.

"How do you feel?" Bella asked.

Archie thought about the question. He thought about the five weeks — the arrest, the handcuffs, the GPS monitor, the trading floor he'd been escorted from, the courtroom, the plea deal he'd refused, the notebook he'd found in his father's desk, the brick through the window, the firefight on the farm road, the three Marines who'd bled for him, the sister who'd confessed, the brother who'd found his spine, the woman standing in the doorway who'd given up her career and her case and her apartment to sit on a dead man's couch in Bakersfield and fight.

"I feel like my father's killer has been caught," Archie said. "And my father is still dead. And both of those things are true at the same time."

Bella looked at him for a long moment. Then she walked to the rocker and sat on the armrest and put her arm around his shoulders.

"Come eat," Bella said. "The pasta's getting cold."

"In a minute," Archie said.

They sat on the back porch together, watching the stars, the porch light burning behind them, the kitchen warm and waiting. The case was closed. The killer was caught. The sister was in jail. The brother was free. And the father — the man who started all of it, the man who loved too much and saved too little and wrote "God help me" in a notebook seventeen days before someone he trusted gave away the key to his front door — was gone.

Esteban Molina would go to trial. Dante Voss would go to trial. Lorraine Butterworth would plead guilty and testify and spend the next decade in a cell, paying for a crime she committed with her mouth and her rage and the information she never should have shared.

And Cyril Butterworth would remain what he had always been — a good man who left the light on. A father who couldn't stop loving. A name in a notebook, written in his own handwriting, in entries that spanned fourteen years and ended with a prayer.

Archie stood up. He took Bella's hand. They walked inside. The pasta was getting cold. The kitchen was warm. The porch light burned.

Some lights you leave on because you're waiting for someone to come home.

Some lights you leave on because turning them off would mean admitting they're gone.

Archie left the light on.

CHAPTER 27: "The Porch Light"

December in Bakersfield was mild the way December in most of California was mild — cool mornings, warm afternoons, the kind of weather that made the rest of the country jealous and the locals complain about. Archie stood in the driveway of Cyril's house on a Saturday morning and looked at the lawn.

The grass was dead. Not brown at the edges the way it had been for weeks — fully dead, the whole yard turned to straw. The sprinkler system that Cyril had maintained on Helen's schedule had finally stopped running. A valve had broken, or a timer had failed, or the system had simply given up the way systems do when the person who cared for them is no longer there to notice.

Archie turned on the hose and watered the lawn by hand. It took forty-five minutes. The water soaked into the dead grass and pooled on the hard soil and ran down the driveway in thin streams that caught the morning light. It wouldn't save the lawn. The grass was gone. But the watering felt like something that needed doing, so he did it.

Bella came out with two cups of coffee. She handed him one and stood beside him in the driveway, watching the water soak into the yard.

"You're watering dead grass," Bella said.

"I know," Archie said.

"Is this a metaphor?" Bella asked.

"It's a hose," Archie said.

She smiled. The smile was small and tired and real — the smile of a woman who'd spent six weeks in Bakersfield and had earned every line on her face. She was going back to San Francisco on Monday. The Hernandez hearing had been rescheduled for the following week. Castellano had called twice, each call warmer than the last, the firm's discomfort with her absence replaced by something closer to respect. She'd fought for a man who wasn't her client. The firm understood what that said about her.

"Come with me," Bella said. "Back to San Francisco. You don't have to stay here."

"I know," Archie said. "I'm not staying. I just need a few more days."

"For what?" Bella asked.

Archie looked at the house. The white paint was peeling near the gutters. The brown trim needed a fresh coat. The hedge along the side yard had grown shaggy — Cyril trimmed it every two weeks, and it had been seven weeks since anyone had touched it. The house was aging in real time, the slow deterioration that begins the moment the person who maintained it stops maintaining it.

"I need to decide what to do with this place," Archie said.

"You don't have to decide today," Bella said.

"No," Archie said. "But I need to start thinking about it. Knox doesn't want it — he told me last week. Too many memories. And Lorraine —" He stopped. The sentence didn't need finishing.

"What do you want?" Bella asked.

Archie turned off the hose. He coiled it on the hook by the garage door — the same hook Cyril had screwed into the wall twenty years ago, the coil precise, the routine automatic. He straightened up and looked at the house again.

"I want it to be someone's home," Archie said. "Not a memorial. Not a shrine. A home. The way it was when Dad was alive. A family. Kids in the yard. Someone who trims the hedge and fixes the sprinkler and leaves the porch light on because they're waiting for someone, not because they're remembering someone."

"That's a good answer," Bella said.

"It's the only answer Dad would accept," Archie said.

Knox came by that afternoon. He and Delaney were back in their apartment, the new locks installed, the security system armed, the paper leaves from the bulletin board still on the coffee table because Delaney hadn't had the heart to

throw them away. They'd set a new date for the wedding —
April instead of March. The original venue had been
understanding. The caterer had been flexible. Cyril's
barbecue plan had been replaced by a buffet, because nobody
wanted to stand at a grill without Cyril beside them arguing
about propane versus charcoal.

Knox sat at the kitchen table with Archie. Delaney was
in the living room, measuring the windows for new curtains
she'd volunteered to hang before the house went on the
market. She did things like that — showed up, measured,
fixed. The kindergarten teacher who ran the world one small
repair at a time.

"I talked to Lorraine's lawyer yesterday," Knox said.
"She's taking the deal. Twelve to fifteen years. She'll testify
against Voss and Molina."

"Good," Archie said.

"She asked about you," Knox said.

"What did she ask?" Archie said.

"She asked if you hate her," Knox said.

Archie looked at his coffee. The surface was still, dark,
reflecting the kitchen light in a small, distorted circle. He
thought about the question the way he thought about a trade
— not emotionally, not impulsively, but with the careful

precision of a man who understood that the answer mattered more than the speed of the response.

"I don't hate her," Archie said. "I'm angry. I'll be angry for a long time. But hate takes energy I don't have. And Dad wouldn't want it."

"No," Knox said. "He wouldn't."

"Will you visit her?" Archie asked.

"Yes," Knox said. "Not right away. But yes. She's my sister. That doesn't change because of what she did. It can't."

"Dad would say the same thing," Archie said.

"Dad would already be in the visiting room," Knox said.

They sat at the table and drank their coffee and didn't say anything for a while. The kitchen was quiet. The clock ticked. The retirement invitations were gone — Archie had packed them in a box with the rest of Cyril's personal items, forty stamped envelopes addressed to people who would never receive them, each one carrying the handwritten message "Hope to see you there."

"Knox," Archie said. "The wedding. I want to be there."

"You're the best man," Knox said. "You have to be there."

"I didn't know I was the best man," Archie said.

"I didn't know either," Knox said. "Until about five weeks ago. But you are. If you want to be."

"I want to be," Archie said.

Knox looked at his brother across the kitchen table — the same table where they'd sat with Cyril and done crossword puzzles, the same table where Reece had built an intelligence operation, the same table where Hale had delivered plea deals and forensic reports and the kind of news that rearranges a life. The table had held all of it. The wood was scratched and stained and marked by forty years of use, and it was still standing.

"Archie," Knox said. "Are you okay?"

"No," Archie said. "Are you?"

"No," Knox said. "But I think we will be."

"Eventually," Archie said.

"Eventually," Knox said.

That evening, after Knox and Delaney left and Bella had gone to the motel to pack, Archie was alone in the house for the first time since the morning after Cyril died.

The silence was different now. Six weeks ago, the silence had been an absence — the hole left by a man who should have been there and wasn't. Now the silence was something else. Not peace, exactly. Something quieter than peace. Acceptance, maybe. The recognition that the house was what it was — four walls and a roof and a porch light and the memory of a man who had lived there and died there and loved there until the love itself became the fault line that broke the family apart.

Archie walked through the rooms. The bedroom where Cyril had slept alone for eight years after Helen died. The guest rooms where Marines had slept and bled and planned. The living room with the new carpet and the plywood window that still needed replacing. The kitchen with the clock and the coffee maker and the stove light that Cyril always left on.

He ended at the desk. The bottom drawer was open — he'd left it that way after finding the notebook. The old newspapers were still there, stacked neatly, the way Cyril stacked everything. Archie reached in and straightened them. A small gesture. The kind of thing Cyril would have done without thinking.

He sat in Cyril's chair. The chair was old — wooden, swivel, the cushion worn flat by forty years of a man sitting down to pay bills and do crosswords and write entries in a notebook nobody knew about. Archie put his hands on the desk, flat, the way he'd done the morning he found the notebook. The wood was smooth and cool under his palms.

He closed his eyes.

The grief came. Not the wave he'd been bracing for since November. Not the river that had hit him in the hospital parking lot after visiting Tommy. Something different. Something that didn't crash or rush or overwhelm. It rose slowly, like water filling a room from the floor up — quiet, steady, total. It filled his chest and his throat and his eyes, and Archie Butterworth, the Marine, the trader, the man who controlled every room he entered and every emotion he carried, put his head on his father's desk and cried.

He cried for Cyril. For the man who washed dishes by hand and mowed the lawn on Saturday mornings and wrote "Hope to see you there" on forty envelopes he never mailed. He cried for Helen, who'd been dead eight years and whose birthday was still the alarm code. He cried for Lorraine, who would spend the next decade in a cell paying for a crime she committed with words instead of weapons. He cried for Knox, who'd carried a secret that crushed him and told the truth when it mattered most. He cried for the Marines — for Tommy's shoulder and Wes's hands and Reece's quiet competence and the dirt road where the brotherhood proved itself in blood. He cried for Bella, who'd walked into his life eight months ago and into his war six weeks ago and hadn't flinched.

He cried until there was nothing left. Then he sat up. He wiped his face with the back of his hand. He looked around the office — the desk, the drawers, the chair, the empty space where the notebook had been.

"I miss you, Pop," Archie said. The words went into the empty room and stayed there, the way words do when the person they're meant for is gone.

He stood up. He walked to the front door. He opened it and stepped onto the porch. The timer had clicked on twenty minutes ago, and the yellow light fell across the steps and the walkway and the dead grass and the driveway where Tommy's borrowed truck had been and Bella's rental and Knox's car and all the vehicles that had come and gone during the worst six weeks of Archie Butterworth's life.

The street was quiet. The neighbors' houses were lit. A dog barked somewhere — the same dog, always barking, the one constant in a neighborhood that had been through a murder and a media circus and a firefight in the almond orchards and had gone back to being a street where people came home from work and ate dinner and went to bed.

Archie looked at the porch light. A single bulb in a brass fixture that Cyril had installed when they moved in thirty years ago. The fixture was tarnished. The bulb was the same kind Cyril always bought — soft white, sixty watts, the warm yellow that made the porch look like a painting of a porch instead of the real thing.

He reached up and touched the fixture. The brass was cool under his fingers. He could change the bulb. He could replace the fixture. He could turn the timer off and let the porch go dark, the way every other porch on the street went dark after the people inside decided the day was over.

He didn't.

He left the light on.

He went inside. He locked the door. He walked to the kitchen and poured a glass of water and sat at the table and listened to the clock tick and the refrigerator hum and the house breathe around him, alive with memory, heavy with loss, warm with the stubborn, irrational light of a man who never stopped believing his children would come home.

In April, Knox would get married. In Palo Alto, Wes would finish his thirty days and start the harder work of living without the bourbon. In Sacramento, Reece would go back to his consulting firm and iron his khakis and never talk about the farm road unless someone asked. In Bakersfield, Tommy would get the sling off and go back to his tow truck and drive past the almond orchards where he'd taken a bullet and keep driving, because that's what Marines do. In San Francisco, Bella would win the Hernandez case and call Archie that night and say "come home" and mean it.

And in a prison somewhere in California, Lorraine Butterworth would sit in a cell and think about a porch light she could no longer see, left on by a father she could no longer call, burning for a daughter who had finally told the truth — too late to save him, but not too late to save her brother.

The light stayed on. It would always stay on. Not because anyone was coming home tonight. But because some promises outlive the people who make them, and some lights burn longer than the hands that turned them on.

Archie finished his water. He turned off the kitchen light. He walked down the hallway to the guest room, the room where Reece had slept and Tommy had slept and Wes had slept, and he lay down on the bed and closed his eyes.

The house was quiet. The porch light burned. And Cyril Butterworth — the man who fixed buildings and loved his children and wrote prayers in a notebook nobody knew about — was, at last, at rest.

THE END

A NOTE FROM THE AUTHOR

I started writing this book because I couldn't stop thinking about a porch light.

Not a real one — an imagined one. A light left on by a father who couldn't stop hoping his daughter would come home. That image stayed with me for weeks before I wrote a single word, and it became the heart of everything that followed. Recently, my daughter passed away, but I still leave the light on.

The Last Whisper of Innocence is a work of fiction. The characters, the events, and the city as I've portrayed it are products of my imagination. But the themes are real — the love between parents and children, the damage addiction does to families, the lengths people will go to for the people they call brother, and the terrible cost of silence when the truth needs telling. I know, because one of my daughters passed away from drug use.

I am a Navy veteran. I spent decades in service — military and civilian — and the values I carried out of uniform are the same values I try to put into my writing. Duty. Loyalty. Honesty. The belief that ordinary people are capable of extraordinary courage when the people they love are in danger.

If this story moved you, I'd be grateful if you left a

review on Amazon. Reviews are the lifeblood of independent authors, and every one of them — long or short, five stars or honest criticism — helps another reader find this book.

If you or someone you love is struggling with substance abuse, help is available. The Substance Abuse and Mental Health Services Administration (SAMHSA) National Helpline is free, confidential, and available 24 hours a day, 365 days a year: 1-800-662-4357.

Thank you for reading.

Jackie L. Smith

ABOUT THE AUTHOR

Jackie L. Smith is a United States Navy veteran and author of fiction spanning thrillers, middle-grade fantasy, and family drama. His writing draws on decades of experience in military service, hospital administration, and Air Force civilian support. He brings to the page the same values he carried in uniform — duty, loyalty, and the belief that ordinary people are capable of extraordinary courage.

His novels include Echoes of 1969, The Customs Conspiracy, The Fractured Path to Emerald Vale, Echoes of Betrayal, Atlas Drummond: Fragments of Deceit, Hank Blankenship and the Longest Fall, Colby Utterback: Finding His Place, Brynn Thornwick: Guardian of the Crimson Crown, and Wilbur Northcutt and the Boonesborough Fall.

He lives in eastern Kentucky, where he spends his time writing, collecting stamps, tinkering with computers, and proving that retirement is just another word for working on your own schedule.

DISCUSSION QUESTIONS

For book clubs and reading groups:

1. Cyril kept a notebook documenting every dollar he gave Lorraine over fourteen years. Why do you think he kept this record? Was it an act of love, accountability, or something else?

2. Knox knew about Dante Voss for eight months and said nothing. Was his silence an act of protection or cowardice? Where is the line between the two?

3. Archie refused the plea deal despite the risk of life in prison. What does this decision reveal about his character? Would you have made the same choice?

4. Lorraine's confession came after learning that Archie refused the plea deal. Do you think she would have confessed if he had taken it? Why or why not?

5. The porch light is a recurring image throughout the novel. What does it represent, and how does its meaning change as the story progresses?

6. Bella gave up a major case and risked her career to stay in Bakersfield. Was this a personal decision, a professional one, or both? What does it say about her relationship with Archie?

7. Wes Draper arrives broken and leaves committed to recovery. What was the turning point for him, and do you believe his recovery will last?

8. Detective Salcedo admits she built the wrong case. How much of her failure was personal and how much was institutional? Should she bear responsibility for what Archie went through?

9. Archie tells Lorraine in the visiting room that he came because their father would have come. Is that forgiveness? Is it obligation? Is there a difference?

10. The novel ends with the porch light still burning. What do you think happens to the Butterworth family after the final page?